Chance Meeting

By

Bidisha Ganguli

"Made me think of Eat, Pray, Love as it's truly a woman's journey of discovery. This book delved into some major issues women can relate to – the pros and cons of staying in an unhappy marriage because of the children and also the issue of body image in a very respectful and personal way. Gives the reader lots of food for thought!" – ***Carol U.***

"After being forced into a profession, getting married and having children, Karina is yearning to shake things up! Join her as she unconsciously follows her own internal compass, stretching beyond what Western society, her family and her Indian heritage might dictate. Be ready for the unexpected in this romantic adventure about inner truth, transition and breaking through invisible cultural barriers." – **Robyn R.**

"It would have been entertaining enough that ***A Chance Meeting*** *explored the instant connection between Karina and a mysterious stranger in the storied city of Montreal. But the revelations of her heart and mind and through the strength of her spirit, we find that a more profound meeting. Between Karina and a self that was always there but pushed aside by expectations and obligations. A self that is reborn and who will be a constant, assertive companion on the journey ahead."* – **S.G.**

"A fun read about unadulterated thrills that you do not dare admit you have dreamed about. Karina takes us on a brave journey of self-discovery and acceptance. Written from an escapist, but relatable, perspective about life's challenges and changes." – **T.H.**

Aka Naksha Books

Disclaimer:

This is a work of **fiction**. Names, characters, businesses, places, events, locales, and incidents are either the products of the author's imagination or used in a fictitious manner. Any resemblance to actual persons, living or dead, or actual events is purely **coincidental**.

Cover Design by Simone Zahradka
Editor: India Hammond

First Edition

www.akanaksha.com

ISBN 978-1-7774215-0-2

To my sister for allowing me to be brave, strong & weak.

To my three boys for encouraging me through it all.

To my husband for supporting my adventure.

To my parents for always being there.

And to the one who awoke the insatiable desire in me.

A Chance Meeting

Chapter 1

Oh, Sunny Day...

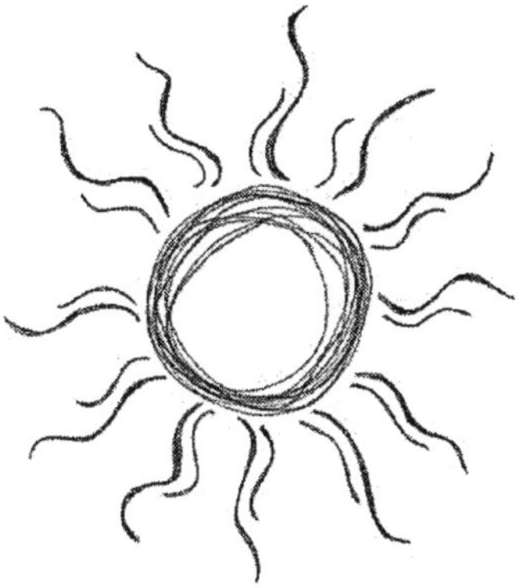

Exactly one year ago, I had made that fateful trip to Montreal with my quiet and traditional husband. A trip full of upset, regret and eye-opening realizations. Who would've thought that the trip that I was so not looking forward to, was going to change my life? So much had happened since. I had learned so much about myself. And this year, I had finally convinced my husband I needed something for myself. I planned the ultimate trip to the Okanagan! I was going with my best friend Carmen and I couldn't wait! A girl's trip that was way overdue.

I sat nervously on the edge of my brown leather couch in the front room, looking out the large floor to ceiling two-storey windows before glancing down at my phone again.

My large but toned toffee-coloured thigh bounced automatically under my summer dress. I was trying to distract myself by looking at the beautiful view of the Rocky Mountain Range with its snow-capped peaks, but it wasn't working. I was holding my breath, so I forced myself to exhale. I closed my eyes momentarily and looked at the phone again. Carmen had said she was going to call me at 1:00 p.m. to confirm a pickup time and now the clock read 1:12 p.m. I was all too familiar with Indian Standard Time (an Indian cultural concept of always being late), but I had no patience that day. I was sure she wasn't working. I stood up and started to pace before deciding to sit down again. Why hadn't she called yet?

Maybe I should text her, I thought to myself. I was starting to feel anxious. I typed a simple message, "All good?" and hit send. I was so looking forward to this trip. I knew that nothing would stop me from going...nothing; yet something was wrong. Call it instinct or a mother's intuition, but I could sense it. I put the thought aside and looked out the window again.

Calgary summer days were incredibly long, and the bright sun kept you company long into the twilight hours. In Canada, when you lived this far up the northern hemisphere, hot, sultry days were some of the rarest to come by even though they were long. But today was one of those exceptions. It was a gorgeous, bright, and sunny day. The temperature was in the mid-twenties and there wasn't a cloud in the sky; the sun's rays beamed in all directions, beating down and brightening everything they touched.

I thought back to earlier in the day, just a few hours before. I had scrambled to get lunch into my three boys and my hubby, packed up all the camping gear into the back of the minivan, and loaded up the bikes on the bike rack.

My fourteen-year-old had planned a boys only camping trip to Waterton National Park in Alberta, Canada and they were going to be gone for five days. Waterton is considered a hamlet with its whopping 108 residents in the entire area. Its backdrop of majestic mountains, waterfalls, trails, valleys, lush grasslands and untouched natural aspen forestry made it ideal for camping and hiking. He had invited a few of his friends from school along with their siblings and dads to join. They had decided to try some difficult hikes, hit the bike trails, do some lake swimming and of course, roast marshmallows.

All the food had been prepared, labeled and packed; their medication and toiletries put into bear safe bags; and the tent and sleeping bags were aired out and ready for the wilderness. I wanted to make sure everything had been taken care of, so my hubby and kids wouldn't have to worry about a thing.

"Ma, I wish you were coming," said my eldest, Arjan. "You know you're tougher than some of the dads going. You would've crushed the trails we picked!" As he spoke, he glanced over at his own dad, knowing he was probably in that category.

"I promise Arjan, I will plan an amazing trip with you and your brothers later this summer," I replied trying to be encouraging. "I'm looking into a triathlon for us to do. But you will have a great time on this trip, although I will miss you dearly. Make sure you do some of the driving and remember to take care of Baba and your brothers. And have fun!"

My middle son Aryan looked at me devilishly, like he had made plans with his buddies that he knew I wouldn't approve of and was glad that I wouldn't be there to foil them. My youngest Arjev, who was almost as tall as me, hugged me tightly and wouldn't let go.

A part of me was sad to see the boys leaving without me; I knew I would be missing out on a great adventure, but at the same time, the thought of spending five days in a tent with three stinky, sweaty boys pushing me well beyond my physical limits in the wilderness was something I was willing to exchange for some chillaxing with my best friend.

As I kissed hubby goodbye, I felt a pang of concern. He already looked tired and conflicted. He wasn't a huge outdoorsy guy; he had never been the athletic kind. I thought some "bonding" with the boys would do him good and I had hinted that I needed some space. I smiled at him kindly and whispered, "Try and have a good time. Give yourself a chance to have fun with the boys.

The trip will be good for both of us, a much-needed break. Fresh air, exercise—it will be great."

I saw Arjan hanging on my every word, making sure I was okay. I smiled at him reassuringly and blew him and my other boys a kiss. It's strange, because I would miss hubby and yet, I was so happy to see him go.

Hubby looked at me wearily, gave me a faltering smile and whispered in my ear, "I could really have used you by my side, to take care of the kids and keep me company at night, to take care of my needs."

My heart sank, an icky feeling coming over my body. Taking care of his needs was his way of telling me it was my duty rather than for fun. At least he hadn't mentioned my trip, the one we had fought about multiple times. I disregarded it as his insecurity and forced a smile.

Our marriage had been strained the last few years. I was struggling. I had set my ambitions aside to be a stay-at-home mom. I loved being a mom and I was proud that I was able to raise my boys, but I had lost myself along the way. Watching my boys grow up, the feeling of obsolescence was becoming more and more present. It was becoming more of a struggle, trying to challenge them, especially since they were getting older—now ten, twelve and fourteen.

Unfortunately, one's success is often measured by one's career, and I had not had one for an awfully long time. My well-educated and focused husband was wealthy, even if his job wasn't always stable. However, his sense of financial insecurity wasn't very healthy. His expectations were difficult to achieve; he wanted a traditional wife to cook and clean and yet he reminded me constantly about my lack of earning, calling me lazy and saying I lacked priorities, which made me feel guilty.

"Why did you give up on your career? You went to school for so many years and worked so hard to get educated and then you threw it all away. You sit around all day eating bonbons and watching soap operas. What has your life amounted to?"

Whenever we had this conversation, he always spoke with a tone of disappointment. I would hold my breath and close my eyes just long enough to swallow the pain I felt. We had made the decision together for the family, but he liked to remind me it was my fault and I was a failure.

It was hard to wrap my head around going back to work full-time. I knew if I really wanted a fulfilling career, I would have to give it my all and I wouldn't be able to have a healthy work/life balance. A part of me also felt like I should be putting my time and talent into something I was passionate about, not a career I had been forced into.

It wasn't just my husband. Friends would ask, "Why be a housewife, why not go back to work? Why take care of your husband and give up on your own success?" I always felt judged, the same narrative repeated back to me, that I had so much "potential", but that I did "nothing" with it.

Even my parents were disappointed. Even though I had done everything they had asked of me, it was not enough. They expected me to do everything at once: juggle raising three "perfect" kids, be a full-time mom, the "perfect" wife, and the CEO of a Fortune 500 company while also volunteering, working out and making Sunday dinners for the extended family.

I felt a lot of pressure to be a lot of different things to a lot of different people while not really knowing what I wanted for myself. I was still trying to figure out "what I wanted to be when I grew up". Even if I tried to defend myself, my place and value in the relationship, my husband couldn't understand. I had lost my confidence and felt unworthy.

At least, my husband and I had always had trust in our marriage, because without it there would be no marriage, but recently even that had been falling apart. I no longer trusted him with our finances and he didn't trust me with my intentions in the marriage. I had lost interest because I felt I didn't have a say in any of the financial decisions. He felt I wasn't committed to our relationship anymore because I needed more excitement and emotional connection. To a degree, it was true. We needed things we couldn't give each other. I felt so suffocated.

Recently my husband and I were becoming steadily more disconnected, both of us feeling betrayed by the other. We needed to find a fix or I feared a separation might be a reality.

I was dedicated to the family. I really was. I wasn't ready to give up on the marriage, and I didn't want to raise my kids alone. He was a good man and a loving father, but he was withdrawn and unavailable.

It hadn't always been that way. We were so happy, so physical. But the burden of married life had started to weigh us down. It was still physical, just not as happy.

I know, life, marriage, time, getting older; it all changes you, but fundamentally, I didn't feel right. I was hungry for change. I didn't know what that looked like, but I knew I needed something. The house I called a home felt more like a prison and I was trapped. I had entered the bonds of marriage and I was tied to them. My life was full but my heart was empty. I felt I was living a lie. Maybe I was going through some sort of crisis, I wasn't sure. But I was going through something.

I needed a break; no, I deserved a break. I wanted some adventures and experiences to call my own. Getting married young and being a busy and tired mom of three, I didn't always have a lot of time to myself. Having five days to myself with my best friend Carmen was going to be amazing. She had this energy that brought out the best in me, and this trip was exactly what we both needed. For the kids' sake, I pretended to be unhappy that I was going to be missing the camping trip, but inside, I was a little excited, no, extremely excited to have some time to myself.

When the boys had started planning their camping trip, I had told Carmen about my idea. Tess and Jenna couldn't make it, but I didn't mind; I was looking forward to some bonding with my best friend. It would be the longest I would be away from the boys since being in hospital, but I wasn't going to let my mom-guilt get to me. We were going to be taking a road trip. Starting in Kelowna, making our way through the Okanagan Valley to see all the beauty of British Columbia. Wineries, orchards, beaches, and even a day trip to an ashram for meditation and yoga. Really, what more could a (middle-aged) girl ask for? No husbands interfering, no parents lecturing, no kids nagging, just us.

Carmen was going to call me any minute now. I was feeling anxious because I was really looking forward to the getaway. In the 20 years of marriage and being a stay-at-home mom, I hadn't had many opportunities to myself. This was going to be the longest I would be away from the boys and I wasn't going to let my mom-guilt get to me.

All my life, I had done what I was supposed to. My parents were conservative and that clashed with my free will and liberal-minded viewpoints. They had moved to Canada from India in the 1970s and brought me up to be a good, traditional Indian girl. I was sheltered and protected from the "real" world, but my heart ached for freedom. Through my mom's eyes, the western world was full of sex, drinking, corruption, and it was no good.

They had a future planned out for me and I had to listen to them. I had no choice; they were my parents. If I did try to find a voice, they never approved, there was accusations, guilt trips and consequences involved. I had no real say over my life, it was dictated for me, but presented as a choice. I had to be obedient, fulfill my obligations, and be a dutiful daughter. My father was controlling and my mother was manipulating.

I had studied to get the degree my father wanted me to have. In his eyes, I needed a professional career, one that was respectable and demanding. There was no time for nonsense like a gap year. Immigrant mentality meant I was brought up with more responsibility, a hard work ethic, and no option to fail. I needed to rise above the rest, be courageous, mature, better.

My mother thought otherwise. "Why do you need to be a doctor or an engineer? Those jobs are for men. You should be a good girl and not so strong. Boys will get scared and not want to marry you; marriage and kids matter most."

My mother just wanted me married, settled and no longer a burden to the family. Even before I had completed my degree, my mother started proposing the idea of an arranged marriage. She tried to console me, "I know I don't always say the right things and the things I say aren't always what you want to hear, but this is all I know. I am doing this for you."

I had protested. "But Ma, must I remind you that we are living in the twenty-first century and not in India? No one, and I mean no one in all of North America gets an arranged marriage anymore. There are no dowries and I can take care of myself, I don't need a man or a husband. And if you would actually look at what's going on in India, you would see that they are more modern than your backwards way of thinking. Why can't I date—take my time, meet someone special, fall in love, maybe even live together to see if it makes sense first? Or not get married at all."

I'm surprised she didn't die of shock. Love was impractical, and living together was worse than sin, if there was such a thing.

It didn't matter how much I argued, the plan was already being hatched back in India. When ads in the local newspaper (I am not kidding) didn't pan out and a friend of a friend's cousin wasn't working out either, my grandmother had been contacted. Surprisingly, she was more practical than my Ma, realizing a typical arranged marriage wasn't going to work for me—a long distance relationship or a man directly from India wouldn't suit me. They needed to find someone who would be modern enough for me yet who understood tradition.

They were concerned that they wouldn't be able to control me much longer. Time was being wasted and they needed to see me married off as quickly as possible. I was becoming a spinster and would be undesirable and too old for children. I was twenty-one.

While attending a business class at university, there had been an industry mentor running some real-life scenarios during lectures. He was very serious about his assignment. He had noticed me and instead of just talking to me, he had decided to torment me.

"Miss Karina, please come up here and show us how you could go about firing an employee." He pointed at me and called me down using his index finger, gesturing to the front of the class.

I was mortified, I had never even had a job, let alone fired someone. I thoroughly embarrassed myself during the exercise, giggling the whole time. I later realised that it was his way to get me to stay after class.

I had mentioned to my mom that he was boring, brown and that he picked on me in class. My mom immediately honed in on him being brown and used the community grapevine to get in contact with him.

Before I knew it, a convenient meeting had been set up by my parents. Outside of class, he was soft-spoken and timid. He was also much older than me. They hoped his calm demeanour would tame my restlessness. They knew my strong personality and boundless energy could be difficult. This way, they could make it seem like they were giving me more freedom, when in reality, I would no longer be their problem.

Too ambitious to settle, I told him I wasn't interested and we went our separate ways. I needed to see what else was out there, behind my mother's back; experience what little freedom I could. There was a brief period I found ways to bend the rules and let myself be me and do what I wanted.

My parents were still determined to have me settle down with the right man, the stable guy who was the safe choice; the one that would take care of me. They weren't concerned that he would limit me. They didn't give up that easily. We "met" up again and started dating (mostly family dinners and chaperoned outings). I wasn't ready for anything serious, I was too young, but things were set in motion. I hadn't even finished school.

The day after graduation, I started working at a company my father had lined up for me. Taking any time off was not allowed. The idea of moving out was unacceptable even though I was earning money; I had to live at home under the watchful eye of my mother. Plus, money was for saving, not for wasting on rent, at the bar, travelling with friends, or on material goods. I tried to live what I could of my own life, but it was hard.

Shortly thereafter, he proposed marriage. There was no romance, no love, but he was a good option, he was the only choice. I knew my husband-to-be wanted an ideal, devoted wife, but he tried to convince me otherwise.

"I know you aren't ready to settle down, but I want to be with you. But no pressure, you should follow your dreams. I will support you. I'm not like typical Indian husbands, I grew up in Canada and understand the liberties of women. I want to make you happy. I cherish you and love you and I want the best for you. I promise I will give you whatever you want."

Don't get me wrong, I loved my Indian heritage, with its rich culture, delicious food and festive ceremonies. I loved preparing meals from scratch and dressing up in colourful ornate saris. I attended celebrations, painted my eyes in dark kajal, and wore bold costume jewelry. But I am not sure how much my wedding had to do with me. I was not ready for a life of commitment, months of preparations, or a hysterical mother. My friends were still single or dating, living life, working on their careers and figuring themselves out. I had barely lived my life; I wasn't ready to share it with someone else.

Yet a wedding date was set. It was a whirlwind six months. It started with a blessing, then the engagement, another blessing, an engagement party, another blessing.

Indian marriage ceremonies are long, complicated and drawn out.

The celebrations lasted a week and no expenses were spared. It was festive, colourful, vibrant and exciting, but there was a process, a show to put on for the extended family, the community, and my parents' peer group. I was put on display. More was spent on saris and jewellery to compensate for me not being skinny or fair, but I was smart, had childbearing hips, and was "homely" (a good quality to have in my culture).

There was a mehndi party, a halud (turmeric) ceremony, a photo shoot, meeting the priest, Aiburo bhath (final meal as an unmarried woman) and then blessings in between each event. There were over one hundred guests assembled for the ceremony in my parents' backyard. The wedding itself was hours with the priest, fires, and rituals. Everything was in Sanskrit. It was epic.

The reception was in a beautiful hotel ballroom the day after with close to three hundred guests. It was supposed to be the happiest time of my life. My parents put so much into it, but a part of me felt like I was only there for the show.

After we got married, I moved into his place. I had never lived on my own or done my own thing. Even the simple pleasures of picking my own linens, dishes, and housewares were robbed from me. His mother had bought it all and gifted it to us, all to her taste.

I know my husband wanted to make me happy, but not at the expense of his own needs. I had to put him first. If I tried to do something for myself, he would get nasty and bitter. I started to give in to more of his needs, but the more I did, the more of myself I lost. After a while, that's all I knew.

Marriage represented convenience and a vessel for children, not love, attraction, or passion. That is the primary reason brown girls get married, to start producing. My husband had said "no pressure", but before I knew it, I was pregnant. Everything had changed too quickly; I wasn't even aware of it happening. My life began to feel like a blur: getting pregnant, buying a house in the burbs, not finishing graduate school, getting pregnant again, quitting my job, trying to finish my degree, getting pregnant again, buying a minivan, trying to find a job.

I had kids, no job and was supposed to live happily ever after. Not quite sure I was doing that. My husband was happy, my parents relieved, which meant happy, for them. My children were a joy but they had broken me to no fault of their own other than from being children who needed their mother.

I had checked off all the boxes. Except now, I no longer knew who I was. I had always listened and supported those around me. I gave, and gave, and gave. But I never got what I was promised. I felt betrayed. I could no longer follow along or listen to others. Something had awakened in me. I needed to reinvent myself. I was done feeling guilty.

My phone rang and brought me back to reality. It was Carmen. I answered and could hear sobbing on the other end of the line.

"Hello, Carmen, is that you?" I asked, confused.

"Hi, Karina, it's me. I am so sorry. This is terrible, but it's my husband!" She sounded really upset and began to speak louder and faster. "He...he, I don't know where to begin. This morning when I was doing laundry, I checked his pockets, and there it was. A pair of pink lace panties that weren't mine! I didn't know what to do. So, I grabbed them and stormed into the kitchen where he was sitting enjoying his favourite breakfast I had prepared. As he was about to smile, I held them up by one finger and dangled them in front of his nose.

"He started to choke and before he could say anything, he grabbed for his chest. Next thing I knew, he was having a heart attack. I dropped the panties and called 911.

"The ambulance arrived and rushed us to the hospital. He's not doing well. In all the chaos, I completely forgot to call you. You know that's not like me, since we've been planning this trip for months. But now, everything is a mess. He's going to be in the hospital for at least a few days. I don't have anyone to help care for him. There's no way I can leave. Everything is a mess! How can this be happening? Everything is a mess!" I heard her take a breath before the line went silent.

I was numb. I didn't know what I was more upset about, my best friend's husband cheating on her, his heart attack, or the fact that she was cancelling this trip that had been so important.

I took a deep breath, ready to drop everything and be by her side. That's what best friends do; they take charge when the other one is falling apart. "Don't worry, we got this. I'm coming over, I'll take care of everything," I said. Although I was afraid, I was also falling apart, but I needed to be there for her.

Carmen's voice thundered on the end of the line. "Are you crazy? There's no way you're not going on this trip!" I could see her longer than shoulder length dark straight hair swaying back and forth and her fiery brown eyes boring into me as she shook her head. "You have to do this, for you. If I can find a way, I will join you. And we'll keep in touch while you're there. You have five days to make this your own thing."

"You want me to go, alone?" I asked, feeling bummed. "How much fun would that be?"

Sounding so practical and full of wisdom even though she was a good eight years younger than me, she replied, "You know how much you need this trip. This is for you to do something for yourself. Think of it as a rejuvenation retreat. You need to recharge; you're so drained, you don't even recognize it. You can spoil yourself, indulge a little, and have fun. You might even make some new friends. You will come back a new person, ready for all the hardships and challenges of being a mom and wife. I know you love your family, but you deserve this."

She took a breath before she continued, "And I will be okay. If I need you, I will call you. You got this. I've got this. We've got this." Carmen said it in such a matter-of-fact manner that I felt like I was the one going through something.

I smiled to myself, thinking back to the day we met. I had joined a baby group, something inexperienced mothers-to-be do when trying to learn a thing or two about becoming a mom. I was reluctant when I had walked into that shabby little room, not knowing what to expect.

A fuddy-duddy, elderly nurse stood at the front. It felt like she was already judging me because she made me feel like she knew everything about parenting. And then, this tiny girl walked in, timid and frightened. She had big brown eyes, lightly tanned skin, and jet-black hair.

She looked lost so I called her over. She explained how she had accidentally gotten pregnant at the age of seventeen. She wanted to keep the baby, and her boyfriend had promised to take care of her. Now, she needed to learn a thing or two about parenting.

We started chatting about the men in our lives, being pregnant and how our lives were going to change in a few short months. We figured that the nurse teaching the class didn't like either one of us and wasn't really teaching us anything. If we were going to survive, we needed to stick together.

It was convenient that we lived close to each other and could carpool and grab a coffee after class. Over time, we became friends, best friends.

Carmen was smart, strong, and beautiful. She had an aura that made you feel warm and comforted when you were in her presence. She had wanted to be a yoga teacher before she got pregnant, and I knew she would be the perfect teacher. She was full of life, energy, and excitement. She wanted to learn new things and teach people how to be better versions of themselves.

After she got pregnant, she was so scared; scared for herself, her baby, and what was going to happen to her. Her boyfriend was so much older, but he loved her and wanted to take care of her. So, they got married.

Unfortunately, things didn't quite work out the way she had planned. About eighteen weeks into the pregnancy, she felt unwell and had lots of pain. Then the bleeding started. By the time I got the phone call, it was over. She was in the hospital, and the baby was gone. She was heartbroken. But she was strong, she would get through it. I was so torn. I was still pregnant and I was trying to comfort her while trying not to remind her of what she had lost, but I knew she could try again.

Six months later, I had a baby boy and she was now married and pregnant again. I couldn't have been happier for her. This time, she didn't even make it to fourteen weeks.

I got pregnant again with my second, and she was a little more broken. By the time I had had my third, she had lost her fourth. She was a shell of herself.

The only thing that got her through it was becoming a second mother to my kids and finding comfort at my place. Each pregnancy drove her husband further from her and she started to lose herself.

She needed something; she couldn't carry on that way. Her home had become toxic and the house always felt empty. She wanted to spend her time with people, connecting with them and helping them to redefine their lives. It was her way of healing.

She decided to finish her yoga training and completed her fitness and Buti certification; she even dabbled in pole and aerial fitness. She focused on her mind and body, wanting to find a way to make herself stronger even when she felt they were betraying her.

The harder she pushed her body—the more it hurt, twisted, turned, stretched, and balanced—the better she felt. The pain was a way to help her cope. And when she pushed past the point of pain, she felt pride.

I was so proud of her for accomplishing what she did. I never had the ability to do my training. I was more brains than body. I took her classes whenever I could, trying new things in her basement studio, usually making more of a fool of myself. Sometimes I did it on purpose because it made her laugh and I missed her smile.

Now, just as she had finally started redefining herself and finding happiness again, her world had been destroyed yet again by her cheating husband. But I knew she was strong enough to get through it as she had so many times before. And she always had me.

Remembering I was still talking to Carmen, I smiled into the phone and said, “On one condition, you take care of yourself as well. Make sure you call Jenna and book an extra-long massage. I know you could use one. I will text you. Love you beautiful.”

“I will,” she assured me. “On another note, was Arj…I mean, was ‘hubby’ happy about the trip, or should I say ‘husband’?”

Even when she was going through so much, she always took the time to make sure I was okay.

Carmen and I had this running joke that I never referred to my husband by name. Culturally, it was disrespectful to refer to your spouse by name; for us, it was an inside joke. When things were good, I referred to him as hubby; when he treated me badly, it was always husband.

I paused, not sure how to answer. My silence was revealing enough for Carmen to understand.

"Husband it is. I can tell. I am so sorry sweetie. Hang in there, we will get through this."

Reluctantly, I hung up the phone. I took a deep breath, looking down at my phone, reading the text she had just sent, "I will be fine. You will be fine. Get in the car and go on this trip for you. Love you. Carmen".

Chapter 2

The Text Message

Buzz. Buzz. Buzz. It was my phone again. I thought it was another text from Carmen, but when I glanced down, it was a message from a familiar number. My heart skipped a beat and made me impulsively smile. It was Marcelo. A friend of a friend I had met once, about a year ago on my trip to Montreal. It was a brief visit—intense, but brief.

My ever so practical husband had convinced me we needed to attend a three-day conference in Montreal for a new idea he had come up with. I have no idea why he had decided to become an accountant because his interest had always been in engineering and electronics. He enjoyed building and tinkering in the garage and basement, both of which he had converted into work stations.

One day, he had an idea. It was the most delighted I had ever seen him. He was bored with looking at numbers and wanted to design something, so he decided to create a prototype. He travelled to factories in China for parts and production and began investing heavily. It was so far removed from anything he had ever done; I was worried he wasn't experienced enough to pull it off. I had heard about con artists duping people with fake factories and facilities. He was a brilliant accountant, but entrepreneurship was not his strong suit.

When I spoke to him about my concerns, he made it clear he thought otherwise. "Woman, your place is in the kitchen, don't worry your pretty little head about it." I didn't want to fight, so I let it go. He also seemed to overlook the fact that I was the one with a business degree.

Tens of thousands of dollars were spent on his design—market research, aesthetics and demand weren't things he had really considered. I tried to reason with him about an untested product, but he was on a mission. And I had dinners to cook and boys to look after.

He figured that the best way to get his product to market would be to attend this "sure thing" conference. I wasn't so sure; it seemed overpriced; I couldn't wrap my head around it. He was determined that the high entry fees would ensure more visitors and customers. I didn't think this was a guarantee, but he had invested over two hundred thousand dollars and needed to continue his mission. Money that we may never recover.

I was never allowed to interfere where finances were concerned. I had convinced myself, that it was never my money. I hadn't earned it, so I didn't deserve to spend it.

We made a choice, that for the children, I would stay home. I put my career on hold, I didn't know any better, that's how my mom had done it. I didn't have anything, no career, no ability to take care of myself. Of course, the money was ours, we were in this marriage together. I worked hard by staying at home and taking care of the family. But I had nothing to show for it and I felt like it could all be taken away.

I started to change my behaviour. My husband earned, I saved. When he lost his job, I saved even more. I let the money take control of my life in a negative way; I didn't spend and I worried. And my husband made sure it stayed that way.

The awful part was that my husband had accused me of not having any financial sense or appreciation of "earning" money. He didn't want me to have any financial freedom. He wanted to control me and if I wanted to do something for myself, he saw it as a threat to the marriage.

Treating me this way wasn't healthy. I always used to be afraid that if I left, I wouldn't know what to do about money or how to support the kids. Now, I felt like I would find a way, because keeping me trapped wasn't going to work.

I hated thinking like that. I always thought we were in it together, wanting the same things, to save money for a common purpose, to spend it on our dreams. Piece by piece, I had given up on me.

I had hoped that this trip away from the kids to a fun city like Montreal, even if it was for a conference, would help revitalize our marriage. Prior to the trip, he had been so focused on research and development that he had started to get lost in it. When he wasn't busy with his accounting contracts, he spent every waking moment building, testing, and implementing. When he wasn't thinking about the design itself, he was distracted thinking about a logo, graphics, the website, or his online presence. He didn't have time for the kids, family, friends, or quality time at home. He definitely didn't have time for me.

The last time we had been to Montreal was just after we had gotten married. I would never have been allowed to travel with a man before marriage. It had been an unforgettable trip; we had toured about Old Montreal, checked out Quebec City, and enjoyed the sites. While we were there, we met up with a few of my friends from university; Daryl, who had moved there recently for a job, and Tess, who was attending a medical conference for the weekend. Both were unattached and in their early twenties. Daryl was full of life, had great energy, and was very charismatic. He was all about the party and wanted to show us a good time. Tess was a sweetheart, but she was reserved and all business. Although we were all friends, Daryl was very into Tess. I knew she had a thing for him, but she was too uptight to do anything about it.

That night was full of surprises. Daryl took charge and tricked us all into going to the infamous Cabaret Le 281. "Let's check out this casual lounge, I think you will like it..." he had said. Well, it turned out to be more than just a lounge, if you know what I mean. The iconic Montreal institution was known for its erotic shows for women. Tess was "educated", and hubby was traumatized and barely survived. Daryl and I enjoyed ourselves a little too much.

After stimulating our senses, we decided to stimulate our taste buds. We found a poutine shop at 3:00 a.m. where we ate greasy, cheese curdy, gravy-drenched fries and enjoyed every bite! I missed those days.

This time around, we would be in Montreal for the conference for four days and I had left the kids with my parents and it would be just me and my husband. Unfortunately, the conference didn't go as planned. The vision of his product did not align with market demand. Few visitors and even fewer customers proved that we had spent a whole lot of money on a whole lot of nothing. For a man with financial insecurities, he didn't know how to manage business very well. I felt more distant and like he blamed me somehow.

As a distraction to the business side of things, the conference hosted a social gathering one evening. Hubby was excited to be able to hang out with his techy buddies, sharing their ideas and not worrying about the finances. He wanted to drag me along.

"It'll be a blast, Karina, I am sure you can find something to do. I am excited to talk about the newest model of the..." He was flailing his arms around as he spoke, thrilled about the latest and greatest. Once he started talking model numbers, he lost me.

Tagging along seemed better than sitting alone in the hotel room, but I was wrong. I was bored, so bored. There I was, in one of the most vibrant and exotic cities in Canada with amazing night life, wicked music and even more wicked night clubs and my husband wanted to talk drones, gaming, mobility, television, VR goggles, space and who knows what else. I was completely out of my element. And I was miserable the entire time. Well, almost the entire time.

That night, Daryl called me, as he still lived in Montreal. We had kept in touch over the years and he was still all about having a good time. I had messaged him before we had left Calgary to let him know I would be in town for the electronics conference.

"Karina, darling, how are you? Enjoying the conference, I'm sure? If you don't have plans for tonight, I would love to take you out. Do you think you can get away from your adoring husband for a few hours?" he said over the phone in his deep, husky voice. He was cute that way, calling me instead of texting.

I looked over at hubby; he wasn't paying any attention to me. I knew he wouldn't miss me for a few hours.

"Daryl, it's so good to hear from you. Yes, I could use a night out, all this tech stuff is getting to me. What did you have in mind?" I could feel myself getting a little giddy at the chance to see something in Montreal outside of the conference.

"Be ready in thirty minutes sweetheart. I'll pick you up. Can't wait to catch up and show you a good time, hun!"

The sound of his voice excited me. And to be going out, I couldn't wait!

I kissed my hubby's slightly wrinkly brown head, wrapped my arms around his pudgy waistline, his pot belly protruding under his untucked shirt, and smiled as he looked at me through his brow-lined glasses. I don't even think he noticed when I told him I would be heading out for a few hours to check out a club with Daryl. He was having a great time. Besides, he wasn't much of a drinker and even less of a dancer. He didn't like lounges or bars, with their loud music and flashing lights. He was also twelve years older than me, so he just wasn't up for going out and partying. In all honesty, I think he was relieved he didn't have to "entertain" me for the night, and he knew Daryl was trustworthy.

Daryl had always had a special place in my heart. I had known him for the better part of my adult life, and although there were sparks between us, he had always been a gentleman. He was patient with me in a way most men would not be. After graduating, our paths had crossed briefly at work. He knew about my parents forcing me to get married and my husband being a home body. I told him I was struggling to find friends, working in a male-dominated field and being the only married girl there. At work, I had to pretend to be one of the guys, always putting up a tough front to fit in and compete. With Daryl, he let me be more feminine. He would take me for coffee, run with me along the river on my lunch breaks, and even introduced me to snowboarding and to golf, which required a special kind of patience. We would use work as an excuse to get out so my hubby wouldn't be able to object as much. I didn't know there were men like Daryl out there.

The first time Daryl took me dancing, my youngest had just turned eight. I hadn't been to a lounge or club in years. At first, I thought I was doing something wrong, being married and going out with another man. But when he wooed me with his loving arms, his fancy footwork, and his affectionate words, I realized he was mine, in a unique way; he was pleasure and fantasy, yet he was completely trustworthy. There was respect, boundaries, and I felt secure. I was his, yet I was his friend. I felt lucky to have him.

Realizing I didn't want to miss out on this opportunity with Daryl, I quietly slipped out from the conference social, went up to the hotel room, and decided to get dolled up. It had been so long since I had had an opportunity to do that. It didn't mean I didn't like doing it, I just didn't get to do it very often. I was out of practice. But I had also learned to get ready efficiently living in a household with four men! So, thirty minutes was an eternity with the bathroom all to myself.

Earlier that day, hubby had been manning the booth, so I snuck out of the silly electronics conference for an hour, hoping to get a coffee. I never believed in retail therapy until I discovered its therapeutic effects when dealing with life. Unfortunately, I couldn't spend a lot of money since I didn't earn much, which made it tricky, so I had to get as creative as I could.

As I walked down a few streets, I saw a shopping district. I saw a Guess store. I had always wanted to shop there but never had. I figured I couldn't afford it, and besides, I thought that such a trendy store would probably only carry things for tall, skinny models. It would never tailor to someone like me, an old, boring housewife. I figured nothing would fit or look good on my tired, jiggly body.

Standing at the door of Guess, I felt like I should turn back. But somehow, I mustered up some courage, stood up straight, and decided to walk in and check it out. I managed to find a clearance rack and fumbled through the hangers sheepishly. Nothing was in my size and it was looking hopeless when something caught my eye—like it was meant to be.

Hanging on the clearance rack was a sleek, sexy, stretchy, black jumpsuit with spaghetti straps to show off your shoulders, a low cut back, a peek-a-boo slot across the midriff, and long slits thigh high up the outside of each leg. It had a "75% off" tag on it. I figured it must have been torn or that the zipper was broken, but when I stepped into the changing room to try the outfit on, as I slowly slid the soft fabric over my body, not only did it fit like a glove, but there was nothing wrong with it! I was so giddy! I am sure the cashier thought I was nuts—there I was raving about some outfit from last season from the clearance rack, but I loved it. I wasn't sure I would get the opportunity to wear it, but I had to have it.

It was certainly a "fun" outfit you could wear to a club, not something you could get away with at a conference like this. I was so glad I had bought it because nothing else in my wardrobe would've been suitable for going out that night with Daryl. I cut the tag off, slipped it on, and took off my comfy conference shoes, slipping into my 4" black wedges. I applied some smoky eyeshadow, carefully lined my big, bright, brown eyes with dark midnight kajal, applied mascara to elevate what was left of my lashes, filled in my brows with powder, added some blush to my already rosy cheeks, and put on my favourite shade of blood-red matte lipstick.

I caught a glimpse of myself in the full-length mirror. Instead of recoiling, I decided to check myself out.

My lips looked so amplified, bold and painted. My brown eyes looked even bigger and sexier outlined in eyeliner. My cheeks were slightly flushed. And the new jumpsuit was slimming and flattering, hiding the lumps, bumps, and unevenness of my body. I actually looked kinda hot! I couldn't help by smile back at myself.

Daryl would be picking me up in ten minutes. I scrunched some volumizer into my hair and spritzed on my favourite perfume, Coco Chanel. I was ready for a night out!

I hadn't seen Daryl in at least two years, but the moment he pulled up his tiny little black hybrid to the curb in front of the hotel, we picked up just where we had left off.

"Hello gorgeous, you look mighty fine this evening," he smiled as he planted a gentle kiss on my cheek and wrapped his arms around me. Kissing on the cheek must be a Montreal thing.

"You look absolutely giddy. Don't get your hopes up, I'm not taking you to a sex club or an exotic massage parlour!" he joked knowing the commotion it had caused the last time.

"I don't care where you take me, I'm just excited to go out and have you on my arm! Besides, we will have to save that for the next time I come to visit and don't have a husband in tow!" I said only half-jokingly as I wrapped my arm in his and squeezed. If only.

I was feeling bold and sexually charged, alive and ready for what the evening would bring. Although I knew it was a simple outing, I felt so thrilled to be able to get away from the family environment and just be myself. I was feeling confident. Dressed up and on the arm of a gorgeous man was making me feel sensual. I knew Daryl's heart belonged elsewhere; he had never really gotten over Tess. He still asked about her whenever I saw him. I also wasn't into him, not like that, but he brought out a confidence in me that I hadn't felt in a while. I didn't need anything crazy, but I loved dancing, which I was hoping to do. That would be enough.

Daryl was easy going and smooth. He had this confidence about him that oozed. He always made you feel desired. Maybe it was his smile or the way he wrapped his arms around you. Or the way he always used words like "darling", "sweetheart" or "hun" in that velvety voice and paid extra attention to details, complimenting constantly. It could be the delicious way he smelled when he stood near you or the stylish dancing shoes that went along with his finely picked outfits. Or the washboard abs that went along with the rest of his toned, muscular, dark chocolate brown body. Whatever the case, I loved being on this man's arm.

And before I forget to mention it, could this man dance! He could spin you around on the floor like a top even if you had no idea what you were doing. He always showed you a great time and made you feel like a goddess, while managing to remain respectful while doing it. He had a gift.

"Speaking of good times, Tess was talking about you the other day," I dropped in casually as we walked to the bar.

"How is Tess?" Daryl asked sheepishly. "I haven't been able to convince her to come visit me, maybe you'll have to bring her someday." For a man so charismatic, it surprised me how shy he was around Tess.

"She's good, always busy with work and too proud and independent to admit she's in need of a good man. You should call or visit; you know she's too practical to visit you."

I walked into the bar on Daryl's arm and felt a weight lift off me, allowing me to breathe and take it all in. The vibe of the busy bar that had its own personality, the energy of the place excited me—the pretty bar staff, an outrageous number of bridal parties with sweet young ladies in tight bodysuits and short skirts with tiaras and veils on and the steady crowd of gorgeous men who were ready to please. I was feeling vulnerable and bold. Maybe that's the definition of desperation, but it felt raw and satisfying. I really wanted to have a good time and felt drawn to the dance floor.

Daryl had invited some of his friends to join us. He had asked me to be "nice", show his friends a good time, and keep them company, mostly because his friends were a little introverted, perhaps even a little geeky. I laughed when he described them as such; since we were all in our late thirties or early forties, I thought we were past all that junior high nonsense. It's a good thing I loved a challenge, and I found men easy to get along with.

Hoping to order a drink, I tried to get the bartender's attention. I was completely flustered by how absolutely gorgeous he was with his Mediterranean features and tight black pants that accented his ass. It had been so long since I had been out. I watched as he rotated his hips as he mixed drinks. I had to remind myself to stop staring. He was way too distracting; a level of sexy that just didn't exist in my current realm of moms and housewives. It would have been fun to dance with him if he were available. He wasn't.

When Daryl introduced me to the "Italian fellows", I could tell right away they were going to be entertaining and a challenge. One of the guys, whose name I can't remember, was gorgeous in his own way; he was ripped with lots of tattoos and a few piercings. He had on a tight button-down shirt that was unbuttoned to show off his gold chain and chest. He had short, dark, spiky hair and sported a thin-lined goatee. He had dark, dreamy, brown eyes and a bad boy grin. And he smelled almost as good as Daryl; just maybe slightly overdone the cologne a little. He was more than happy to show off his tattoos and get up close and personal. As much as I was enjoying the attention, when the conversation drifted from travel to cocaine and fetishes, I knew I needed to move on. I wasn't ready for that level of intensity.

Then, Daryl introduced me to Marcelo, and I knew I had my work cut out for me. He was so shy and unsure at first. But I had been instructed to be nice, so I was going to do my best. There was something intriguing about him and I was curious to see what he was all about. He had this hidden confidence about him. Even though he looked nervous, I could tell he was sizing me up from the moment he laid eyes on me. I didn't feel that it was necessarily in a physical way, almost in a healthy competitive way—like he was evaluating whether I was worthy enough to talk to him. He seemed like an intellectual, not arrogant, but reserved. I could tell he was curious about me as well.

I was determined to have some fun with this guy. I figured he might try and push me intellectually, but I would push him physically. I wasn't afraid to be a little provocative and flirty. It was just one night, and I knew I had Daryl to rescue me if I couldn't handle myself.

At first, I couldn't tell if he was pale because of the lighting in the bar or if the colour had drained from his face because he had to talk to me. He had a smooth complexion and a clean appearance, with faint stubble along his chiselled jawline, gorgeous gray-green eyes, dark hair, broad shoulders and defined biceps. He was wearing a simple, blue golf shirt that rested on his broad shoulders and dark blue faded jeans. I don't think he was wearing sneakers, but I couldn't tell you for sure.

He was a man of few words. He was poised, sophisticated, and well mannered, while being thoughtful and mysterious. He was some sort of Ph.D. in some technical field: physics or pharmacy, something that started with a "ph". I was so intoxicated by the vibe in the bar, that I lost focus on what he said he did. He was clearly very intelligent and specialized in his area of expertise. He had written and published many papers and had presented at multiple conferences—flying around the world, all expenses paid. He mentioned genomes and double-blind studies, which oddly enough interested rather than bored me. When meeting new people, I felt I was always more attracted to how knowledgeable they were. It was actually a turn on. I was charmed by his clever yet subtly sexy manner. It's what had initially intrigued me about my husband.

Once, my friend Tess had joked with me, "You know what you are, right? You're a sapiosexual. You find people's minds attractive." She loved to label things with her medical ideas and figured I had a condition.

"Yah, you are probably right, I find intelligence to be incredibly sexy." I had laughed, "but I prefer the term "nymphobrainiac", it sounds smarter!"

"Whatever it is," she had replied, "you definitely have it. Now you just have to find people who can challenge you on that level. You need a man that can stimulate your mind and your senses. Not sure hubby is doing either these days!" The look she gave me made me realize she was right. Maybe I would someday.

I looked over at Marcelo and thought maybe I had met my match; I was mesmerised with all his talk about his work and the research he was doing. I was in awe of his lifestyle: the freedom, the respect he had in his industry, the success. He wasn't showing off at all, but whatever he was talking about got technical pretty quick. I did my best to keep up, and then I thought I could fake it, until I couldn't because he was losing even himself talking about his research. It was adorable. And I was losing myself staring into his gorgeous eyes or following his hypnotic yet cryptic smile.

He laughed nervously when I worked dancing into the conversation. He was intrigued but embarrassed by my forwardness. He laughed at my jokes, made eye contact, and held my gaze when we spoke. When he asked about my kids, he didn't make me feel like a tired old mom, but someone who was successful and ambitious in the way I was raising them. He didn't see me as boring and useless when I told him I filled my time knitting when I had nothing else to do; he made me feel important and smart. He saw me as educated and independent. He had a different perspective on life and on me; it was refreshing.

He had a quirky sense of humour. He talked in puns and innuendos and made comical connections that most people wouldn't recognize but which made me smile. I had never met a man who could be so smart and funny at the same time. I was enjoying his company, and I was excited about getting to know him better.

I think, above all else, it was his attentiveness that really caught me off guard. From the moment we laid eyes on each other, I felt something. There was something intriguing about this man but I wanted nothing more than an evening of fun and harmless distraction.

Daryl had ordered me a dark Appleton rum and coke, knowing I wasn't capable of ordering or finishing a drink. I had no clue what Marcelo was drinking except that maybe it was clear.

I was not a drinker. My friends all made fun of me for being a cheap drunk because I was done after about two sips of alcohol. I loved to dance and talk dirty. Give me some good beats and provocative conversation and I could entertain you all night. Moving to the beat, dancing, sweating, bodies teasing, aching—it gave me a high like no other.

Daryl wrapped his arm around my waist, pulling me aside and giving me a wild grin. "I thought I should mention that Marcelo doesn't dance. So don't expect much."

"At all?" I questioned, placing my hand on his flexed bicep, knowing he was messing with me. It was impossible for someone not to dance.

"Well, in the fifteen years or so that I've known him, I have never seen him dance. And I doubt you will be able to get him off that barstool." Daryl was challenging me. We both looked over at Marcelo, he did look comfortable with a drink in his hand.

That was all the more reason I was determined to get Marcelo on the dance floor. Besides, I wanted to get a better feel for this man (no pun intended) and dancing would do just that. The eye contact, the fluid motion of our bodies, keeping the rhythm—I could learn a lot about him.

Marcelo was adamant about not getting on the dance floor, he was enjoying himself from the barstool. I decided to play along and sat down next to him. But I was still adamant about getting on the floor because I couldn't stop swaying to the music as soon as we had walked in. I didn't want to charm him or win him over that night, I only wanted to loosen him up a bit. Above all, I really wanted to dance. I am sure Daryl was laughing at my efforts and I knew I could dance with him anytime, but like I said, I enjoyed the challenge. And there was something about Marcelo. When I stared into his eyes, his gorgeous gray-green eyes, I felt like I would get lost in them. There was something haunting there, I just couldn't quite pin it down.

As it grew later and the bar became even busier, I couldn't sit any longer. I scooted closer to him, propped my elbows against the bar top, eliminating the distance between our bodies, while holding his gaze. I turned to Marcelo with an intentional look and gently placed my hands on his thighs, grazing them with my fingertips and swaying to the music while giving him an impatient yet determined look. He tried to hide his amusement, but his alluring smile betrayed him. I moved my hands back, leaning away but gently placing my leg in between his, gently nudging and spinning his chair in the direction of the dance floor. I was teasing him and coaxing him with my big brown eyes to join me on the dance floor. He was hesitant but it was clear he was intrigued as he reached out to caress my forearm.

Eventually, Marcelo was tipsy and curious enough to give me a chance, allowing me to drag him to the dance floor. When he stood up, I realized he was taller than I expected but had a great frame. He held my gaze and clasped my hand even tighter, slightly fearful as I led him to the floor. He looked so out of his element at first. I didn't want to torture him, so I eased him in gently, taking the lead, holding him close enough to feel my presence, allowing him to move with me, feel the union of two bodies. Guiding his hand, I placed it on the small of my back, allowing him to follow my flow, pressing my body against his. He was impressed at how well I could move, I was taken aback by how well his body responded. I allowed myself to close my eyes and enjoy the moment.

He undeniably surprised me that night, because what I thought was going to be awkward turned out to be mesmerizing. He was receptive to every move, paying attention and even attempting to impress me. He held me close to his body, wrapping his arms tightly around me, diminishing any space between our bodies, crouching down to make the embrace even more intimate. There were moments when I felt lost in his arms, our cheeks brushing against each other. I could feel his breath against my neck, and although I wasn't sure, his deep inhales felt like his eyes were closed, taking it all in as he squeezed me tighter against him.

He got more daring and allowed his hands to roam my body, the soft material making it easy to feel my curves under the fabric. I also had free reign to his hard body pressing up against me, spinning me around or pinning me to a bar stool. I would run my fingers across the back of his neck, down his shoulders, across his butt, and make my way back up his chest before encircling my arms around his neck while tangling my fingers in his hair. I didn't have to try at all to make him look good on the floor and I noticed women checking him out. Although the attention was probably tempting, he stayed focused on me.

"You are way more fun than Daryl made you out to be!" I said, giving him a playful smile.

"Not sure what that means," he laughed, leaning into me to get close enough for me to hear him.

I pressed my lips up against his ear, letting them brush ever so softly against his earlobe so he could hear me over the music. "In case you were fishing, it means that you are really sweet and I am having a great time hanging out with you. Not 'just' a geeky friend of Daryl's. And a super fun dancer for a guy who doesn't dance!" Although I didn't mean to, my lips brushed against his neck as I pulled away from his ear to look him in the eye. I caught my breath at the intensity of his gaze. I felt feelings awakening in me that I didn't even know existed. My husband couldn't dance and Daryl had always treated me well but never made a move on me. Marcelo stimulated me, I could tell he felt it too, the way his body was responding to mine, pressing into me, not ready to let go.

"No, not fishing, but thanks. It's fun hanging out with you too," he replied, smiling down at me. My head was spinning and I was glad he didn't let go of me.

Being introduced to Marcelo that night in Montreal had been serendipitous. A chance meeting. I wasn't sure I would ever see him again. What had started out as innocent and playful that night had become confusing; nothing had happened that I didn't want, yet there were so many things left unsaid.

The next day I had asked Daryl for Marcelo's number—I didn't have the nerve to ask him myself. Making up an excuse, I texted him the next day telling him I got his number in case I needed to find a bagel shop while in town. I was surprised when he texted back and offered to help if I found myself lost or bored.

When I had got back from Montreal, I immediately texted Carmen. Meeting at Second Cup, armed with lattes in hand, she gave me one look and said, "Honey, what's wrong? Something happened in Montreal, I can see it in your eyes, spill."

I didn't know where to begin, but I found myself blurting out, "The conference was a failure. Hubby was his usual self. I saw Daryl, I met a man, ate too much poutine, and missed the kids so much I couldn't wait to get home."

Carmen knew me too well. "Wait a minute. Look at me. That's it, that's what I see. I can see it in your eyes. You met a man? Who is he?"

I didn't feel ready to explain the intensity of what I had felt that evening to Carmen. "He's just a friend of Daryl's. It was nothing, just a silly infatuation; we danced, that's all. I'll probably never see him again."

She knew better. “That’s not all. I hope you got his number; I haven’t seen you like this in fifteen years. I hope you don’t mess it up, whatever this is.” She smiled and raised her eyebrow at me. “Sounds like love at first sight, and don’t tell me you don’t believe in love.”

I rolled my eyes at her. “Okay! I had fun. I enjoyed a man’s company, that’s all. But I *don’t* believe in love! I will probably never text him,” I covered.

Carmen countered, “Which means you already have. I’m happy for you., Don’t be afraid to think with your heart, something you have never done.”

I sat back, looking at my phone. So, there it was, a text from Marcelo. I bit my lower lip gently in anticipation of what he would have to say. I was a little surprised to hear from him but I enjoyed getting his texts. I sometimes wouldn’t read them right away, not because I was ignoring him, but because I looked forward to savouring them when I had some time to myself.

We had had this instant connection that I couldn’t quite explain, which is why I didn’t delete his contact when I got home. I found myself texting him the odd tidbit here and there. His texts usually had to do with the weather, cars, or work. Most of our conversations were short and light, but that’s what made them appealing. I think I liked that we had no history, so the situation was easy; there was no thinking or explaining required. And yet, he was witty and interesting and considerate. He was my little escape from reality.

I think, after the first few months of texting, I started to develop an obsession towards him. Don't get me wrong, not stalkerish or anything weird like that, more of a healthy obsession, something to think about on nights where I wanted to run away from the reality of my life as a large chunk of my time went to me playing chauffeur, chef, or referee to my boys. My husband was either busy in the basement, staring at his stock investments on the computer, or horny and needing attention. I fulfilled his demands in one way or another, giving myself fully without getting anything in return. He didn't recognize it, but there was a chasm growing between us. Even though the house was filled with family and there was rarely a dull moment, I felt alone. No, not alone, as I didn't mind being alone when I could find an opportunity, but I felt lonely. I longed for comfort, a sensual caress or an affectionate word; but there was only detachment and harsh conversation.

I needed distractions to keep me sane. Yes, there was running and coffee with the girls, but sometimes I needed a little more. Sometimes I was looking for a level of intensity where *my* needs might be fulfilled, but unfortunately, it only existed as an escape in my mind.

I usually developed an "obsession" every six months or so, be it a cute dad at after school pickup, a well-built sensei at the karate dojo, or a strong, flexible girl at the yoga studio. It was fun to fantasize about what it would be like to be with them. It was never serious and nothing would come of them—they weren't real. Marcelo was just the new guy to obsess about. And his intelligence added something new to the mix. And he was pretty...really pretty, which added to the charm.

Sometimes, I wondered, what if I could have him? No—who was I fooling? Maybe one night with Marcelo would be enough to make up for a lifetime of loneliness. Even though our conversations over that past year had moments of intensity and intimacy, it sparked false hope. I wanted him more than I would ever admit. I wanted the experience of him and what his life represented: independence, success, brilliance, exposure, it was far more fascinating than mine could ever be. But I wasn't prepared for him.

We often texted a lot of nonsense. I would send him all kinds of random notes if I was happy, stressed or overwhelmed. I didn't mind opening up. Marcelo was a bit of a closed book, not up for sharing much. Or maybe he was being cautious or scared? I was always a little more daring. I was even bold enough to tell him (well, text him) that I thought he had the "kindest eyes" I had ever seen. Of course, this was true, but admitting it to him was strange.

Initially, texting hadn't felt like flirting but like intellectual foreplay, but then what started off as fun and light started to become more personal and immersive.

Then one day, we had been exchanging text messages and he just stopped. Weeks went by and I heard nothing from him. I had sent a couple of messages, trying not to look pathetic or crazy. I thought for sure I had done something wrong. Dealing with high stress and chaos in my life, I was looking for some comfort, instead I got nothing.

I could feel an icky kind of desperation coming over me, which made me feel even worse, because not only did I not want this man to have that kind of power over me, but I also didn't want to want him to feel good about myself. That feeling of worthlessness and despair is hard to rationalize, and even though he wasn't a part of my life, I felt unfairly judged and neglected. It wasn't even like I knew him that well; I felt conflicted and confused.

When I finally had the courage to write to him again a month later, he replied like nothing had happened. Yet there had been underlying tension. Maybe we were getting too close or I was too much for him to handle.

In the last month or so, things had been quiet between us, I haven't heard from him other than a quick message. There was this heaviness in the air which we both ignored, like how we had left things in Montreal. I felt like our meeting had been too brief and somewhat unfinished. With all the traveling he did, I had hoped he would visit, but it hadn't worked out.

Coming back to reality, I decided that with the house empty and Carmen busy that this would be a great time to read what Marcelo had to say. His text read, "Hey, how are you?"

Before I could reply, there was another, "Guess what?"

I decided to bite. I replied, "Should I guess, or are you going to tell me?"

He wrote back, "You know how you are always telling me to come to Calgary."

"Yah," I replied.

"Well, I am here."

Here? I tried to register what he had just written. He was in Calgary. Why was he telling me this? What was he doing in Calgary?

I wrote back, "What do you mean?"

"I need a favour."

He continued, "I am stranded at the airport and need a ride."

A ride? From me? And why did he have to come into town the five days I was planning not to be here?

He wrote again, "Would you mind helping out a friend?"

A friend? He considered me a friend? Of course, I was his friend or at least a friend of a friend. And I guess I could help him out. *Why not?* I thought. My plans had fallen apart and I had nothing better to do. And that's what I was good at anyway, right, helping people?

I wrote back, "Of course, I could come to your rescue. I can pick you up in 30 minutes or so. See you soon."

My bags were already packed in the trunk of my car and I didn't feel like unpacking. I just hoped he didn't have a bunch of luggage. I grabbed my purse, phone, keys, and a light running jacket. I pressed the button to open the garage door. I couldn't help but pause every time I looked at the triple car garage. As the door opened, it allowed the sun to cast a warm glow and perfect reflection. There was an empty space for where the minivan had been. Beside it was a midnight jade SUV that belonged to my hubby.

Beside the SUV was a gorgeous, brand new, custom-wrapped, deep pink Audi RS5. This was my baby. I had bought it after being completely fed up with driving the minivan for the past twelve years. I knew my husband would never approve of such an extravagant purchase. Afterall, I was only a housewife and didn't deserve anything nice, especially if he had to pay for it. And I didn't want that either. When I finally found the courage to find a job, I was good at and that paid well, I dedicated myself to saving up for a down payment and be approved for a loan on my own terms. It was important to me. I had waited a long time and saved up. All for this car. This car that brought pure joy to my heart.

Every time I started the engine it purred to life, and when I cornered, it glided, hugging the road. I had driven a minivan for so many years that I had forgotten the thrill of driving until I had gotten back into a sexy, sporty sedan. Everyone tried to convince me to buy an SUV or a crossover, something higher off the ground and a more comfortable ride. I wasn't going to have it. I wanted something low and racy. I compromised on the two-door because that would be cruel for my boys and their long legs; besides, I didn't want them folding and marking up the seats every time they needed to get in and out. The new RS5 was a sport back, super sleek, and not to mention the 444hp beast of an engine.

I hopped into the low, racer, leather bucket seat with upgraded diamond stitching, feeling it hug my legs. As I started the engine, the vibrating massage seat came to life. I gripped my hands around the leather-wrapped steering wheel, twisting my wrists slightly to feel the smooth leather in my palms.

I pulled out of the garage and headed for the airport. It was a good thirty-five-kilometre drive but I didn't mind at all, I loved to drive the city's eight-lane ring road, which was a high-speed highway. I could easily do thirty over the marked speed limit and not even feel the road.

I had the tunes playing loud as the sun shone through the panoramic moon roof and warmed the interior. I felt oddly light and relaxed although weight had always been an issue for me. Hippy, busty, curvy, strong, and voluptuous were usually the words people used when they didn't want to say chubby. But I was okay with it; I had always been a bigger girl, well-proportioned, big thighs, and hips that wouldn't lie! I had been working out hard these past few months getting ready for this road trip. But you have to play to your strengths, right?

As I pulled into the airport, I found the exit for arrivals. Slowing down, I scanned the long airport sidewalk. I hadn't seen Marcelo in a year and when I had seen him last there had been drinking involved in a dark-lit bar. I remembered his eyes, which didn't help much when you were trying to scan a busy airport terminal. I needed to look for a tall, white guy with dark hair, possibly in black rimmed Ray Bans (as I recalled from his profile picture).

I should've asked for a door number or something. I did remember he was cute, not that that was helping. At least he was flying domestic, so that cut things down to just one airport terminal.

I had often wondered what it would be like, to see him again. We had had one awkward, confusing and incredible evening together. I felt like we were strangers yet connected as we had been texting for the last year. Those texts, although silly and mundane at times, meant the world to me. And for whatever reason I still don't understand, no matter what I wrote, whatever problems I was having or ridiculous things I said to him, he had always been there for me, not that I had ever expected it. He comforted me. He was kind, attentive and, in a long-distance, text-only kind of way, a good friend, until he couldn't, which is why things felt strained recently. I didn't know what it would be like to see him in person again.

After a few minutes of driving through the airport arrivals, I had convinced myself I had missed him; then out of the corner of my eye, I caught a glimpse of him. There he was, Marcelo, waiting outside, with a goofy yet somewhat irresistible smile on his face.

Chapter 3

So, We Meet Again

Marcelo obviously didn't recognize the car; he was probably expecting a minivan and was surprised when I pulled up next to him. I hadn't had a chance to tell him about it yet. Although I was feeling a little nervous, seeing his goofy smile made me feel good. Pushing my insecurities aside, I jumped out of the driver's seat and walked over to him, arms outstretched. I was a hugger. Even in my four-inch wedges I had to tip toe to embrace him as he was a foot taller than me. He reached around my waist, embracing me tightly, pressing me into him and holding on for a little longer than I expected. I felt him inhale deeply before letting go. I was unsteady from the sensation of our touch.

He took my hand in his as he took a step back, making it obvious that he was checking me out. He wasn't being creepy about it, just admiring.

I hadn't spoken to him in over a year, so when I heard his deep, serious, and commanding voice, I felt a shiver run up my spine.

"It's nice to see you again, Karina." He looked me up and down again. "Wow, you look amazing! You have been working out. And you smell good too, like you stepped out of a field of flowers and fruit."

It's a good thing my toffee-toned skin colour didn't blush because I was extremely embarrassed. Where was the nervous man I had met at the bar, the unsure man I had left behind in Montreal? This Marcelo was acting confident and assertive. And I wasn't used to being complimented. My husband barely even noticed me anymore.

Granted, I had put on a cute, fitted, cream-coloured summer dress that highlighted my waist and hips that came up just past my thighs. It was accented with large peach flowers. I had done my hair so that my dark curls rested just above my shoulders and put some makeup on, including my favourite shade of matte dark pink lipstick. I had spritzed on some Oscar de la Renta Rose perfume before heading out. I thought I was going away with Carmen and I liked dressing up when I could.

If he had seen me in my usual mom sweatpants and my hair up, he would not have been as impressed. I had been trying to lose some weight, the ever-vicious cycle I was continually on. I had started yoga and running more regularly. My legs were a little more toned, my waist a little smaller and my breasts a little more accentuated.

Marcelo looked quite charming himself. He had broad shoulders and muscular legs. He was wearing a simple navy-blue cotton tee shirt and fitted khaki shorts, an outfit that was flattering on his tall, slim, yet strong build. His short, dark chocolate brown hair was only slightly disheveled and he had a slight five o'clock shadow. He had great features, a straight jawline, pursed lips, and defined cheek bones.

He did have big ears. They didn't stick out or anything, but they were prominent, making him look wise for his age. I know, silly, but my mom had told me that big ears were a sign of intelligence, and, well, he was brainy. They suited him, balancing out the dorky and sexy.

And when he smiled, not only was he more irresistible but he had this mischievous look, like he was hiding a secret, but not on purpose, just made you feel more curious about what he was thinking. But by far, his best feature were his eyes. He had the nicest gray-green eyes I had ever seen. When I looked in them, I felt a sense of gentleness, a soothing calmness I couldn't really explain.

I didn't know what to say, so I said, "You still have the kindest eyes I have ever seen." I had never said that to him in person, so it seemed more intimate than intended. I didn't mean to embarrass him, but he turned a little red. He looked over at my ride.

"Check out that car! I see you aren't driving your minivan." He whistled, changing the subject. "You did it, you bought your dream car. What a beauty. And damn! That's quite the custom wrap. Not a lot of people could pull off that shade of pink, but you are rocking it! And it matches your lipstick." I couldn't tell if he was being sarcastic, but I went with it. I loved my car and its colour made all the difference.

The car, my car was a big deal. I had driven that minivan for so long and I couldn't do it anymore. And being in this car was exhilarating. If it weren't for Rebecca, I wouldn't be driving it right now and I wouldn't have a job to pay for it.

I clearly remember the evening I met Rebecca. While scrambling to get dinner on the table, looking at the kids' homework, preparing them for their guitar lessons, and doing laundry, my phone had buzzed. I looked down to see a reminder that I had a school council meeting. How had I forgotten? Probably because of the twenty other things I had going on. I kissed hubby on the cheek, grabbed my notebook and headed to the school. Rushing in as I was running late, I ran into someone. I was so embarrassed.

"I am so sorry; I didn't mean to bump into you!" I said.

"It's okay, no rush. I'm headed to the council meeting as well. I'll walk with you. My name's Rebecca."

We bonded instantly. It turned out she had a son and a daughter the same age as my kids. They were in debate club, band, and played basketball together. Rebecca was well-educated and smart.

"My partner and I have decided to create a small start-up," she told me, "So it's exciting and busy times. What do you do?"

"I'm a stay-at-home mom," I had said. I hated telling people I was a stay-at-home mom. It wasn't that I was ashamed, I just felt that people took my time for granted because they knew I would always be willing to work for free. It was thankless, difficult and underappreciated. "But I have business experience," I continued. "Not to mention an engineering background. It's just been a while." When I said it out loud, I almost impressed myself. It really had been a while.

After sitting through a painful council meeting, I said to her, "I am so glad I didn't get caught up in yet another volunteer role. Everyone expects me to step up because I don't have a real job, but I'm busy and I want to do something that makes me happy. And that is not it."

What Rebecca said next surprised me. "Well, if you're looking for a great paying job, flexible hours, and want to work from home, let me know. We're looking to expand our company and are looking for a marketing manager. And your technical background would be a great asset."

I shook my head in disbelief, was she offering me a job? Did she say I could be a great asset? This was absolutely something I was looking for.

"Come by our home office on Saturday afternoon and we can talk. See you then."

We exchanged numbers. And that was that.

That Saturday afternoon when she called me over to her house, I wasn't sure what to expect. Especially when she said she wanted to meet in her office and proceeded to lead me to her bedroom. It's not often that I am led upstairs for an interview. I caught myself thinking about what kind of undies I had on, which almost made me laugh out loud.

At first, I was a little confused because she led me right into her bedroom, but the office was attached off the bedroom in a spacious room to itself. I met her lovely wife, who was not only the "brains" of the operation, but absolutely stunning. Her intelligence was mind-blowing and she was so capable. She took me seriously and offered me a real job, one that paid and had expectations and deadlines. She had a passion about teaching and made you excited about whatever it is she was working on. It was nice to be treated with respect, and she appreciated that I was educated and skilled. This was so foreign to me, to be seen as more than a housewife with childbearing hips!

Bumping into Rebecca that night was the best thing that could've happened for my career. She was an amazing powerhouse of a woman and her appearance suited her personality; she was easily a head taller than me and a dominatingly large but fit and attractive lady. She knew how to be direct and get things done, she was smart and assertive but kind and caring, and she had a sweetness about her that made you feel safe. I nicknamed her "mama bear" because I felt when I was struggling to find any external value, she took me in as one of her own.

Nothing bothered her, Rebecca always found a way to make things better and never had anything negative to say. I could never figure out where her pot of optimism came from, but she always inspired me. When she wasn't being a super mom or working, she had her book clubs, wine trips through the country sides of Europe and cruises. She lived in a beautiful home which she designed herself. Logical, practical and always wore a smile.

I once asked her what her secret to her optimism was and she answered with one simple word, "Priorities!"

Rebecca had become the person in my life that I wanted to live up to. If there was ever a person I wanted to be more like and admired by, it was Rebecca. She turned out to be way more than just an employer to me. She was my friend and my mentor. She allowed me to see what I could be capable of again.

Getting my "first" paycheck after all those years was a strange feeling. It's like I wanted to save it and spend it at the same time. Obviously, I decided to spend it.

I started small, taking the kids out for specialty hot chocolate and fancy dinners. Eventually, I gave myself permission to spoil myself a little. New shoes, a new wallet, a purse to match, fun clothes, lots of lipstick, theatre tickets, and more shoes—all on sale, of course! I saved just enough each month to buy my car. It was the best purchase I ever made.

I must've been lost in thought because Marcelo was staring at me and looking over at the car. I said, "I do love my car!" and grabbed his bag and popped the trunk open.

"I guess we should get out of here. You're a busy and important person—I'm sure you have lots to do!" I said to him and smiled, feeling that fluttered excitement from the last time we met. As I loaded his suitcase, he threw his carryon in the trunk, and laughed. "Just the busy part, but even then, I am not that busy right now."

He noticed my packed bags.

"Planning a trip?" he asked, looking a little disappointed.

I opened the car door for him and he walked around and climbed in. "I'll explain in the car. Why don't we get out of here and grab a coffee and catch up, unless you have somewhere to be, that is?" I felt that sense of hurriedness that this might be the only chance I would get to see him.

Before he could answer, I walked around to the driver's side and slid into my seat next to him. My dress inched up a little higher than usual and I hoped he hadn't noticed. As I looked over at him, I caught him looking me up and down again. His boldness caught me by surprise.

Our only other interaction had been by text and every text had been proper and decent and kind. I don't use that word much...kind, but he was genuinely kind. I thought things would've been more awkward in person, but he felt more like an old friend than a stranger I had met only once. But the way he looked at me, perhaps reminded him of the physical tension between us that night. And seeing him after all this time, definitely heightened some of those sensations and memories for me.

As his gaze slowly trailed up to meet mine, he replied, "It would great to grab a coffee." I smiled, happy he had the time and pulled out of the airport.

"Wow, listen to that engine, this is a beast of a car! I would love to drive it," he said more like a challenge than an assumption.

"No one can maneuver her like I can, but you're welcome to try," I said, enjoying the healthy competition.

I didn't mind him driving my car, although I couldn't remember if he owned one. "Do you have a car?" I asked. "I hope it's sexier than a minivan!"

"I have a VW Arteon, looks like this," he said, holding up his phone for me to see a sleek yet practical, metallic blue, four-door sedan.

"You own an iPhone?" I groaned, disapproving of his choice.

"So, what if I do!" he said laughing, giving me a look that told me iPhones were better.

"I am strictly an Android girl." I pretended to give him a disappointed look while shaking my head for effect.

"But that's a sexy car. Love the colour. I would've taken you for a metallic dark gray kinda guy." I teased a little.

"Well, I am full of surprises," he turned to me, eyeing me mischievously. "I thought about gray but I wanted something a little less boring."

"How come you didn't get an SUV?" he continued. "Or a Subaru for those Calgary winters? It's cold when the temperatures drop and there's so much snow."

"I didn't want an SUV; I'm so done with driving boats. I would do a BMW over Subaru. I know, impractical, but I have done practical forever. I needed something fun," I explained.

"I like the A5, might have to get an Audi next, even with the silly pricing. BMW works too. Not a big Mercedes fan, too pretentious in my opinion," he stated, although he looked at me to see if I would agree.

"Well, I guess I got really silly, which is why I got the Audi RS5; the engine does purr real pretty. I love the BMW z4 but a two-seater with three boys really wouldn't have worked! I agree, Mercedes' are too showy." At least we agreed on that. He looked satisfied.

"Yes, this is a really nice car, almost feels like it would be wasted on the comically bad Quebec roads though. Probably makes more sense out west," he said logically.

"We do get eight months of winter, which means salt and rock chips, but we do have decent roads, so I guess so," I said.

I was enjoying the banter. It was pleasant talking to him. "So, how is work going, anything new?" I asked.

"Nothing unusual," he replied, "but I have had a few challenges recently. Hit a bit of a wall, but I am sure a fresh perspective and a break will help with that."

Even though I knew what hitting a wall meant, for some reason I pictured him pinning me up against a wall while trying to sort out his frustrations with work. What was wrong with me? Too much obsessing? Or maybe it was all the glances he kept throwing at me.

I must've been lost in my fantasy because he asked again, "So, how are the boys doing? Keeping you busy, I bet."

I tried to focus on what he was saying. "Yes, the boys are good. Very busy. They're on a camping trip at the Waterton National Parks for a few days. The fresh air and activity will be good for them." I couldn't remember if I had mentioned it in one of my texts.

"Have you been dancing lately?" he asked unexpectedly. The look on his face told me he was thinking about the night we had met. I wondered what else he was thinking about.

I laughed, "The last time I went dancing was with you. I tried asking a few of my mom friends, and by a few, I mean twenty-five of them, and only one responded; she said no. I will have to go with you, at least I can drag you onto the floor!"

Marcelo laughed heartily at my comment.

"Are you seriously laughing at my pathetic social life?" I said, pretending to be hurt. "And that was for my birthday. You are so cruel. You might have to make it up to me." I was flirting with him, and I liked the way it felt.

"I was just laughing at the 'dragging' part," he replied. "And you're involved in a million different activities. Not pathetic at all."

We drove to the nearest Second Cup, my favourite coffee shop. We ordered a couple of lattes, found a quiet table in the back, and sat down. We sat for a moment in silence; I felt like he was figuring out what to do or say next.

"I still can't believe you're in Calgary," I started as he chimed in almost simultaneously, "Where are you headed? Road trip?"

I smiled. "You first," I said. "What are you doing here? Lots of work meetings? Presenting a paper?"

"It's a funny story actually," he replied. "I was planning on heading out to a BBQ later this afternoon to visit family in town, I think I mentioned I have some family in Calgary? But it turns out they got a last-minute invitation to house boating at the Shuswap, which is why I needed a ride. Thank you, by the way. Now, I'm in town for a week with nothing to do. I was hoping to hang out with you but now it looks like you aren't going to be around. I hope I didn't interrupt plans by asking you to pick me up?" He shifted in his seat, holding his breath.

Sipping my favourite coffee, staring at the man across the table from me, I thought to myself, should I tell him about the road trip and about Carmen cancelling on me? Should I invite him to take her place? Although I was sure I had mentioned the trip in a few random texts, he probably didn't remember. I fought with myself internally—I couldn't deny that I wanted to spend some time with Marcelo, since I had only seen him once a year ago and it would be great to hang out. Our last visit had felt so rushed and unfinished. But at the same time, I needed this trip more than anything and I didn't want to give that up. Maybe a coffee with him would be enough and I could try and meet up with him once I got back. I could drop him where he needed to be and head out on my "personal journey".

Before I could fully decide, I found myself telling him, "Funny story actually," mimicking his response, "I might've mentioned it, but I planned a road trip with my best friend Carmen to visit BC for five days, but she is in full drama and crisis mode and cancelled on me last minute. So, I was planning to go on my own and was about to head out when I got your text. I wish you had told me earlier you were going to be in town, I would've like to spend more time with you—"

He cut me off before I could finish my sentence, "Sorry. Work has been nutty the last few weeks, I didn't get a chance to text you, not that that's a good excuse."

"Were you really going to come into town and not tell me?" It slipped out before I could stop myself; I was feeling a little hurt, more than I expected to.

Marcelo looked guilty when he replied, "It wasn't intentional, just a timing thing. You had mentioned your trip, I wasn't sure when it was and I didn't want to bug you. I only took a chance and texted because I was a little desperate. Besides, I wasn't sure you wanted to see me again."

This took me by surprise. "Why wouldn't I want to see you?"

"Because of how we left things in Montreal. I know we've been texting. I guess sometimes it's easier to stay connected without it getting complicated when it's not face to face, although I think there was some miscommunication there too. Sorry." I was taken aback by the look of concern on his face.

I wanted to reach over and grab his hand, but it didn't feel appropriate. I looked into his eyes. "Montreal was incredible," I paused and took a deep breath before continuing, "and your friendship has meant a lot to me. It's okay—there's always miscommunication over text." I paused again. "Look, I would have loved to spend more time with you, but I need to go on this road trip."

"The road trip sounds amazing," he said enthusiastically. "I can't remember the last time I went on a road trip to BC. And it's so amazing and scenic; nature's playground. If you could use the company and an extra driver for those long stretches, I would be happy to join you." He looked at me with that adorable smile.

Did he just invite himself? I thought. I didn't recall inviting him, although I had thought about it. Even so, it hadn't been a serious thought. After all, he was a friend of a friend; he sometimes even felt like a stranger. We had enjoyed one memorable evening together. Yes, we had exchanged text messages, but that was a little different to wanting him to join me on a five-day road trip. Not that I wouldn't enjoy the company, but I was a married woman and to spend five days with another man?

Although these thoughts flooded my mind, I found myself feeling excited and curious. I thought back to the night I had met him in Montreal. Should I be worried? Was he weird or repulsive in anyway? No. Was he creepy that night? Not at all. Did he try to take advantage of me? Not really, nothing that I didn't want. Did I allow him to seduce me? I had, but only because I wanted it.

I allowed my mind to travel back to our first meeting. I felt the swelteringly hot summer night as I sat with Marcelo at the crowded bar and heart pounding beats filled the air.

"So, you really won't dance with me?" I said, staring him straight in the eye with a mischievous smile on my face.

Buying time, he ordered a drink. Daryl's friend bought us a round of shots. He looked back at me suspiciously. "Maybe you should dance with Daryl? He looks lonely." He accidently downed my shot along with his drinks before ordering another round. I haven't touched mine.

"Daryl is a big boy; he can take care of himself. I can dance with him anytime, I want you all to myself," I teased. He looked flattered but flustered.

"Maybe you could check out a hot yoga class while you're here, Daryl mentioned you were into it," he said, trying to change the subject.

So, Daryl and Marcelo had discussed me. I wondered what they had discussed but wasn't about to ask. I looked Marcelo up and down, he didn't really seem the yoga type, and definitely not hot yoga.

"You may be fit, but you don't seem that flexible, but if that's how I'm going to see you half naked, then I'm all in." I grinned and bit my lower lip. Of course, I was teasing him; I wanted to talk a little dirty to get a reaction out of him.

He was visibly uncomfortable and stumbled with his reply, "I wasn't trying to get you to—"

"But we don't need hot yoga for me to see you showing off your moves," I said, eyeing the dance floor, swaying in my seat and raising my eyebrow at him. "I'm just teasing!" I laughed when he didn't respond. "Because I can see your moves right here, on the dance floor."

"Good plan. Forget naked...I mean hot yoga and maybe the dance floor too, let's just hang out and talk," he stumbled.

"Let's get on the dance floor first and then we can talk all night. What did you have in mind exactly?" I asked. The bar atmosphere was getting to my senses.

"Do you mean like a one-night stand?" He asked so earnestly and unexpectedly that it threw me off; and that never happens. Was he trying to out-tease me or was he seriously asking? Did he know I was married? *I need to be more careful with what I'm saying*, I thought.

"Whoa! Sorry Marcelo, I'm not one for one-night stands. Definitely not drunk enough for that—I'm not even drunk! I just wanted to dance, that's all." I told him.

"No, I'm sorry. I just thought that maybe you were in an open marriage." So, he did know I was married but I couldn't deny that I was surprised by his question. He had seemed uncomfortable earlier. Maybe it was the alcohol talking.

Unexpectedly upping his game, without breaking eye contact, he asked, "Are you in an open marriage or did your husband give you a hall pass?" He glanced down casually at my left hand. I realized that he had picked up on the fact that I wasn't wearing a wedding ring.

The wedding ring—of course—it symbolizes union and commitment. For many reasons, including it being a cultural thing, not wanting to conform to societal norms, and having a cheap husband, I didn't wear a wedding ring. My husband didn't care to spend money on jewelry. He just knew I belonged to him, that he owned me.

Now I understood where he was coming from, he wasn't upping his game, he was curious about the ring or the lack thereof. Of course, I wasn't in an open marriage, but the idea of a hall pass was interesting. I could not imagine my husband ever agreeing to that. And one-night stands were not my thing. I like to know the person I am getting into bed with. Not that I was getting into bed with him. I wasn't sure I was ready to share my thoughts on this with this man.

I explained, choosing my words carefully, "I am married, I'm not in an open marriage and I don't have a hall pass. I just don't wear a wedding ring; it's a cultural thing. But that doesn't matter, I don't want to talk about my husband or my marriage. I want to hang out with Daryl and his friends and have a good time."

"Are you having a good time?" he asked, looking past me towards Daryl, perhaps looking for guidance from his friend.

"I am enjoying your company but this is one of the strangest conversations I have had with someone I just met; but perhaps that's what happens when you are drunk and horny and trying to..." I said without thinking, making a fool of myself.

Before he could answer, I said, "I am so sorry, I can't believe I just said that. It's been a while since I've gone out. It's probably the alcohol talking." Even though we both knew I had barely had a sip.

"Please don't be sorry, I am enjoying your company too. I wasn't trying to..." He said, trailing off intentionally while smiling at me reassuringly.

I looked over at the dance floor again. "Well, I am trying to get you onto that dance floor. I'm lucky if I can get out to a club once a year, I really don't want to waste it sitting on this barstool. And since you're stuck with me, you will have to dance with me!" I told him, gently placing my hand on his knee, urging him with my eyes.

"I'm not much of a dancer, but I'll see what I can do." He grinned trying to convince himself more than me but staying planted on the barstool.

Even though the alcohol seemed to loosen him up a bit, Marcelo was a tough read. Our conversation was all over the place that night, he didn't talk much about himself. He was trying really hard not to tell me anything about himself. When he did mention something, it was almost like he slipped up and wouldn't finish the story. I think he wasn't used to it, all the attention. He did have some great stories to tell about Daryl and his friends, which kept me entertained.

At one point, while Marcelo was sitting at the bar waiting for another drink, he rolled his shoulders; and cranked his neck to one side. I instinctively stood up behind him, placed my hands on his shoulders and began to rub them. Why instinctively, I don't know. I could see he was tense and I wanted to make him feel better. He was this stranger in a bar and there I was, rubbing his shoulders. I felt so in-tune with him even though we were all over the place.

"Why do you think my shoulders are so tense?" he asked.

I couldn't tell if he was being serious or not. I needed to assess the situation better. I continued to massage his tense shoulders and pretended I couldn't hear him over the loud music.

I pressed my breasts into his back, wrapped my arms around his neck to rest on his chest let my lips hover against his ear, and asked, "What did you say, I couldn't hear you?"

He turned his head, our faces inches apart from each other and he locked his gorgeous grey eyes with my big brown ones. He held our gaze and for a second I thought he was going to kiss me.

Instead, he let his lips brush past my cheek and asked again. I couldn't come up with a practical answer, so I found myself teasing him more; fueled by our connection and underlying foreplay. I slid my face away from him, not daring to look at him and squeezed his shoulders a little harder, letting my lips linger against his ear, I slowly let my lips hover against his ear, and said, "It's because you aren't getting enough!"

I couldn't see his face, but he stiffened under my hands before recovering quickly, spinning around on the barstool. There was an intensity in his eyes that I wasn't expecting. It made my heart pound. "Well, is there anything you can recommend..." he was cut off as his friend asked me to dance but Marcelo looked at him disapprovingly. His friend pulled me away and I thought Marcelo looked upset. It didn't last, I wasn't interested in his friend. But our conversation was interrupted and lost. As the evening progressed, things seemed to intensify between us, we were inseparable on and off the dance floor. Daryl looked over and raised an eyebrow, checking in on me; I smiled back, I was happy. Marcelo was enticing but safe. It's not often I find an intelligent guy who can carry a conversation and a beat, so yes, it was fun to hang out with him that night.

The smell of the coffee brought me back to the coffee shop. Meeting a guy like Marcelo had been incredible and I enjoyed his company, but could I do it for five days? More importantly, should I?

He was staring at me so intently that I almost forgot he had invited himself. Those eyes, those gorgeous eyes, those gorgeous gray-green eyes, I could feel myself drowning in them. How did he do that? I felt so connected to him, and as I stared back, I recognized the haunting look I had seen in Montreal; a distant sadness that was drawing me in, because I felt that same kind of deep sadness myself.

I needed to give him an answer before the silence got awkward. I looked down at my coffee, swirling the coffee stick although it didn't need stirring. I sipped my latte again. Should I have him tag along? How bad could it be? He was nice, and I was fairly sure he wasn't a serial killer because he was a friend of Daryl's. I could use the company and it might be nice to have someone to talk to, someone that didn't know me that well and wouldn't judge me.

I thought to myself, "Do I want to finish what we started on that dance floor, that night? Yes. Should I be worried about Marcelo's intentions? I don't think so.

What would that look like? I don't know. Would things be different if I weren't married? Of course, but I am married. Would anything actually happen? Probably not. Could we still have fun? Yes."

I found myself answering, "Well, if your plans fell through and you don't mind spending a few days with a boring, old housewife, you could probably join me. But we can't just talk about the weather the whole time—I'm looking forward to a relaxing break."

"That sounds great Karina, and I'm sure we'll find lots to talk about. And I'm already packed," he said light-heartedly.

"I do have to warn you though," I continued, "I planned this trip with my girlfriend, so I hope you're up for some good old-fashioned girl power entertainment."

Even though I had planned out every detail, asking him to join me was the most spontaneous and risky thing I had done in twenty years. As I finished the last sip of my coffee, I realized I was now committed to spending the next five days with this guy. I hope I had made the right decision.

We could go on this trip without crossing any lines, I thought to myself, *we're friends*.

He smirked, and for a second, I felt like he had read my mind. "So, what's on the agenda for the trip?" he asked. I knew his question was because he knew how organized I liked to be. All my friends made fun of me for how organized I was. Personally, I think I was just really good at faking it, because I always had at least twenty things on the go, so maybe I had no choice. Me and my spreadsheets, calendars, and journals. I liked writing things down, and I used them for everything. This trip was no exception.

I pulled a notebook out of my purse and slipped the folded five-page printed spreadsheet across the table. As he reached for it, our hands brushed, and I felt something tingle between us. I looked up and caught him looking at me. He quickly looked down, pretending to be very interested in the itinerary.

"Well, we better get on the road if we are going to fit all this in today. You always have lots on the go, even when you relax, you're busy! Do you want to drive the first shift or should I?"

I found myself letting go of my usual control, handing him the keys. He had been eyeing the car since he laid eyes on it, this was an excuse for him to try it out. Why was I so trusting? Maybe he just made me feel that way.

"First stop, Radium Hot Springs. Time to destination, two and a half hours. Do you need to pee before we leave?" he asked. I glared at him, feeling oddly comfortable to have him in my presence and annoyed by his candor. These flip flop feelings were new to me.

I did need to pee, so I threw him my purse and journal and told him I would be right back. I realized in the washroom that I had handed over my entire life to this stranger and I might come back to find everything, including my car, missing.

Just then, my phoned buzzed and there was a text message from my mom saying, "Have a safe trip honey, and tell Carmen I say hi!"

The thought of my mother finding out that it wasn't Carmen going on this trip but a man she didn't even know existed freaked me out. It didn't seem to matter that I was an independent woman in her forties, I always struggled with my mom's ideas and values and following societal norms. I had never been much of a rule follower when it came to fulfilling my wishes. I knew she would never see things from my perspective anyway.

I typed carefully, "Just heading out, looking forward to a break and will text you when I get back. Love you."

What am I thinking? I asked myself. And I realized, I wasn't. I was just going along with the flow of what had been presented in front of me. I still wasn't sure I could go through with it, having Marcelo join me, my confidence in myself waning. What if he had taken off with my stuff? What if I couldn't trust him? What if this was the wrong decision? I had to stop. Heading back from the washroom anxiously, I couldn't help but smile when I saw him; he was still standing there, holding my purse.

Chapter 4

Road Trip!

I slid into the passenger seat, since he already had the car keys; oddly comfortable with the idea of him driving my baby. Perhaps I could let go a little. Carmen said I should try it. "You want to see how she drives, now is your chance to try her out!" I said.

He had to adjust the seat, mirrors, pedals, and steering wheel before we headed out to accommodate for his long legs and height. As he eased into driving the car, I could see him grinning from the exhilaration of driving this perfectly engineered machine.

He gripped the steering wheel and wrapped his fingers over the leather. He was enjoying the ride; the way the engine roared while he maneuvered. I could almost see the cogs turning in his brain while he calculated the velocity and acceleration required to push the car just as far as he wanted. I had a feeling this "test drive" would consider him to upgrade. Nothing drives like an Audi.

"This baby really purrs when she wants to run, doesn't she?" he said as he accelerated around a bend while passing a few cars.

"She's not the only thing that purrs when she's ready to go," I said out loud. As soon as I had said it, I covered my mouth, but it was too late.

What was I thinking? The sheepish grin on his face told me I wasn't. He made me feel giddy and good and he was giving off this intelligent yet sexy vibe and I just couldn't help myself. I was feeling a little reckless. Maybe it was the pheromones or being in a tightly enclosed space with this attractive man. But I didn't want to scare him off, I meant no harm.

Playing with my hands, I tried to recover, "What I meant was—"

"No worries, I'm glad we can have some fun. Seriously, I am very curious about the purring now," he said, chuckling.

I still didn't know how to justify an answer, so I didn't. He seemed more confident than I had remembered from the last time we met, but I liked this side of him. I was so glad for the superior sound system in the car because the music was a great distraction. And honestly, I needed to think things through a little before figuring out what to do and what I had gotten myself into.

The control freak inside me was screaming. I wasn't one for surprises and this whole day had thrown me off. I probably should've texted Carmen to let her know about the situation just in case I got into any kind of trouble. But I didn't want her to judge me. Not that she ever would. The one thing that Carmen and I understood about each other was our non-conforming way of thinking. Each of us had faced more adversity than we had ever imagined and had to adjust not only our way of thinking but our way of accepting and believing. It didn't always make sense to others, but it worked for us. I was sure she would be cheering me on if I told her.

I also didn't want to bother her; with everything she was going through. I would text her once I was more settled. I pulled out my spreadsheet to see what we had planned. We had decided to head into Radium Hot Springs, a tiny little mountain side town that was so perfectly old-fashioned that it belonged on a postcard.

One of Tess's friends owned a cute little motel and we had planned to stay there. Carmen and I had planned a nice soak in the natural fed hot springs followed by good conversation and dinner at a charming little place down the street from the motel before chilling in the room for the night. I could handle that.

Or could I? Our accommodations popped into my head. If I were spending the night with Carmen, it wouldn't matter where we were sleeping. We were very comfortable with each other and I could share a room or even a bed with her if I had to. But Marcelo, that was another story. I felt a little panicked. I quickly pulled out my phone and emailed the Piccadilly Motel. I asked Penny, the owner, if I could change my reservation to have two rooms. I waited anxiously for her response.

She replied, "No can do Miss Karina, we are sold out, but I can make sure you've got a room with two queen sized beds."

That would have to do. There was no way I could share a bed with him.

Marcelo broke the silence. "Here I thought I was going to take care of you, but you rescued me from the airport, whisked me up in your fancy sports car, and have an amazing trip planned. I'm going to have to up my game." He smiled, just the edges of his mouth turning up slightly as he ran his fingers through his hair.

It had been so long since someone had appreciated my efforts. I felt my hand involuntarily reaching for his face, but I stopped myself. I didn't realize how much I had missed seeing him. I sounded silly but I said it anyway, "I wanted to make you smile, I have missed it." He gave me a bigger smile, which made me laugh.

I continued, "No need to up your game, just be your kind self." I love taking care of people, it's what I do best. And this is fun and you are easy to please, so watch out, because I'm long overdue for showing someone a good time!"

"I'm looking forward to it. I'll do my best to keep up," he replied.

"Seen any good movies lately?" he asked. I don't think we were ready to talk about anything serious. We also weren't quite ready for comfortable silence, and I did enjoy the sound of his deep voice.

"Well, I haven't seen anything new, but for fear of dating myself, I watched Dead Poet's Society with my boys this weekend. So many powerful messages. It's such a classic," I replied.

"Wow, Dead Poet's Society, been a long time since I saw that. And you aren't dating yourself. Carpe diem, it's a great movie!" he approved my choice, that was a good sign.

He slipped his Ray Bans up, looked over, raising his eyebrows as if testing me and asked, "Have you seen the movie 'When Harry Met Sally'?"

Of course, I had seen the movie. Every woman my age had seen it. It was a classic from 1989. It was infamous for a few key scenes. Almost immediately, the three that came to mind were the "I'll have what she's having" where Sally fakes an orgasm in the restaurant, "Just friends" where Harry and Sally discuss whether men and women can be just friends and the "Dream" scene, which you either remember vividly because of its ridiculousness or live in ignorance forever. I wasn't sure where this conversation was going and I wasn't sure I wanted it to continue down any of these paths.

I tried to be casual when I answered, "Of course! That was a great movie! One of my favourites. Although I haven't seen it in a while." I started playing with my hands again, feeling a little nervous.

"Do you think men and women can be friends without the sex part getting in the way?" he asked as he looked over at me, before turning his attention to the road. And here I thought we weren't ready to talk about anything serious.

I could feel myself started to panic again, which was weird, because usually I was the risqué one. I was almost wishing for small talk. In a way, I was glad—I wanted to clear the air with him if I could. Lots had happened between us and the nagging feeling of not knowing what it all meant was bugging me.

"Well, we are friends, and you're a man and I'm a woman, so yes, I think they can." I didn't want to talk about sex with him, I'd barely spent an hour with him. This had to stop. I wasn't sure my heart could take more stress right now. I felt like I was trapped in the car, just like in the scene from the movie when Billy Crystal was having the same conversation with Meg Ryan.

"Honestly, I don't know," I continued, "I've tried being friends with men in the past and it hasn't always worked out. Especially married men. I don't have a problem with it, it just seems to get complicated and messy. If you can't decipher between what's real and what's flirting and not intended. If we could just be friends without problems, I would have more male friends in my life," I concluded, feeling conflicted.

"It's a good thing I'm not married, gives me a better chance." He replied. A better chance at what?

I figured he was just testing the waters and trying to see what I would say. Normally, I wouldn't be bothered as I am comfortable with my sexuality. I liked to be a tease and have a little fun. Now, I felt the tables were turned. And I was rambling, perhaps he had stuck a little too close to home.

I didn't want to ask what, so I said, "Besides, I believe there's a big difference between intimacy and sexuality and each play an important role in any relationship or friendship. And sexuality isn't the only type of connection, it can be physical, social, emotional, or even intellectual. Depending on what you are looking for, you can be intimate and still stay within the limits of your friendship."

"Limits? Like ground rules, or boundaries?" He took his eyes off the road momentarily to make eye contact.

"Yeah, I guess. I mean, like I said, you can be intimate with someone without ever being sexual. And you can have meaningless sexual interactions without ever getting intimate. Things can be physically, emotionally and intellectually stimulating without ever crossing any lines." I was rambling even more, repeating myself and trying to think out loud. I was feeling a little shaky.

"So, what are the rules for this trip? Where do we draw the lines between intimacy and friendship?" As he spoke, he deliberately put his hand on my knee and as he mentioned drawing lines, he used his finger to indicate lines along my leg, inching his way slowly from my knee up to my thigh, daring to let his fingers trail under my dress. I swallowed as I felt a sensation run through my body, making me very aware of the man beside me—a sensation I hadn't felt in a long time. I casually moved his hand away from my leg, although his hand lingered against mine momentarily. I had to get a hold of myself. I wasn't some silly teenager. And I couldn't act like one.

I sat up straighter and tried to sound serious, "Look, if this had been like twenty years ago and I would've been allowed to feel as liberated as I do right now, I wouldn't have had any rules, we would be two young kids enjoying a road trip together. We could've done anything and everything. No strings attached."

"And now?" he asked.

"Now, things are different. I'm married. I can't just do whatever I want," I said.

If only he knew the truth. It wasn't just about being married. I didn't trust myself anymore. I thought I knew what I wanted, but bit by bit it was stripped from me; my ambitions disappearing, my body betraying me, not knowing the truth about loving someone other than out of obligation. I couldn't tell him about twenty years of pain.

"I will admit, I was fascinated by you when I first met you. You're so intelligent, funny, charming and good looking. As you know, I have a family, three adorable kids that need me. I still find you curious but have no love interest, I can't. My life comes with baggage. You know that." I said sadly.

"I get it," he said softly. "But I thought that part of this trip was to try and let go of some of that baggage, or at least not to have to think about it so you can focus on yourself. For you to have a taste of freedom and maybe even try some missed opportunities that you wished you had done in your twenties?" He spoke with so much insight that it threw me off. It was like he was reading my thoughts; I was pretty sure our small talk texts never covered this kind of stuff.

"I might've glanced at your notebook when you were in the washroom and read a page or two," he admitted.

I suddenly felt sick, like I had been sucker punched in the gut. My notebook was like a diary to me. I had started writing it when I was going through some tough times and was trying to evaluate my life. The fact that he had read any part of it and knew personal, private details bothered me. Journaling was my therapy. It helped me feel better and look at my problems from the outside, to evaluate them and come up with a plan to solve them. I shared my journal with no one. It was for me and me alone. I felt so vulnerable. My writing was very raw and included my innermost secrets. The look on my face must've told him how awful I was feeling.

"I am so sorry," he apologized. "I didn't realize what it was until I opened it. When you handed me your things, I figured it was a part of your planning, that you were logging your mileage or expenses. I didn't mean to invade your privacy. It won't happen again. You know you can trust me with anything you want to say or do."

He sounded genuine and I found myself blushing again. I never blush. I was normally a sensible and practical person. Accepting that he had read a part of my journal and to let him in in that way, even though it wasn't by choice, forced me to let go just a little bit of that control. It was new to me. I didn't like feeling helpless and I wasn't sure how to deal with it. I knew I wasn't ready for it. I tried to close my eyes and take a few deep breaths to calm my nerves. It didn't work. I could feel my defences coming up, he should not have read my journal and he needed to know where I stood.

"Rules. You want rules? Fine, I will lay them out for you. One, we are friends, just friends—not friends with benefits, not bed buddies, just friends. Two, no sex! Three, no nakedness, no naughtiness, no nothing!" By this point I had lost track of numbering. I took a breath and continued, "If you want me to satisfy your erotic fantasies, it's not going to happen but we can talk, we can hang out, eat! We stick to the schedule and do the planned activities and that's it."

He could see I was upset. “I meant it when I said I was sorry, I wasn’t trying to snoop.”

“I was just a bit uncomfortable.” I sighed.

“I didn’t realize I made you uncomfortable. I was just a little hurt because I thought we were friends already.” He explained.

“It’s okay.” I breathed out. “I’m sorry too. That might have been a little too harsh.” I was flustered and tired of defending myself. “Are we good?” I asked and he nodded yes.

I couldn’t look at him. Was he questioning my intentions without letting on anything about his? Why did I feel so upset? If I allowed it, I would probably tear up. I didn’t. I was past that. Obviously, there was more going on with me, but I needed to sort that out for myself.

He put his hand on my knee again. I tried to pull away, but he grasped and squeezed. This time the physical sensation wasn’t intrusive or sensual, so I let it be.

He tried to console me as he said with a soft tone to his voice. “Can I ask why you’re so worked up? You invited me on this trip, I thought you wanted me here—”

I interjected, “I did not invite you, well, whatever, and I do want you here, to spend some time with you, but...I just feel a little flustered.” I decided honesty was the best way to handle things. I put my hand on his.

“How do you feel about men and women being friends, does it work?” I needed to know, to hear it from him.

The jerk reaction as he pulled his hand away told me he was now feeling uncomfortable. I don't think he was expecting the question. Usually, with our texts, if he didn't want to answer something, he just avoided it—it wasn't so simple now.

"Honestly, I don't know. Since I met you, I have always welcomed the interest and I wasn't trying to question your intentions. But it's hard for me to open up; I'm not good at sharing. I think we're on different wavelengths, like you said, you are married with a family. Knowing you belong to someone else makes it confusing..." he said sincerely.

I didn't know where he was going and so I blurted out, "What, did you think I would automatically want to sleep with you?"

"No, I never thought that at all!" he said defensively. "I do remember the night we met. I thought you were flirty when we talked about one-night stands. A little strange for not drinking. Insightful and playful for saying I wasn't getting enough while you massaged my shoulders. You...didn't seem to have so many rules that night. I remember the way you looked at me at the bar. I was impressed by the way you danced with me on the dance floor. You were adamant about going back to my apartment. Curious about the view from my rooftop. I wasn't sure what you wanted or if I could give it to you..."

He took his eyes off the road again for a split second, searching my gaze for confirmation.

I needed to say something. "Yes, I was adamant about going back to your apartment because 'what's his face' was stupid drunk and I wasn't about to let him drive home." I paused. "I was curious about your rooftop, but I really didn't have any expectations, I...just got caught up in the moment. Look, you're sweet and sexy and smart, you can go drinking at the bar on the weekends with your buddies and pick a different pretty girl to dance with and get her panties wet with your charm, leaving with her on your arm if you wanted it! That night, on the dance floor, I was overwhelmed. I was caught up in the moment and vulnerable. You affected me in a way you don't even realize. The way you affect everyone around you. I never feel that way. I am just another pathetic and desperate housewife to you."

Now it was his turn to defend himself. "I don't go out that much. It's not really like that, it's not some kind of routine. I was being genuine that night. I'm not this charming guy you think I am. You bring that out in me, which is why I like being with you."

He continued, "Although, I think I owe you an apology. I'm sorry, I drank way too much that night and we seem to have different recollections. That night was special to me too. I just wanted to see if anything had changed. Seems like it has."

"Don't apologize. You didn't do anything wrong. It doesn't matter if you had too much to drink. Your "drunken" recollections from that night seem to be intact. Your being here with me right now, it's just a little unexpected. That night...you were always more of an escape than a reality." I confessed.

That night had been intense, unreal in many ways. Perhaps it was only meant to happen once and be forgotten. Perhaps inviting him on this trip had been a mistake.

"Are you okay? You know you can talk to me," he said.

Our conversation was bringing up all kinds of memories from that night.

"I think you're great, and when I am ready, I know I can talk to you. There's a lot going on and this is all a little sudden, it's going to take me some time to figure things out," I explained.

"I know, it's complicated," he said. "There were a lot of things left unsaid, that night and in our texts. I was hoping we could figure out where things stand, but it came out wrong. I want to be friends; I want to have fun on this trip."

I sighed. I was frustrated. He was right. I decided I did owe him some sort of an explanation. I began to try and explain things to him. I had been a different woman in Montreal. I felt like I was under a spell that night mesmerized by the allure of Montreal and what she had offered, not a woman trapped in a marriage. I felt so conflicted. When I attempted to explain all this to Marcelo, he listened and nodded in silence.

After a brief silence, he said, "You messaged me a while ago and it's been nagging at me ever since. You said,

'I don't know what is going on, but truth be told, I miss the man I met on the dance floor...' Do you remember that?"

Of course, I remembered. I said to him, "You wrote back, 'I just can't be that person right now...maybe someday.'"

At the time, I had felt so hurt. I had stopped trying after that. He was good at pushing me away. I thought that meant that he didn't want to have anything to do with me. Then I got the feeling that maybe he was conflicted about how he felt, with me being married and what that meant. I know he wasn't good at sharing. I couldn't expect him to be my person, I never expected that of him. The fact that he was there for me at all didn't make sense, but the "maybe someday" talk? I was so confused. I didn't want to think about it. I just wanted a friend.

He tried to comfort me, "This might be that maybe someday. We will figure this out. I made some mistakes—I wasn't prepared for you either. And this last year has been confusing for me too. I just want you to know I am here for you now.

"Perhaps it's time for a change for both of us. It looks like you're moving in the right direction to find yourself, perhaps, you just need to keep going. Your kids sound amazing, you have friends who love you, a new job, and a husband who's trying. This path you are on is going to lead you to where you need to get to. It might just take a detour or two to get there. Besides, I'm pretty sure you're still the same sexy, crazy, fun-loving girl I met in Montreal!"

Did he just call me sexy? I was feeling a little embarrassed.

He continued, “You, my darling friend, are going to have an amazing five days of freedom! And this will give us a chance to figure things out between us, whatever that means.”

I smiled, although I wasn’t sure I believed him. “Let’s just take it one step at a time,” I said.

This was all so confusing. I was feeling exhausted and drained from all the talking but also glad to have him here, which made no sense. My mind starting racing. This trip was supposed to be calming, and now I felt more aggravated than ever. I couldn’t stop twisting my thoughts. I was afraid I was losing my mind.

I was so relieved when I saw the “Welcome to Radium Hot Springs” sign on the side of the highway. It was just past 5:00 p.m. when we had arrived at the motel in Radium. I explained to Marcelo how this quaint little place belonged to a friend of Tess. The Piccadilly had a fully operational, freshly painted red double decker bus and a red phone booth as part of its décor. Penny gave me a warm hug as she came out to greet me, surprised that Carmen was not with me. I explained without getting into too much detail that there had been a last-minute change and that my friend Marcelo would be joining instead. She showed us to our room and I was relieved not only to see the two separate queen beds but also when she didn’t ask too many questions.

I slipped into the quaint and cozy room while Penny showed Marcelo around. It had a little sitting area with couches and a table. There was a mini fridge and the two beds had cozy plush mattresses. It was clean and nicely decorated. It was one of my favourite places to stay.

I washed up and grabbed a bottle of water out of the mini bar. I picked out my bed and unpacked a few things. I set out some snacks to nibble on and wine in case we wanted to chill in the room if we didn't want to go out right away. I polished off half the bottle of water, my throat feeling parched from all the talking in the car. And then I flopped onto the bed, feeling spent.

The thrilling sensation I had felt earlier in the day had somehow drained out of me and I felt lost. I had been so excited, then rocked by Carmen's situation, questioning what I should be doing. Then Marcelo showed up, our conversation confused me, scared me and excited me all at one. My hubby was off having a great time with the kids and this trip was intended as a break. And that's what I needed to do, relax.

When Marcelo came back to the room, I quickly sat up. I grabbed a bottle of wine. I was antsy and immediately started asking questions.

"Are you good to go to the hot springs? If you are hungry, I brought snacks. We could share a bottle of wine, freshen up and head over to the pool. Or we could walk around for a bit, grab a bite to eat, and then head over to the pool. Or…" I rambled when I was nervous and making decisions was never my strong suit. Apparently, neither was relaxing.

"Karina, it's been a long day for both of us. Let's relax for a bit, have a drink, have a nice dinner, and then check out the hot springs. I have heard they are really pretty and relaxing at night." He said, making the decisions for me. I couldn't argue with that. It had been a long day; my nerves were shot and it was nice to have someone else take some control and made the decisions. More importantly, decisions that made sense that I was okay with, because my control freak wasn't quite ready to let go.

He grabbed the bottle of wine from my hands, found the corkscrew, and poured each of us a glass. I took a sip and placed my glass on the table and collapsed on the bed again. He sat on the edge of the other bed. He looked even cuter and kinder, if that was possible, maybe it was because he was taking charge. He let me rest.

Finishing my glass, Marcelo said, "I didn't pack a swimsuit. Don't think they are going to let me into the pool without one." An image of his gorgeous naked body without a swimsuit flashed before my eyes which I dismissed immediately. Then I remembered I had a spare.

"I got you covered, sweetheart, I have Arjan's standby swimsuit in the trunk. I always keep a backup pair in the car in case he forgets his for swim meets. They should fit. Good thing he's never needed them; they are brand new, you can keep them." What I hadn't told him was that my son's backup shorts were short boxer brief speedos.

"Penny told me about this Austrian restaurant we can check out," Marcelo said. "Come on, freshen up, grab your stuff, and let's head out. I have a feeling we're going to have a grand evening!"

We walked to the car, and I found the bag with the swimsuit in it and handed it to him. He opened the car door and let me in, taking my bag and tossing it in the backseat with his. He was taking charge, and it felt good to be taken care of.

"Don't think for a second that this is your car!" I told him playfully as he sat in the driver's seat next to me.

"Trust me, no one thinks this is my car, it's just not my colour!" he winked back.

Chapter 5

Testing the Waters

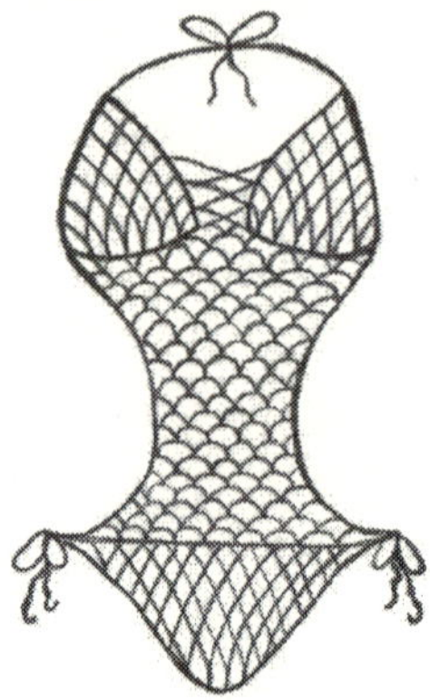

We headed over to the restaurant for dinner. It suited the rest of the village with its rustic yet elegant ambience. The décor was inviting, like a chalet. It was family run and its food was authentic and absolutely delicious. Our waitress was adorable and tough all at once. She looked like she belonged in a biker gang with her long, straight, jet-black hair with bright red streaks, her almost leathery tanned skin, her tattoos, piercings, and her strong demeanour. She smiled at me, looking at me excitedly with her green eyes.

She walked us to the table and we sat down. She gave us a warm smile, and as she described the evening specials, she placed her hands on my shoulders. In my sleeveless blouse, I felt self-conscious having her touch me, although I think she was trying to make me feel more comfortable. There were too many new sensations. I was probably overwhelmed and not used to people paying attention to me.

I also think I was hungry. I had skipped breakfast and lunch as I often did when I got busy with the family and forgot to eat myself. The turmoil of the day and all the surprises had worn me out and I was feeling shaky and lightheaded. Finally getting some food into me made me feel calmer.

When the waitress was out of earshot, Marcelo looked at me knowingly. "I think she's into you."

I laughed, "May I remind you that I am the boring, old housewife."

He smiled, "Well, I am here to remind you that you are far from boring and don't look a day past 29."

He sure knew how to make me feel good, even if it wasn't true.

"Fiery, dangerous, and flirty are some of the words I would use to describe you," he continued, blushing slightly.

I looked at him puzzled. He thought I was fiery? How could he possibly?

"So, how can you trust me if you think I'm dangerous?" I asked, giving him a fake serious stare while smiling shamelessly.

He raised an eyebrow, cocked his head to one side, and replied, "How do you know you can trust me, Karina?"

"That's easy, you are so strait-laced and kind, you are the type of guy who would go out of your way to help old ladies cross the street." I replied giving him this look that told him I thought he was easy to read and could be trusted.

When the bill arrived, I naturally reached for it, but he quickly interjected, "What do you think you are doing, paying for dinner as well? Will you not let me do anything for you?" Our hands lingered on the check, each of us pretending to take it away from the other.

"Well, I did promise to show you a good time, let me take care of it. I am sure you can come up with something later to make it up to me!" It came out more alluring than intended.

"That I will..." he said as he stood up and pulled my chair out for me.

"Why don't we walk around for a bit and watch the sunset before heading to the hot springs?" he suggested as we stepped out of the restaurant. He took a chance and reached for my hand, letting his fingers brush against mine. The sensation made my heart ache slightly and I looked up at him, trying to read him. I couldn't, so I took a chance too and slipped my hand into his. It felt oddly familiar, with the same warmth I had felt in Montreal. I had longed for my husband to hold my hand so many times; it never happened. How did it come so naturally for us?

He led me down a path past the restaurant that eventually led to a beautiful ridge. Far below you could hear the river roaring through the carved canyon snaking its way through the land.

Standing on a green, grassy knoll overlooking nature's beauty, with the sun slowly setting to the west behind us, I felt calm. Marcelo grabbed his phone and took a few pictures. He captured a couple of me, and we attempted a few selfies, but we kept messing it up due to our height difference. I stepped up on a fence board and stood on my tiptoes, grabbing his arm tightly while his outstretched arm held the phone, trying desperately not to fall over. It was entertaining for people passing by. I thought I would be more worried capturing any evidence of us being together on camera, but a part of me liked having the memories. Besides, we were two friends, enjoying a nice evening together.

As I stood there, staring down at the darkness of the water far below us, feeling the last of the sun on my skin before it set, I felt Marcelo behind me, just millimeters away. I felt a chill go down my spine and so I crossed my bare arms, hugging myself in an attempt to warm up. He came a little closer and embraced me in his arms. His warm breath brushed against the nape of my neck; his five o'clock shadow along his jawline felt rough against my bare shoulder. I tilted my head back just slightly, so I could rest it against his chest. I could feel his heart beating and I could feel mine aching. What was I doing here with him? There was this connection I couldn't deny and it scared me. How could someone that felt like a stranger make me feel this way? An image of my family flashed before my closed eyes and I jerked forward slightly. I was married, with kids!

"We should get going or we're going to miss the hot springs," I reminded him as I slid out from under his arms and headed back to the car. I had to find a way to stop feeling.

By the time we arrived at the hot springs, the sun had just set. The natural hot pool was built with an open-air concept, so you could see the night sky and feel the cool breeze as you soaked in the warm waters. The moon and the stars were bright in the sky. There wasn't a lot of artificial lighting placed around the springs intentionally, which made the night sky even more brilliant. In the main hall, I split one way and headed to the ladies' change room and Marcelo headed towards the men's.

As soon as I started to change, I felt self-conscious. Trying to cover myself up, I attempted to slip out of my clothes. Then, two cute, giggling, twenty-something girls walked into the changing room. One of them stripped down to nothing almost immediately. She started bouncing about with her perfect, perky breasts and well-groomed body—she looked like she didn't have a care in the world. They continued to change as I stood there even more awkward than before. How was I going to show my old, chubby, scarred, and stretched-marked body now?

I looked at the suit I had packed, regretting my choice immediately. When I thought I was coming with Carmen, I didn't care about what I was bringing. Being brought up in a traditional Indian home and being a bigger girl, I had never felt comfortable showing off my body or being proud of it. My mother would constantly tell me to not show cleavage, to cover my toffee-coloured skin and not attract attention. It wasn't the right thing to do.

When I went on vacation, my family would be in tow, and although I knew I shouldn't care and that it was my body, somehow, I would always bring the most conservative outfits and kept things simple.

The suits I had packed for this trip, Carmen had convinced me to buy. Carmen was all about body image and not body shaming. She helped me get past a lot of those stigmas. For me, it was a little more complicated. Carmen got me through a very painful and difficult time in my life when I had had to undergo breast surgery ten years ago and many more surgeries and treatments thereafter. She helped me see myself as a woman again, attractive, whole, and beautiful. She bought me scarves when my hair fell out, she taught me how to draw in eyebrows and use eyeliner to make me look like I had lashes, she forced me to eat when the thought of food was so nauseating, I wasn't sure I would ever eat again. She helped me rebuild myself, finding new styles for my uneven body. And although the rebuilding had begun, it wasn't the same. And I wasn't ready to let Marcelo know about my difficult past. I was scared he would see me differently. And I didn't want more sympathy, not now.

This suit wasn't a bikini (I wasn't quite ready for that, although I had packed one), but a one-piece, black, lace, cut-out suit overlaid on top of a pink, green, and white bikini. The "bikini" bottom was cut high in the butt and hips, but still had ample coverage. The "bikini" top cupped my breasts and tied around my neck. The lace attached the two pieces by starting at the cups of my breasts and my midriff was covered only in lace with semi-circular cut-outs making an hourglass figure with the lace continuing to the bottom half of the suit. There was no material covering my back or sides.

Even though I was self-conscious, this suit was one of my favourites because it was sexy and flattering, hiding my scars and stretch marks and accenting my curves in just the right places. I had never worn it out of the house. I guess I had no choice but to slip it on. I tried not to think of those other girls, trying to muster up my own confidence. I barely glanced at myself as I tied my hair into a high messy bun, took a quick rinsing shower, grabbed my towel (too shy not to cover myself up), and headed for the springs.

I was hoping to have beat Marcelo to the pool so that I could slip into the water before him, but he was standing close to the door, waiting for me. I figured I could just walk up to the edge of the pool and slip the towel off at the last second. Instead, Marcelo grabbed the towel from me, pulling it off my body in one quick gesture, almost spinning me. Before I could realize what had happened, the cool breeze hit my body and I almost screamed from the chill. I tried to cover my body with my arms, but Marcelo reached out and grabbed my hand before I had a chance to. I noticed him looking at me.

He gave me the widest smile with a look of approval and said, “Smart and gorgeous, I am a lucky man tonight.” I almost rolled my eyes, thinking he was being sarcastic as my husband often was. But no-one had looked at me the way he was looking at me right now.

I had been so worried about what I looked like, I had forgotten about him. Marcelo was wearing the suit I had given him. He looked like Daniel Craig from the ocean swim scene in Casino Royale, a level of sexy that only exists in Bond movies.

He was standing there in the pale blue, tight, boxer-style shorts and there wasn’t a lot left to the imagination. They were probably a little small for him; they hugged his tight butt, lifting it slightly, and squeezed around his hips, the faux fly stretching over his...well, you know. It was extremely flattering. The black band sat under his navel, accenting his pelvic bones. It was outrageous—he looked very much like a swimsuit model. Tall, broad shouldered, muscular, fit, attractive. The blue suit brought out the grey in his eyes. I tried to stop staring, but I couldn’t. And the steam from the hot pools was wafting behind him, giving off a smouldering feel...okay, I am exaggerating but there he was. Here I thought I was going to get the better of him by giving him this suit, but he had managed to pull it off and look gorgeous.

I couldn't help but look him up and down and take in the image presented before me. Almost impulsively, I reached out and touched his chest and abs, wanting to see if he was real. I let my fingers brush his chest before stopping myself and getting too carried away. He was real. He was standing in front of me. He was here with me. He put his arm around me and gave my shoulders a squeeze. Then he held my hand and led me to the pool.

I slipped into the inviting 37-degree hot water, allowing the liquid to pool around my body and cover me in warmth. I started to relax and found a seat with a jet to massage my lower back. Marcelo sat next to me. As the natural spring-fed, mineral water started to do its magic, I lay back and allowed my body to accept it. The pool was large, a good sixty feet from end to end. There were varying depths and an island in the middle with seating all around the edges. It wasn't overly busy, so we had space to ourselves and some privacy.

"Not that you don't already know, but you look really good too, have you been trying something new?" I tried to say casually.

"Well, I did spoil myself with a new spin bike. And I love the house music playlists you sent me, keeps me motivated," he said modestly. He looked a little more defined than I recollected; the spin bike was obviously being put to good use.

"I'm looking into a biking and wine tour in France, if you think it's your thing, maybe you could join me." I couldn't believe I was proposing another trip together.

"Sure, sounds like fun. Not sure you could keep up with me though," he said, daring me as he smiled.

"Well, when I won't be kicking your fine ass, I will be enjoying the view, either way I'm motivated," I countered.

"And I'm sure you will be sporting all kinds of cute outfits. Only one way to find out. So, one year from now, you and me in France?"

"I don't know about next year, but promise me that in this lifetime, you and I will do something fun. Make it happen someday?" I had no idea where I would be next year, but I did want to do this with him.

"Deal. We will have to find a way to make it happen. Maybe next year? But definitely!" He said playfully as he traced his fingers down my arm. He felt surreal.

I replied "I guess that's a definite maybe! More definite from you and less maybe from me and we might just get there." And we left it at that.

Sitting in the hot pool brought back memories from my younger days. "When I was in my twenties this was all the rage—do people even use that word anymore? Anyway, everyone went to the hot springs. On the rare occasion I was allowed, my friends and I would drive up to the mountain village of Banff for the evening. We'd soak in the hot springs, find a lounge or club to hang out at all night long, and then drive the 90 minutes back to town at 3:00 a.m. I miss being young sometimes, being impulsive like that."

He smiled at my spontaneity. "If you love adventure, let me tell you about an amazing natural hot spring I visited," he said. "It was during my trip to Fiji. They're formed by volcanic springs underground, and they're rich with minerals. They flow back to the surface creating waterfalls and naturally cratered pools. Surrounded by jungle vegetation, serene beauty, and fragrant tropical flowers, they say it's rejuvenating and holds mystical healing powers."

I looked at him quizzically, not sure he was making up this story.

"No, really," he continued "I have never experienced anything like it. I would love to take you sometime—show you all the amazing botanicals and rich culture. What do you think, would you let me take you away, Karina?"

The way he said my name in his deep, husky voice, relaxed from being in the hot pool—I loved it. It was the way he said it; he didn't have an Italian accent, but he rolled the "r" just slightly, making my name sound like a purr. It felt like he was alluding to something naughty even though it was just my name. I completely forget the question, but I nodded absent mindedly.

I loved hearing his stories about the exotic and interesting places he had travelled to. He would always have an interesting spin on it: how dangerous the weather conditions were during landing, how many pints he could drink, how the locals always made him feel welcome. Sometimes I felt like I was traveling there with him. He had been all over the world and his lifestyle seemed so exciting. I wanted to be transported to all of the places with him, and to not fear, worry, or feel anxious about what it would mean.

Was he being serious in wanting to take me? Even if he were, it's not like I could ever make it happen. For now, I just wanted to listen to his hypnotic voice and adventurous tales.

I looked around the hot springs. They were always impressive to me, with a huge, wet rock wall face, large boulders, and the perimeter lined with deciduous and pine trees. There weren't fragrant tropical flowers, but the minerals combined with the pine created a natural earthy scent which was soothing. This must have seemed like an average community pool to Marcelo in comparison I thought.

He continued, "I love exploring and trying different things. Every place holds a little mystery and magic." He brushed a few curls away from my face, which was feeling flushed from sitting in the warm water and listening to his stories.

He looked over at me with those kind eyes and said, "Come sit with me, let me rub your shoulders, help you relax." He reached for me and pulled me even closer to him.

He guided my body towards his and held me by my hips. I couldn't see him but I was very aware of him. I kept thinking back to the night in Montreal, going back to his apartment, up to his rooftop. It brought up feelings I hadn't allowed myself to indulge in. I pushed them aside and allowed myself to escape in the moment.

My husband had never understood sensuality, comfort, or tenderness. He had needs which had to be met. There were no gentle caresses or lingering sensations. No kissing or affection. Marcelo had this way of making me vulnerable, allowing me to trust him, to explore and feel secure. I wanted to surrender to him. He slowly slid my body onto his thighs and held me in place. His hands deliberately moved up my bare waist towards the sides of my breasts and his warm gentle fingers traced their way along my shoulder blades and rested on my shoulders. I was tense, between all the events of the day and feeling his presence, and I was holding a lot of my stress in my shoulders, I could feel it. They were so tense that when he started rubbing them, I lost all regard for the fact I was sitting on his lap. As he slowly moved his thumbs along the ridge of my shoulder blades, I felt them relax. I almost moaned audibly, catching myself and pursing my lips shut. I had ached for his touch again since that night.

He was so gentle and yet so deliberate with his hands, working my shoulders with precision and effort. He started to work on my neck and gently slid my body closer to his. My eyes were closed and the things I was imagining in my head were so much naughtier than what was happening to me. I hadn't allowed myself to feel that way in so long and it felt so good. I know I should've stopped, the thoughts and his hands, but I couldn't, he knew how to knead and release and add just enough pressure to make me catch my breath.

I was being transported; forgetting my worries, only pleasant thoughts were drifting in and out of my mind and warm sensations were flowing through my body. The inviting hot springs, the amazing scenery of the night sky, the mountain skyline, the twinkling stars, the crisp night air, the warm waters and his comforting hands. This wasn't real. He wasn't real. I kept my eyes closed in case I opened them and it was all my imagination. Caught up in my thoughts, I lost my sense of balance momentarily and bobbed in the water. Trying to regain it, I reached down with my hands, looking for the seat to steady myself. Instead, I felt his muscular thighs. I tried to use my legs to stand up but slipped back and instead found myself pressing my back up against his legs and torso. And that wasn't the only thing I felt. There was a firm poke against my lower back. I froze. It felt impressively large and very hard, perhaps the thin layer of our suits was not hiding much.

As stupid as this sounds, I didn't recognize it at first. After twenty years of marriage, sex was often scheduled, quick and routine. I knew what to expect, when and how. The adventure was rarely there and the passion had dwindled. My husband was older, he was comfortable, he was content. The few times we had tried to surprise each other or be spontaneous, it hadn't really worked out. Don't get me wrong, there is nothing wrong with familiarity; we knew what worked, but that spark was gone.

Feeling Marcelo in the hot springs was more than I could handle. Like something you would find in an adult toy store. Impulsive, thrilling, pleasing...it was all too much. I knew he was having an effect on me, but obviously, I was having an effect on him too. I pressed up ever so slightly against him, just for a second, to see if what I was feeling was real and not just my mind playing tricks on me. It was very real. I had to slip away before things got out of hand. I regained my composure and slid off his thighs and found the seat pulling my knees up against my chest and wrapping my arms around them.

I couldn't look at him. I didn't want to embarrass myself. It took me a minute to calm down and let my arms and legs relax again. He could tell I was uncomfortable, but it wasn't his fault. I just wasn't ready for all of him. We didn't speak, it was odd, but the silence between us was strangely comforting. He slid his hand over to mine and our pinkies touched. For now, that was enough, all I could handle. We sat in silence for the rest of the time and enjoyed the night air.

"Let's grab a drink before going back to the room," he finally said when we were both done soaking. I was so relaxed, I wasn't sure I could move, but I nodded, it was time to go. Somehow, I managed to drag myself out of the water, changed, and met him back out by the car. I don't think I was ready to go back to the room quite yet, so a pub was a good idea.

We found a local pub and decided to check it out. It was quite simple yet quaint, like everything in the town, with dim lighting, wooden floors, a nice large bar, country music playing in the background. There were a few people scattered about. We grabbed a couple of seats at the bar and ordered.

"I will order us a few white beers or blanche as we call them. Do you like Belgium Moon?" He stopped when he saw the confused look on my face. "Don't worry, I will find something you will like. On second thought, let's do an Ol' Beautiful Brass Monkey Blood Orange Blonde Ale."

I honestly thought he had made up the name, being not at all familiar with beer. It was more fun to say than to drink, but it was a nice crisp citrus ale. A few sips in, my head was spinning, so I slid the pint over to Marcelo to finish. He smiled his irresistible smile as he finished up the drinks. I was so relaxed and so aware of this man. My body was tingling.

He looked at my flushed face and gently brushed my cheek. "You are so beautiful and full of life. I get why Daryl loves your company. Pretty, smart, and strong. Your husband is a lucky man."

I looked down, embarrassed, feeling self-conscious. My husband never saw any of that in me and definitely never told me. I didn't believe Marcelo either.

As I looked up, he was staring at me like he wanted to share more, but he couldn't. He masked his expression, but I could see a longing.

I held his gaze and gently touched his shoulder. "I'm not sure I believe you; you are the sweetest thing to be there for me," I said softly, "and you have been so kind, amazing and supportive I don't deserve you."

As we stared at each other, I felt the tension between us increase. I had to lighten the mood, "You're not so bad yourself, kinda gorgeous and charming. Now, let's get out of here before it gets to your head," I whispered as I gently punched him in the arm. I was done for the night and wanted to have a real conversation with him, which wasn't going to happen in the bar.

"Just kinda?" he said playfully as he nudged my shoulder with his. He reached for my hand, helped me off the barstool and we headed out.

I don't know if it was the soaking in the hot springs, the night air, or the unexpected turn of events, but I wasn't feeling like my old, tired, housewife self at all. I felt a kind of determination come over me. I wanted something. All the confusion from earlier in the day was gone and I felt completely in-sync with him.

As we stepped into the room, Marcelo said he was going to hang the suits to dry and stepped into the washroom. I decided to quickly slip into a spaghetti strapped, purple tank top, shorts, and a hoodie. I set up a Bluetooth speaker on my nightstand and pulled out my phone so we could listen to some music. As the bathroom door closed behind him, I jumped at my phone as it made the most obnoxious sound. Instead of my music, it was a strange notification sound Arjan had set so I would know when he was texting. Something between a loud fart and a sound an alien would make. It did it again, and again, and again.

I felt a slight sense of panic, quickly checking my messages, worried something was wrong. He had sent me a few pictures of his arm with a big bloody gash in it. My heart stopped. He was hurt! Why hadn't someone called me? Would I have to go to the hospital? Before my thoughts spun out too much, there was another message saying, "Don't be alarmed! Gotcha!" Boys and their pranks.

He'd also sent a series of photos from their day: the tent, the mountains, the campfire. It looked lovely. There was another message from Aryan; he'd sent a video message of himself playing a clip from "Stand by Me" on the guitar. He was so talented; I could listen to him play anytime. Then my phone started to ring. When I glanced at the name, I saw it was my husband.

My husband! I had forgotten all about him, and I hadn't told him about Carmen. And now he was calling me. Of course, I had to answer. When I did, I thought for sure the truth was going to come spilling out.

"Hi honey," I said as I picked up, "how are you? How are the boys? Having lots of fun, I am sure. I got a little worried when I saw the texts Arjan sent—"

"Hi Karina," he said, cutting me off. "The kids are fine; I needed a nap after the long drive. Thank you for all the food you made and packed. Not sure about exact plans but the kids will be hiking tomorrow and will have limited cell reception." He sounded tired and disengaged.

"Anyway, have a-good night. Arjev wants to talk to you." My youngest son's voice suddenly filled the phone as he told me he loved me about a hundred times and missed me and wished I was there to tuck him in, then he hung up the phone.

I didn't get to say bye to hubby. He didn't apologize for the arm gash prank. He didn't ask me about my day, what I had done, or if I had plans. He simply assumed that my mundane housewife life wouldn't be eventful enough to talk about. And he forgot that I too was on a trip. He didn't even say he loved me.

My music started to play through the speaker and it was as if nothing had happened.

When Marcelo opened the bathroom door, he was wearing nothing but his boxer briefs. He had "accidently" gone into my toiletries bag and found some satsuma-scented massage oil. I think he liked going through my things, but it was super annoying to me. I glared at him, letting him know that I was not impressed.

"Why you would pack massage oil is a mystery to me, but lucky for me you did. And you did mention you wanted to give me a massage some time ago, so this works out." He had a boyish grin on his face, making him even more irresistible. He pulled the covers back and lay down on his bed, face down, holding the bottle up in the air. I didn't recall him being so playful in Montreal. Something had changed and I was determined to find out what.

"Do whatever you want to this body, as long as it involves massage oil!" he said, still waving the bottle.

By this point I had taken the massage oil from him and instead of warming it up in my hands first, I deliberately drizzled the cool oil along his back. He flinched at the chill.

He was about to turn around when I hopped on the bed and straddled him, pinning him down so he couldn't move or make a mess of the oil. I stripped off my hoodie and slowly started to slide my hands over the oil, warming it with my palms and spreading it more evenly over his entire back and shoulders.

It occurred to me that I didn't know if he was single or not. I had teased him about it in Montreal, but a lot can change in a year. I asked him casually, "Your shoulders don't seem as tense, do you have a girlfriend I haven't heard about, to relieve some of that tension?" Not that his shoulders were any less tense.

He grinned. "Are you fishing? You could just ask me if I have a girlfriend."

I wasn't prepared for his answer, probably because I just figured he was single and I wanted to be selfish to have him to myself. I couldn't just ask him, fearful of his response.

"I am not seeing anyone. And will you relax your grip a little, you are hurting my shoulders." He said to my relief. I hadn't realized how tightly I was holding on.

"What is going on with you? You're definitely not the same geeky, shy and unsure guy I met in the bar in Montreal? Or the normal everyday conversation guy I have been texting for the last year. Do you have an evil sexy twin you never told me about?" I asked him. He seemed lost in the massage.

I pressed my knees into his sides to get his attention. I asked again, "So, darling, what has changed? I recall asking you when we met if you were drunk and horny and you were too embarrassed to answer. And now you seem to be both and not hiding it at all. What gives?" At this point, I was sitting just below his waist, straddling him between my thighs perhaps with a little more skin to skin contact than I should have allowed. I couldn't see his face, so I had no idea what he was thinking.

He took a deep breath and said, "Life is short, and you should go after the things you want. And right now, this is what I want."

I wasn't sure where he was going. Surely, he didn't want me. My life was complicated, I was a mess and he didn't need that. I wanted to know but I didn't want to ask.

As I massaged the oil into his back, I thought about what it would be like to be with this man. And how different it would be, fewer distractions and complications. I wondered what it would be like to make love to him. I imagined his hands as they washed over my naked body as his mouth enveloped mine in a deep kiss, connecting on a level of intimacy that was real. I knew I had to stop thinking like this but I just let the thought linger in my mind while my hands continued to move along and massage his body. It didn't matter if I wanted to fantasize, they were just thoughts.

As I applied the massage oil and began to work his back inch by inch, using my thumbs, fingers and even elbows to work the tight muscles, I could feel him relax beneath me. What I thought would be an awkward night fueled by sexual tension gave way to comfortable intimacy, easy conversation, and therapeutic contact. I found knots hidden in his shoulders, by his shoulder blades and down his back. I worked his lower back and even worked up the courage to work the upper glutes. Each time I picked a new point on his shoulders or back to work on, he talked a little more about himself. It wasn't overly personal and often silly, but we talked, laughed, and talked some more. I felt connected to him.

He started telling me about his childhood, his mom, his sister, his life, but with no specifics or details. This was like an art for him, to be able to talk so much about himself and reveal nothing. He also told me more about his travels and some of the more interesting things he had seen and experienced. He told me about his work and some of the papers he would be presenting. It was so interesting to hear about his life, his life was inspiring.

The sexually charged man I had seen a few hours ago was now putty in my hands, literally. I was glad we had talked in the car and sorted out some of the uncertainty and doubt. Even though things were not necessarily clearer, I felt like we were on the same wavelength. I shifted my position to lean against the headboard and carefully crossed my bare legs.

"Can you flip over and lay your head on my lap?" I asked him.

He obliged, gently placing his head on my calves, his hair grazing my thighs and tickling me. I could see his jaw and neck muscles relax as I worked my hands from his shoulders to his neck. With intention, I used my fingers to work his scalp, pressing and working my thumbs back down his neck. I pressed firmly on his chest and pecs, purposely moving my hands in a circular motion, feeling him let his body go completely against my legs.

As much as I enjoyed having this man between my legs while my hands roamed, I knew I eventually had to stop. I wasn't ready for anything more. I allowed myself to rest my arms against his chest and felt him breathe deeply as his heartbeat steadily under the pressure of my hands.

He took my hand and gently interlaced his fingers in mine. As he traced a finger from his free hand up and down my hand and wrist, he explained, "Fun fact: when two people hold hands with their fingers interlaced you are stimulating each other's pressure points. It's a trigger that increases the senses, connected to your vagus nerve".

I clung to every word he was saying, like he was dripping honey on my tongue. His words were like an aphrodisiac. "The pressure from the touch lowers your heart rate, decreases hypertension, and puts you into a relaxed state of mind. The interlacing increases the stimulation."

There was definitely an increase in stimulation and it wasn't only between our fingers. The intimacy of the situation was arousing, the physical touch was heightening, but the sexual urgency wasn't overwhelming. When my legs felt they had lost all feeling, I scooted out from under him and lay my head on his bare chest, more playful than sensual. I was a hugger and a cuddler.

"Karina," he started as he gently curled strands of my hair around his fingertips, "I want to know more about you. This trip feels like an escape from your life, your opportunity to think about what you want," It was clearly my turn to open up. "What do you want to get out of this trip?"

I decided not to dodge the question. "I feel like I missed out on opportunities," I began slowly. "I led a sheltered life and followed all the rules, never figured out who I was. I was that girl who used to be afraid of nothing and wanted to do everything. Yet, I limited my outlook because of artificial limitations, my parents' and society's expectations, a mistake I won't make for my kids.

"I got married young," I continued. As I opened up to him, I found comfort in confiding to him. "I had one partner for such a long time. I regret not taking more risks, experimenting more. There were many missed opportunities. Now, I feel like an anomaly—trying to fit in and please everyone else in my life, all the while being torn up."

I paused, and the room went silent. He lifted my head off his chest, got up and got a drink and got me a glass of water. He sat back down on the bed and leaned back, resting his head on the headboard, his long legs outstretched in front of him. He looked at me patiently, giving me the space to continue if I wanted to. I had a sudden urge to straddle him right there, but I didn't dare, it wasn't right. Even now, I felt torn about what I wanted, but I couldn't tell him. Grabbing a pillow, I placed my head close to his thighs instead, which felt more cozy and not as intense.

"As for this trip, I just want to be true to myself, not sure what that looks like, but so far, things have been perfect." I finally said.

"I am glad to hear it and happy I can be here with you, I feel like I am being true to myself too.," he replied. I still couldn't tell if he was mocking me, I was not used to talking openly like this.

It must've been 3:00 a.m. before we even thought about going to sleep. Things were getting hazy and the exhaustion of the day was starting to take over. The bliss and comfort of just talking, being honest, intimate, and physically comfortable with each other was so satisfying; it surprised me.

Here we were, in bed together, but we didn't sleep with each other. I was so worried about what might have transpired, but we hadn't done anything. It felt right to talk, laugh, and vent. Not having to worry about my husband or kids or being judged was a relief, like a heavy burden had been lifted off me. I was feeling genuinely happy.

And yet, a part of me was feeling like I was lying to myself emotionally. There was something nagging at me. But for now, this would have to do.

Chapter 6

Decisions, Decisions

As a beam of bright light shone through the crack in the curtains onto my face, I knew it was morning. It took me a minute to realize where I was. I was in Radium. When I rolled over in bed, I was relieved to see I was the only one in it and that I still had my clothes on. It took me a minute to recall what had transpired the night before. Across the narrow gap in the other queen-sized bed lay Marcelo.

I rarely slept alone and it felt weird not to have someone to cuddle with in the morning. I was so tempted to sneak into Marcelo's bed, just to feel the warmth of his body, but I knew better. The night before we had come a little too close to crossing lines that I wasn't quite ready to cross.

Because the summer days were so long, I figured it could be anywhere between 6:00 and 10:00 a.m. My phone told me it was 7:30. I had slept in. It was nice not to have the kids demanding my time or having to scream at them to put their electronics away so they could eat breakfast.

I quietly grabbed my phone and took the opportunity to check in on Carmen. Her husband was stable; she was shaken but she was doing okay. She wished she were anywhere but by that hospital bed. I wished she were there with me. At least she was okay.

Marcelo was still fast asleep. He looked so relaxed, like he didn't have anything to worry about. He was shirtless and I could see the light playing off the muscles along his back and shoulders. His strong arms looked so inviting. I really wanted to be held, but I wasn't sure he had anything on. And I wasn't about to find out.

I crept out of my bed, trying not to make any noise and made my way to the washroom. I looked in the mirror and barely recognized myself. I expected to have dark circles and blotchy skin, but somehow, I was radiant. Even my makeup hadn't smeared as badly as I would've expected it to after sleeping in it. I cleaned up and was about to step out when the door opened.

The sound of Marcelo's voice saying, "Good morning, Karina," awakened me in more than one way. I knew he had gorgeous eyes, but his deep, raspy morning voice just added to his charm.

Marcelo almost knocked me over as he brushed past me, the touch of his bare chest, hot against my skin. "I seriously have to pee..." He started pulling down his shorts before I had had a chance to leave.

How had he become so comfortable with me in such a short time? I quickly shut the door behind me and decided to get dressed. Only problem was, there was no separate room to dress. And I didn't need him coming out of the bathroom to see me half naked.

I quickly grabbed my things and headed for the closet to try and gain some privacy. I slipped on some blue polka dot panties and a super cute skirt. I removed my nightie, throwing it on the bed and reached for the matching bra when I noticed it on the floor between the bathroom and the closet.

Could I get to it before Marcelo came out of the bathroom? I could hear the water running, so I covered myself the best I could and dashed for the bra. Just then the door opened and there was Marcelo. As he stepped out, he deliberately stepped on my bra strap. He looked down and picked up the bra, eyeing it and then looking up at me.

He quirked an eyebrow. "Missing something?"

Although my arms were doing their best to cover me, my breasts were not doing a splendid job of hiding themselves; it was like they had a mind of their own. He knew all too well, as I did, that if he threw the bra, I would have to reach out to catch it, and although he was okay to be topless, I was not. I wasn't ready. I could see him staring at my scars, something I really wasn't ready to share with him either. It had never come up, and I didn't want to tell him and make him a part of my pain. He could see the distress in my eyes. He walked up to me and told me to turn around so that my back was to him. I was so embarrassed. I sunk my head down and looked to the side.

He pressed his chest into my back, embracing me gently as he reached around tenderly so I could carefully move my arms away from my breasts and slip them through the straps without exposing myself. He slowly moved his fingers up each arm, caressing them as he moved the straps up to my shoulders. He lightly moved his fingers across my back, tracing the outline of the garment along my shoulder blades. He then proceeded to clip the bra in place, taking his time to clip each clasp. I still had my head cocked to one side, holding my breath. He bent over and kissed me softly on the neck and held his lips against my neck for a second, so I could feel his breath against my skin. He lingered, tracing his fingers down my arms again.

A charmer, a seducer and a gentleman. Who knew?

It reminded me of that fateful night again and triggered a memory I hadn't allowed myself to really think about. That night in Montreal, not only had I lost track of time, as it was probably 2:00 a.m. when we left the club, but also all sensation in my feet. When we had finally stepped out into the night air, the warm breeze and the pain hit me all at once. I hadn't worn heels in an awfully long time and definitely not for four hours of dancing!

My feet felt like they were being squeezed and every step I took, they ached a little more. I could barely walk straight from the throbbing and needed support. I looked over at another one of Daryl's friends who couldn't walk straight to save his life. His name slips my memory right now, but he was very Italian and very intoxicated by the end of the evening.

He had wanted to drive home, but there was no way I was going to let him do that. Luckily, Marcelo lived close by, so I made an excuse that we should all walk to his place and hang out until his friend sobered up. Part of me wanted to walk arm in arm with Marcelo because I wasn't ready to let him go. Part of me wanted to see where he lived. But mostly, I couldn't let a friend drive home drunk.

The cobbled streets didn't help my case. I was so ready to take my heels off and throw them out. Daryl's drunken laugh told me he found it extremely amusing to watch me hobble, but it was an excuse to hold onto Marcelo the whole way there. I held onto his arm tightly, allowing him to wrap his arm around my waist.

My mind was playing tricks on me, I had barely had a drink, but I felt so intoxicated. Every few steps I would fall into him, and he put up with it, assisting me the whole way. If only I hadn't been in so much pain, I would've enjoyed it more, but having him hold me made it bearable.

We walked up to a grand eight-storey sandstone and brick building with elegant columns and double doors that greeted you as you entered. The historic architecture of Old Montreal was majestic compared to most of the cookie cutter houses scattered about Calgary neighbourhoods.

We made our way up the elevator to the fourth floor. As soon as we stepped in, I threw my shoes off. Stretching my toes, I felt a little relief.

The apartment was gorgeous. He had an open concept one-bedroom suite, but it was enormous. It had a newly renovated modern kitchen with stainless steel appliances, a spacious and well decorated living room, a contemporary four-piece bath including a turquoise blue tempered glass vessel sink, an office with mahogany built-ins and a bedroom large enough to house a king-sized bed with stylish bedding and matching furniture.

It was unusually hot in his apartment, almost uncomfortable. There had been an unusual heat wave that week that made it feel even warmer and muggier. I could hear the guys turning on the tap in the kitchen to grab water and then cooling themselves off on a single window air conditioner unit in the bedroom. I didn't trust myself to go into the bedroom, with three drunk men and one very large bed. I noticed Marcelo lying on his bed at one point as I walked by and I wouldn't have known what to do with myself if I walked in.

I made myself comfortable on the large comfy sofa in the living room, listening to them laugh at their own jokes while trying to sober up. I walked over and stood in front of the large living room window, gazing out at the amazing view of the St. Laurent River, Old Montreal with the La Ronde in the background. It was so picturesque.

"It's so stuffy and warm in here. Do you want to get outta here? I want to show you something. I think you will like it." Marcelo asked, sneaking up behind me as I stood there, looking out at the view as he pressed himself up against me, his hands on my shoulders.

"What do you want to show me?" I asked, liking the way he felt.

"Do you want to check out the rooftop? The fresh air will be nice and the view is amazing" He murmured in my ear.

"More amazing than this? I would love to, but what about your friends?" I asked, pinching myself slightly as none of it seemed real.

"They're too drunk and they've seen it before. Let me take you, grab your shoes." He reached for my hand.

"Shoes! I can't put those things on again! But I still want to check out the rooftop. You sure you aren't too drunk?" I smiled.

"It doesn't matter, you don't need shoes. Not too drunk, I can't keep up with them. Let's go." He took my hand in his and we snuck out of the apartment as he led the way, heading up a set of stairs to the rooftop, leaving his friends behind.

The stairwell was oddly dark, so between reaching out for a railing, trying not to trip, and holding onto Marcelo, grace wasn't my strong suit. I felt his free hand slide from my shoulder to my lower back used to guide me until we reached the top. He grabbed the door and held it open for me. As I stepped out onto the unlit rooftop, into the pitch black of night, I caught my breath. As my eyes adjusted, the night sky twinkled with millions of bright stars. The view of the city was captivating and the silence was oddly deafening. There was no one around, we were so isolated. In the darkness of the night, I couldn't make out anything more than a silhouette of Marcelo, afraid that if he stepped away, I would lose him. I closed my eyes momentarily and soaked it all in, it felt like a dream.

Marcelo reached for my hand and held it in his. He gave it a little squeeze, reassuring me that he wasn't going anywhere. Just a few hours ago, he had been jumpy at my touch and confused by my openness, but now, he was taking charge. He was more confident and attentive. I was a little confused by it all and caught up in the excitement.

He turned towards me, "Look at me, really look at me, look me in the eyes." I couldn't do it. Every time I did, I saw what I wanted and knew I couldn't have it; it was torture. If I closed my eyes, I could capture every moment and hold onto it. Create a memory that would last a lifetime. I knew we had only just met and had only known each other for a few short hours, but I wanted it. Anything he was willing to give me. I bit my lower lip, anticipating what might happen. I let the silence and lingering torment me until I couldn't take it any longer.

"Marcelo..." I whispered his name, breaking the silence, caught up in the moment of being with this gorgeous man who was intoxicating, charming and who was seducing me on the rooftop of the building.

Before I could say anything else, he embraced me from behind, allowing his lips to trail along my neck, the faintest smell of alcohol on his breath as his hands began to explore my body. For an instant, I was lost in the ecstasy of his touch, his need, his desire. I needed it too. I allowed myself to press into his body, have him take me away from reality. This was Montreal after all, the sin city of Canada. And I was falling into her mercy.

We were two shadows, dancing in each other's arms, like on the dance floor, but without any music, which made it more intense. As I held his hand in mine, his left hand slipped up my waist, over my ribs and rested on my tender breast. I felt his palm press up, taking the entirety of my breast in his hand, squeezing it gently and then more firmly, pulling at the material so his fingertips touched more skin.

As we couldn't see each other, my other senses seemed even more heightened. I thought I would be more alarmed that he was touching me in this way. I had been poked, prodded, and touched hundreds of times, by doctors, nurses, interns, lactation consultants, oncologists, but my husband had stopped touching me like this years ago. Now Marcelo was not just touching me but awakening sensations and making me feel like a woman he desired. He hadn't even realized the asymmetrical anatomy, that I was missing a part of me. Bearing three children and a diagnosis from ten years ago had left me scarred. He didn't even notice.

I was so caught up in the sensation that when he began to unzip my jumpsuit and slide it down my body, I was even more entranced. We were caught up in some intoxicated fantasy. He had undone the zipper on his pants and when I felt his fingers grip my hips as his thumbs hooked onto my black sheer mesh panties, I jolted. What was I doing? This had to stop. Now. But it felt so good to be held, touched and wanted.

As much as I wanted it, I was not prepared for it or the possible consequences. I didn't think he had wanted this either, he had seemed so nervous and innocent. I hadn't planned for this, don't know if we had misinterpreted things. I could feel the warmth of his body against mine as he bent me over. His hands travelled up the length of my exposed back, all the way up to my shoulders and over to gently cup my breasts, which were barely shielded by the sheer bra, before moving them down again. His lips roamed my neck and back as he began to slip the panties down my hips. Before he got a chance to do anything else, I placed my hands on his and held them in place.

For a moment, I hesitated, allowing myself to take it all in, feeling this man against me. Thinking about what was about to happen if I let it. But I couldn't. Not like this. I didn't believe in one-night stands. I held his hands more firmly and slowly and intentionally helped him slip the black lace back up again. I pulled away just enough to compose myself as I pulled my jumpsuit back up, covering my exposed body.

I allowed him to zip me up again. We hadn't said a word to each other the whole time. I hated myself, but I wasn't sure why. Was it because I felt I had betrayed Marcelo, my husband, or myself?

I let Marcelo hold me, just grateful he still wanted to even though I felt like I had just rejected him. I would've stayed the night. I would've stayed forever at that moment, feeling so vulnerable and protected. My heart hurt so much; I was so torn.

I had a life to sort out first. A husband waiting for me. A husband! Just then, the door opened and Daryl stumbled onto the rooftop, slurring slightly, "I called you an Uber, you have ten minutes to get your butt downstairs and back to your hotel."

Ten minutes was all I had. And then it would be over and I would be back on my way to that hotel room, to my husband and my life. What had just happened? I didn't have time to process.

Marcelo broke our silence. "We had better find your shoes and get you home. We wouldn't want your husband to worry, now, would we?" He said it without feeling, like he had to go through the motions of being a good host. I wasn't ready to leave, but I had no choice.

We made our way back through the dark to his apartment where I gathered my things. He and Daryl walked me out of his apartment, back into the elevator and through the lobby. The Uber was already waiting for me when we stepped outside. With shoes, my purse and my phone in my hands, it was awkward to even give Marcelo a proper hug goodbye.

He whispered in an attempt to hold onto me so that Daryl could not hear us, “Friends, please?”

“Of course,” I reluctantly whispered back.

“I just...misread the situation—” he tried to cover.

“No, you didn’t. And I do want us to stay friends...” I confessed and covered, but it was too late. Clearly, both of us were confused, there was so much unfinished business and we had no time to figure it out.

Daryl was staring at us, trying to figure out what was going on, but he was too drunk to comprehend. I gave Daryl a hug and he squeezed me tight, like he was comforting me although he had no idea what was going on.

“Thanks for organizing a fun night out Daryl. I’ll tell Tess you say hi...” I said, distracting myself.

I embraced Marcelo quickly one last time, said a meek goodbye, stepped into the car and didn’t look back. And just like that, Marcelo was gone. What had I done? The only thing I could.

I had thought about that night so many times after it had first happened. What had I been thinking to go up to the roof with him? How did I let it get so far? And why did I stop it? I wanted to know what he would've done to me. I had thought about it until I couldn't think about it anymore. And then I had to stop, stop thinking about it. It was too painful for so many reasons.

Even though Daryl had been intoxicated, he had picked up on our vibe. The following day he had texted me, "Great seeing you last night. You alright hun? You seemed a little down when you left."

I wrote back, avoiding bringing up Marcelo, "Sad to be leaving. I love Montreal, thank you for making it special. Although I missed you on the dance floor! Didn't quite get my fix."

"Hahaha...as I remember it, you were getting a fix of dancing alright!" He was teasing.

Playing innocent, I replied "Was I? From whom? It wasn't you..."

"Marcelo would be disappointed you don't remember. Lol!" He teased back.

"Would he? Well, you know me, wouldn't want to disappoint." I decided to change the subject, "You know what would cheer me up? A picture of you in your underwear. And no dick pics, so not my thing!" I wasn't sure why I wrote it. I needed to change the subject, anything but Marcelo conversation. And I guess I needed a laugh.

"That's funny...cause that's just what I was thinking of doing, lol!" he replied.

"No, don't!" I replied quickly, "not sure I can handle it. Talk soon, sending hugs and kisses."

I reached out to Marcelo the next day, sending him a text to make sure he was okay, “Thanks for last night, hope it wasn’t too late and you survived. I had so much fun! Anyway, I’m in the area and was wondering whether you could recommend a cafe on my last day here? Daryl gave me your number in case I get lost.” I was trying to be casual and avoid any mention of what had transpired on the rooftop.

He was always the nice guy, “Surviving lol :) Not too sore…Hope your feet are okay. Go to Tommy, they have great pastries. Not sure I’ll be around unfortunately…But keep me posted in case you need help getting around. Have a safe trip home if I don’t see you. It’s been an eventful 24 hours, feeling old and tired.”

I had no idea what he was implying, he hadn’t mentioned the night before either, yet he cared enough to write. And that was that. Montreal was over. And we never spoke of the rooftop incident again.

Maybe he felt regret about the night on his rooftop? I had fantasized about that man in more ways than I ever should have. I refused to wash the jumpsuit right away when I got back to Calgary. I felt like I would be washing away the memories of that night and what we had shared. Seems silly, but I needed to hold onto that, that feeling, the smell, the touch of that man.

Marcelo had this way of making me feel so good and so bad all at once. From the moment I had laid eyes on him at that bar, there was this constant play on feelings. He could be so into me and then so cold. I couldn't figure out what it was. Maybe he was nervous or scared or unsure.

Sometimes he would text me multiple times a time and then he wouldn't write to me for weeks. I would wonder what I had done wrong, not realizing he was just busy. He had a life that didn't include me. I was trying to figure him out and what it all meant. Sometimes I would ramble, a lot, especially when I was stressed out. And he always tried to be there for me, it wasn't fair of me to expect anything more from him and he was a good guy.

Maybe he was being careful; I was married after all. I knew I was sending mixed messages; he was the perfect fantasy and I wanted to experience it, but I knew I couldn't have him in reality. It was torture, but I felt like I couldn't let go. And he was an emotional rollercoaster for me and I was struggling to stay on.

I couldn't figure out why I gave him so much importance in my life, well at least in my thoughts. How could spending one evening with him have affected me so much that sometimes it felt more important than twenty years of marriage? I felt like I needed him to be important. Or maybe I needed him to be an escape when I didn't want to face reality. Over time, I had learned to mute the carelessness of my husband, but I wasn't ready to deal with losing Marcelo. Yet I still wasn't sure how real our connection was and what it all meant. There was still so much that hadn't been said.

And now, somehow, Marcelo was back in my life. We were in a hotel room in Radium. Even though my bra was clasped in place, his fingers were still touching my arms. We both took a deep breath in unison, maybe he was thinking of that night as well. I had to step away.

We dressed in silence and when we did make eye contact, there was yearning in his eyes, like from that night. But we were friends. Just friends.

My memories and thoughts were set aside as my stomach began to growl, hungry for food. We were going to have breakfast with Penny because she was the most gracious host and always provided the most delicious homemade croissants and eggs bene this side of the Rockies.

Unfortunately, that wasn't the only thing I was hungry for. Sipping on my coffee, I was lost staring into his gorgeous eyes, and every time his arm brushed mine or he held my hand, I had this ache deep in my belly, wanting more.

The conversation or perhaps even confession from the night before played over in my mind. I was worried about how I was going to get through the next four days with all the intense feelings and sensations that were washing over me.

The drive from Radium to Kelowna was about five hours. It was incredibly scenic and picturesque with its winding roads, rolling hills, deep valleys, and rushing rivers. There were bridges and tunnels built with unique designs. The mountains were carved to make for narrow roads and snaked along blue-green lakes so big, you couldn't tell where they started or ended. The fruit trees, vineyards and abundant vegetation added to the beauty of the drive.

I grabbed a coffee to go (I would need the extra cup after the late night we had), gave Penny a squeeze goodbye and we hopped into the car. It was my turn to drive and I would get us there well before five hours. Driving long stretches of highway without traffic or time commitments was so freeing; I loved the thrill of the ride.

The comfortable silence was welcoming. I was in my own world, lost to the music, the scenery, and the serenity of the surroundings.

That had been the point of the trip, to get away and let my mind calm. The chaos of the last fifteen years of my life were slipping away. Ever since I had met my hubby, my life had been full of challenges. We shared many beautiful memories and had had fun, but there was so much turmoil.

Every time a new obligation or difficult event occurred, I lost a little bit of me. Everyone needed me, used me and asked me to do things. No one ever wanted me. No one appreciated me. No one desired me. I had no self-worth and there was no validation I figured, as long as I didn't want me, no one else would either.

The life I had been leading came crushing down on me. The expectations to be a perfect wife, mother, and daughter weighed down on me. I was a disappointment to myself. My mind crumbled with all the responsibility that I could not break free from. And my body; my body took on the turmoil, the strain, the stress, and the fear until it finally betrayed me, ridden by disease, leaving me broken and scarred. It had taken me this long to find the courage to start taking care for myself and not feel guilty.

Mid-thought, I saw Marcelo reaching for my journal. I was mortified. "What are you doing?" I asked, alarmed, my voice high-pitched.

"Don't worry, I just wanted to look at the cover. The symbol on it, what does it mean?" he asked, pointing to a hand drawn picture in deep pink of the Tree of Life I adopted for my logo. I calmed down a little. He was interested and wanted to know more. This was new to me, someone interested in my work, it made me smile, even if I was going to embarrass myself.

"There are lots of meanings to it, from the Buddha meditating under the Great Banyan to the connection of realms and creation. But for me, it's a sign of growth, wisdom, strength and beauty. It connects your roots to your branches and allows you to flourish. It also shows that there are many paths from one source, so one person can be, need and do many things. Too deep?" I wasn't sure what kind of answer he was looking for.

"Not at all," he replied, a sincere look on his face.

Without prying, he continued casually, "Would you tell me more about the journals you've been creating? They look amazing." He turned the journal over in his hands admiringly.

Journaling was something I was intensely passionate about. I had recently rediscovered the practice and it had allowed me to escape from the real world. It was sometimes therapeutic, sometimes artistic and often just allowed me to explore raw and dark thoughts I needed to deal with.

It had all started a few years prior when Rebecca suggested a girl's weekend up to her friend's cabin in the picturesque mountain resort town of Canmore. She had this beautiful space with large two-storey floor to ceiling windows with a breathtaking view of the Three Sisters mountains. Six of us, overworked, exhausted and somewhat frustrated girls decided to spend 48 hours away from our families. And it was by far the most rejuvenating 48 hours of my life. We relaxed, ate, talked, drank, complained, gave advice, vented, walked and talked some more.

As we were chilling in the living room, comparing notes about work and family life balance, my dearest friend Tess, who has inspired me in so many ways with her tenacity, creative outlook, ambition and drive told me about a medical conference she had been attending. And then she pulled out this remarkable notebook. At first glance, it looked like an ordinary leather-bound journal. But when she opened it, the watercolours, mind maps and artistic captures were like nothing I had seen. She was a doctor by day, but definitely an artistic, creative soul by night. She would capture information during the conferences and "take notes" by drawing with different coloured pens, emphasizing points through diagrams and cartoon figures. Each of her pages told a story about what was going on and I thought it was brilliant. To design a creative, visual, open-concept wellness journal. I didn't need it to be daily or perfect, but free flowing and ad hoc, to be done when needed most. And not just for myself, I wanted to design them for others to use as well.

"Journaling, mentoring, I can see you doing that, I'm sure you're good at it too. What was your inspiration?" he asked, looking genuinely interested; it was sweet. It was actually a tougher question to answer than I thought it would be. A lot of my inspiration came from a place of pain or weakness, which I found a way to transform into strength. And, of course, from the people in my life.

"I guess it's a combination of things. I really want to be able to help people if I can," I said quickly. I wasn't used to talking about myself.

"What do you do when you're stressed out?" I asked him. I could see that he got uncomfortable at being on the receiving end of questions too. But it was his turn.

"I'd say exercise and fresh air as a first option." It felt like such a typical thing for a single guy with no commitments, kids, or baggage to say. Not that I was making fun of him. His depth of stress was very different from mine.

"Yah, well, when I'm stressed, my first option is usually hiding in my pantry and binge eating, chips, cookies, chocolate, pretty much anything that starts with a "c"!" I replied.

He chuckled before he said more seriously, "Limit stress eating to twice a week." He was so adorable when he said it, obviously oblivious to mommy, female, emotional, hormonal, raging stress!

"Let me guess, you only worry about work and meeting up with your buddies for beer," I said, slightly mockingly.

"That's not fair; I have w ork, deadlines, groceries, you know." He was trying to sound serious.

I tried to be sympathetic, "Okay, I get it, big shot at work. But groceries, come on! Besides, don't you order in most nights or have your mom cook for you?"

"My stresses are real," he said seriously, "we all have things we are dealing with."

I interrupted, concern in my voice, "Of course, I'm sorry." I turned to look at him. "What are you dealing with? You have been there for me. I wish I could do more for you. You can get so quiet; I do worry."

He looked at me sympathetically. "You know it's hard for me to open up, but it means a lot to know you care about me. This trip is helping me already." He stopped and looked out the passenger window. "I just hope you can find what you're looking for." And we left it at that.

Chapter 7

Orchards & Vineyards

Driving down the breezy Okanagan roads, we had been silent for a while when Marcelo turned to me and said, "Karina, don't panic, I know you're driving. I need you to keep your hands on the wheel."

He was so hesitant in his manner as he spoke, "I want to ask you something, but I in no way want to invade your privacy."

I shook my head; this couldn't be good. I took a deep breath, preparing for what he had to say. I hope it wasn't another movie related question.

I tried to sound casual when I replied, "Go for it, what's up?"

"Although I didn't mean to, when I looked at your journal, I saw you had a topic on cheating? What's that all about?"

Cheating! He had to see that page. I was seriously beginning to wonder what else he had read.

I held my breath. At least it wasn't as intimate as some of the other pages in my journal. This I could fake. I decided to dive into the topic more from a psychological perspective than personal. I think I could explain it without embarrassing myself too much.

"Cheating is not a simple concept," I began. "It has to do with more than just cheating on your girlfriend or spouse. It might start that way for some people, but there are more facets to it than that."

"How so?" he asked with genuine curiosity in his voice.

"Whenever I have a topic in one of my journals, I look at it from different perspectives. Perception is a powerful manipulator. Cheating could be external, but I would focus on internal dilemmas as well. I would then ask, how am I cheating on myself? To which answers could be thoughts, food, fitness, effort, relationships, money, drinking, drugs, even work," I explained.

"How do you know you are cheating?" he asked.

"That's where things get tricky," I replied. "If you are chasing a fantasy and it is not attainable because nothing can be better than that fantasy, then what is your reality? Are you cheating on the reality or the fantasy?"

"I guess that depends on which one you want more or which one is more attainable," he said. He was a quick learner.

I explained, trying to use ice cream metaphorically, "Or say you have only ever had vanilla ice cream all your life and all you crave is chocolate, what do you do, stick with the vanilla, or be tempted and try the chocolate, metaphorically speaking?"

He smiled, probably picturing his choices for ice cream.

"So, are you cheating?" he asked directly and harmlessly.

I wasn't sure how to answer. I mean, here I was, a married woman on a trip with a gorgeous, unattached man whose company I was enjoying even though I was unsure of our intentions. I felt like I hadn't allowed myself to enjoy an emotional connection like this for a long time. I was caught between doing the right thing and the right thing for me. I didn't think I was cheating, but I also knew it wasn't that simple.

I answered, mostly avoiding the question, "Well, I have been accused of cheating. That's what happens when your so-called best friend says he wants to be friends but can't figure things out. And is selfish, only looking out for himself although he makes himself emotionally available while juggling his wife's jealous outbursts."

I was talking about Brad. He was an old friend, and we had an extremely complicated relationship. I began to explain Brad's situation to Marcelo to see how he would react.

Brad had rushed into marriage shortly after I got married, compensating for my absence in his life. He wasn't ready to settle and realized that married bliss wasn't all it was cut out to be. He and his wife weren't compatible. He wanted to travel, work, and start a family. She wanted to be a clingy trophy wife. Things started falling apart quickly, and the more he struggled at home, the more he reached out to me.

They visited when I told Brad about my diagnosis. As I tried to explain the procedure to him, the intimate gestures between us, his gentle caresses and compassionate embraces, were mistaken for more by his wife. She thought she had "caught" us in a more intimate connection and assumed the worst. My eight-week-old baby in the room didn't seem to phase her. After they flew back home, Brad told me what had happened. She was outraged and had accused us of having an affair.

She had stated that although our connection wasn't sexual, we had an emotional connection—which she perceived to be having an affair. She accused him of being involved with someone outside of the marriage.

Things got worse after that incident. She would take his phone to look for "evidence" or read through our personal messages. When I realized she was reading intimate details not intended for her, I felt so betrayed.

They were private messages; why had Brad not stopped her? True, maybe mine and Brad's friendship wasn't typical, but I thought we could make it work. Now the bonds of our friendship had been broken. I felt violated and hurt.

"Wait a minute," Marcelo interrupted. "Did you just say your best friend was a guy? How does that work?" After everything I had said, that was what Marcelo had picked up on.

"Yes," I answered, "he was. I guess, if I use Brad as the example, it doesn't work, men and women being friends. It's complicated, but were we cheating?"

When he didn't answer, I changed the subject. "Marriage, relationships, boundaries, even infidelity can be viewed and defined differently depending on the situation." I tried to share my reasoning with him but he gave me a puzzled look.

"Let's put it this way," I continued, "hypothetically speaking, let's say you have a wife, and she is happy because all of her needs are being fulfilled, either through you or because of work, hobbies, kids, or otherwise. You, on the other hand, are not happy because although you are married, you are not satisfied." I paused to see if he was following.

"So, now, if you seek support elsewhere, are you cheating on her? Does it matter what it is or who you are doing it with? Man or woman? Or are you cheating on yourself by not seeking it and staying unhappy? For myself, I want people in my life that make me better and I want to do the same for others." I said.

"Well, marriage sounds complicated but as does cheating or not cheating..." Marcelo replied. "As for you, the girl I met a year ago was confident and seductive on the dance floor but scared, hollow and sad in life. I see something has changed since then, you have made me better, I hope I have done the same for you." He thought I was seductive, hollow and sad?

"Having you in my life has been interesting and I'm just glad you are willing to put up with me!" I said jokingly, shielding my true feelings. We needed to change the subject before things got more intimate.

"Your coffee is getting cold," Marcelo said, changing the subject for me and pointing at the coffee cup in the cup holder. I went to reach for it and it slipped and poured onto my thigh. The hot liquid had luckily cooled down enough not to burn me, but it sent me into panic mode. I tried to maintain control of the vehicle and it veered slightly before I was able to grab the coffee cup and get my hands back on the wheel.

"Are you okay? Did the coffee burn you?" Marcelo asked, concerned. I was fine. I was so glad my husband wasn't there; he would've been so upset with me for being careless and making a mess. I was more worried about my car than my legs. Marcelo tried to pat my thigh and chair dry but that seemed to make the situation worse.

We pulled into the nearest rest stop and stepped out of the car to assess the situation. My skirt was drenched and my legs covered in coffee.

But my seats! Leaning into the car, I grabbed whatever paper napkins I could find and attempted to clean the seats, which were soaked. Opening the door as wide as I could, I bent over the low bucket seats, frantically wiping the diamond stitch leather.

"My husband is going to kill me, he's actually going to kill me, what am I going to do?"

Marcelo came over to my side to try and assess the situation but I was in the way. "Calm down," he said, "it's going to be okay. I got this, we'll get your seats fixed up. And your husband isn't going to kill you."

I was so upset I was shaking. "Well, he might not kill me, but he will make me pay for this mistake. I'll never be free of it, of him and all the mistakes he blames me for."

Marcelo went to the trunk and pulled out a t-shirt from his suitcase, which he soaked with some water. He could see the look of concern on my face and replied, "Don't worry, let me take care of this." He ever so gently placed one arm around my waist and held me from behind. It was comforting to feel his presence.

He put his hand on mine and took over wiping the seats with his shirt. He didn't care that he was ruining it, his shirt, that is. He slowly slid my body out of the way and knelt over the seats to wipe them down properly.

He turned away from the car to assess how badly the coffee had soaked me. Still kneeling, he began to tenderly clean the coffee off my leg, slowly moving his hand between my thighs. I couldn't move. He was so nurturing with his touch. No man had ever tended to me that way, especially not in a situation which was my fault and that wasn't sexually gratifying. I wanted to kiss him, tell him how incredible he was, but I couldn't. At any other time, this intimate position and his touch would have awakened sensations inside me, but right now I was distraught, flustered and needed to be taken care of.

He stood up in front of me and whispered in his soothing voice, "I will fix this. I would never want anyone to make you feel bad because of an accident. No man should treat a woman like that. I'll clean the seats properly. And no one, including your husband, will be the wiser. Go and change into something dry."

He wasn't real, how could he not only be forgiving, but want to help me fix my mistakes? I am surprised I didn't start crying.

"Are you okay?" He said flustered by seeing me so upset.

I was so shaken up by the incident, the questioning conversation and how caring he was towards me, I felt overwhelmed. "This is going to sound ridiculous, but can you just hold me? I could really use a hug." I needed to be able to feel him and feel safe at the same time. At this moment, I needed to feel less frazzled. The look on his face confirmed he knew how I was feeling. He wrapped his arms around my waist. He held me tightly, my head resting gently against his chest, the rhythm of his heart calming my nerves. He just held me. And I squeezed, hugging him back, feeling warmth and comfort and safety. I wanted him to never let me go. And he didn't. He had his arms wrapped around me, so he could even squeeze me a little. I felt so incredibly secure.

"Deep breaths are like little love letters to your body," he whispered. I am sure he had read that in my journal too. This time I smiled, a little. He continued to hold me as I took a few deep breaths. I closed my eyes and inhaled his scent of oak, amber and pepper. I recognized it.

"They're even lovelier when you smell this good," I said, smiling, feeling a little better, but not quite ready to let go. "What do you have on?"

"I think it's called Bourbon," he laughed, "I found it in the glove box. It's nice. Thought I would try it." He really did like going through my stuff.

"You should keep it, smells really good on you." It was a gift my husband refused. It suited Marcelo better.

I could feel my nerves relax and my breathing calm down. Feeling his steady heartbeat pound against me gave me a sense of stillness. I felt a comfort I hadn't felt in years.

For so long, whenever someone needed a hug, I was the one doing the comforting. I always had to be the strong one. I couldn't remember the last time I felt like someone had held me to make me feel better. I released my grip a little.

"Thank you, I needed that. It's been a long time since I found comfort in someone's arms. I feel I can be myself with you." Before he could answer, I continued, "I should change and we should get back on the road."

When we found our way to the Kempf Orchards, we were pleasantly surprised by the majestic beauty of the fragrant scents and varieties of cherries. There was nothing more charming than fresh air, nature's bounty and warm sunshine. Marcelo casually slipped his hand into mine and we walked around hand in hand. I couldn't understand why he felt so good. I think it's because for the first time in a long time he made me feel good about myself.

Walking through the orchard, we came to a row of large cherry trees. The sun was shining bright and the trees provided just enough shade to make you comfortable. We picked a pail of cherries of different colours and varieties. Climbing ladders to find the best ones, we went from tree to tree. We were allowed to sample as much as we wanted. We plucked the cherries off the branches and popped them into our mouths. The experience of tasting plump fresh fruit as the sweet juices burst in our mouths, the fruit effortlessly falling off the pits, allowing us to spit them out made us feel like kids again. I probably ate more than I picked, but Marcelo made up for it, picking an entire pail. He said it was for my boys but I think he was just enjoying himself too much.

The orchard was beautifully landscaped and so well kept. The people at the family-owned farm were kind and generous. We got to try some peaches and purchased some of the best unpasteurized honey I had ever tasted.

Our next stop was checking out a few vineyards, the first being Summerhill Pyramid Winery. Their reputation for high quality, uniquely blended, and perfected recipes for their wines was something I was excited to partake in. The wine tour was like nothing I had ever experienced.

I indulged in the sharp and delicious cheese pairings, and settled on a light, fruitier rosé. The atmosphere of the vineyard is what made it so charming. The old oak barrels, the rustic buildings balanced with modern sleek lines and stunning views. Spacious and inviting tasting rooms with more wine than you could ever imagine purchasing.

Marcelo looked relaxed. His shoulders weren't as tense. He was casually resting his arm on the back of his barstool with that mysterious smile on his face. He was in his element. He tried all the different samples as we sat at the large maple-topped bar. It was clear he was enjoying himself.

Whatever insecurities I had been feeling earlier seemed to fade as I took in the charming ambience of the multi-generational, family-owned winery. The sights and sounds were soothing on my nerves that had felt so jagged before we had arrived.

Looking over at him, he had a little cheese on the side of mouth, so I reached over and brushed his face gently with the back of my hand, feeling his stubble and jawline as my thumb pushed the crumb away. I smiled warmly.

"What are you thinking about?" he asked.

"I was thinking about the time I was stress texting you about a dinner party I had to host," I told him. I would sometimes text Marcelo menus I would be preparing for parties or new things I baked for the boys.

My husband never appreciated the effort I would put into finding new recipes or presenting a more sophisticated meal. He liked his lentils, rice and chicken curry. He liked to have his meals prepared, plated and presented to him every evening like clockwork. Simple, basic, no utensils required. And he expected me to cook every day. If I were distracted with something else, he would "remind" me to get into the kitchen by summoning me with a high-pitched whistle, like I were his obedient dog. It was so hurtful and degrading. Yet, I obliged, a dutiful wife.

To escape the pain, I had often thought about cooking for Marcelo and dazzling him with my culinary skills. I knew he would appreciate it. Having him at my large wooden dinner table, candles lit, sharing a delicious meal and colourful conversation. We would share and enjoy each other. Dessert would involve getting naked and using the dinner table as a prop while he had his way with me. Of course, I never shared the last part with him.

"Yah, I remember," he replied, "you were nervous about a dinner party and decided to make a roast beef with gravy, Yorkshire puddings, baby potatoes and asparagus."

"What, you remembered the whole menu?" I said, puzzled. "It sounded delicious; how could I forget? I wanted to be there to enjoy it with you," he remarked.

"You wanted to come over and have dinner with my family?" I asked again, even more puzzled.

"Selfishly, I wanted it to be just me and you. And, if I had had a choice, I would've picked the double chocolate brownies with ganache for dessert." He smacked his lips for affect. "You would've had to twist my arm, but I might have even tried the whipped coffee with Baileys. Although I usually prefer to separate my alcohol and coffee." I saw the purist in him visibly cringe, although the way the corners of his mouth turned up made me smile.

"I would enjoy tormenting you by mixing flavours, and if you stayed over, I would serve you strawberry almond muffins for breakfast..." The last part slipped out before I could stop myself.

"Breakfast in bed? You really do know how to take care of your guests!" Marcelo smiled, knowingly.

Recovering, "But would you try one?" I asked, already knowing he would try it, for me.

"Well, I would enjoy whatever you prepared for me." He grinned like he was reading my mind.

"From what I remember from your texts, you told me that you are a pretty decent cook. Isn't your specialty veal parmesan for when you are entertaining the ladies?" I reminded him.

"No, not for the ladies. And from what I remember from your texts, you said the next time you come to visit, we could cook together, I was looking forward to it. Except you never did come to visit." He looked disappointed.

"Did you actually want me to visit? I thought you were just being polite." I asked, confused. *Besides, it's not like I could just visit Montreal so we could cook together*, I thought to myself.

"I mean what I say," he replied. "How come you didn't visit?"

"Honestly?" I looked at him incredulously. "It's not like I could just visit Montreal so we could cook together." I say out loud. "How would I explain that one to my husband?" I looked down. "And anyway, even if that wasn't an issue, I wouldn't want to be a burden."

"A burden?" he replied. "You just offered to make dinner with me, how would that be a burden?"

"And also..." I trailed off. I was blushing again, but he couldn't tell.

"What? Also, what?" He looked at me intently, curious as to what I had to say.

I didn't want to tell him. I was so embarrassed. I couldn't believe the conversation had even gotten this far and that I had mentioned things I shouldn't have. I pulled back in my seat, visibly uncomfortable. I was squirming at the idea of telling him what was going on in my head.

He leaned towards me and probed, "And what...please, tell me." It was the please that caught me off guard. I felt a sense of intimacy and intrigue in his voice.

"I couldn't do it," I confided, "visit and cook with you. Because as soon as you were good with it, the first image to pop into my head was you opening your front door wearing nothing but an apron and I'm not sure I could've handled that!" I covered my flushed face with both hands as I finished my sentence, so embarrassed by my admission that I couldn't look at him.

He reached over and slowly slid my hands away from my face with both of his. Still holding onto them, he pulled me off my barstool and into his embrace. He tilted my head so he could see me, although I was still self-conscious.

He smiled that irresistible smile as he leaned in close to me, his lips close enough to graze me as he whispered into my ear, "Is that why you had that look on your face? You were fantasizing about me? Well, if you want me to be honest, I imagined you showing up on my doorstep wearing one of those tan-coloured, sexy, short trench coats with nothing but something black, skimpy, and sheer underneath. And for dessert, you'd be wearing nothing but whipped mascarpone, chocolate sauce and that adorable smile of yours." He didn't break his gaze.

Hearing that, every part of me wished I had gone to see him, that I'd done something wild and stupid and crazy. I had always played it safe and it had made me so unhappy. Maybe I would have to change that. Too bad I hadn't packed any chocolate sauce.

Chapter 8

Confessions...

On our way to the quaint little hotel, instead of reminiscing about the delicious wine tasting, decadent cheeses and souvenir shopping, I kept playing our conversation over and over again in my mind. Here we were, having fun and sharing our fantasies but where was all this going? What did I really mean to this man and what did he mean to me? I needed some time to sort out my feelings without distractions.

Telling Marcelo to settle into the room, I figured I needed a little time to myself and decided to go for a walk.

I stepped outside, enjoying the sunshine on my skin and took a deep breath. Considering this was supposed to be a self-journey, I realised that since I had started the trip, I had not spent a moment alone. I took another deep breath and held it, filling my lungs as much as they could. When I exhaled, I let everything go. I found a quiet path lined with trees and decided to wander. I let my mind wander as well, seeing where it would take me, yet I remained present and aware of my thoughts.

The first thought to drift into my mind was of my husband. It felt negative. He tried to be a sweetheart, being there for the family, being a working man, at least he thought he was trying, the only way he knew. I thought that getting married would intensify his intimacy towards me and my feelings of love for him. It never did. I thought that maybe I would change somehow and accept that the safe and stable choice was the right one for me. I thought if I could figure out how to please him in every way and tried hard, he would want to fulfill me too and not take me for granted. His considerations turned into demands, mine were forgotten. I wanted to feel fulfilled and loved but I felt ignored and insatiable. My body ached for desires it had put on hold for too long. I couldn't think about it anymore. I let the thoughts go and tried to clear my mind.

My mind wandered back to the day when I was on the flight home from Montreal last year. Glancing over at my husband who had passed out and snoring slightly—he was relaxed, content with life, nothing bothered him, he was easy to please because he always got what he wanted. Yet I was so unhappy and lost. It was the lowest I had ever felt. I had finally hit rock bottom. Sitting on the plane, I had put my head in my hands and wept. My chest hurt from the pressure of the life I was leading; I was suffocating myself with my life and I knew that things needed to change.

It was the turning point in my life. I couldn't allow myself to feel like that anymore. As I wept, I recalled my time in Montreal. The girl I was there for a few short hours on that dance floor, in that outfit, it was a glimpse of a life I could've had. A glimpse of a life I wanted more of. Where was the powerful, fiery seductress I used to be? I had been extinguished. I knew I had responsibilities but I wanted to balance my kids, my husband, my family, and my work. I wanted to be liberated from the prison I felt trapped in. I needed to free myself from my own mind as much as the outside world—to give myself permission to be strong and find time to do things that made my heart happy. Dressing up, dancing, talking the night away with people who made me feel good. Travel more to escape the everyday routine. I could do all of that.

I had to push the negativity out of my mind and think about what I needed. I deepened my breathing as I walked, unaware of where I was going.

The next thought to creep into my mind was of Marcelo. There was one moment that kept haunting me and regret washed over me. I hadn't been prepared to be affected by a man like Marcelo on the dance floor that evening. I thought I would be more torn by the situation, but in reality, I felt betrayed. Had I made the right decision that night on his rooftop? This trip that I was on with Marcelo could be a life-changing experience. Was this a do-over of that night or was karma going to bite me in the ass?

I felt conflicted; the next thought that drifted into my mind was lessons of my childhood. Brown girls had to behave properly. Good girls don't create mischief or stray. I had never been allowed to date or be wooed or wanted by a man. I had never known love. I wasn't perfect, but I was expected to behave like a lady. Acting improper and being disrespectful were not permitted.

Then, of course, there was the fact that I was married. I wasn't interested in a new relationship. I didn't want a replacement for what I already had. I did not want another husband. Marcelo was gorgeous and sweet. I wanted him, but there was no place for him in my life in any capacity I could imagine. Even being friends was proving to be complicated. He wasn't mine to keep.

I pushed all these thoughts out of my mind and focused on clearing all my mind. I wanted to think about nothing. After a moment, when things felt calmer, I imagined the Tree of Life, it was my Zen place. I would see the sun shining brightly behind it, casting a large shadow. By the tree, sat a girl, content and free. That girl was me. There were three boys in the distance, but the focus was on the girl, happy and independent. That's what I needed to be. I closed my eyes for a moment, just to focus on that thought.

I felt a hand on my shoulder and I jumped and screamed. My thoughts disappeared and I was back to reality. I turned around abruptly to confront my intruder; hands up guarding my face while I positioned myself into a fighting stance.

"There you are, I was worried about you. Oh no, I didn't mean to frighten you. Please don't hit me!" Marcelo said, trying to defend himself, half pretending as he covered his face with his hands. I pulled his arms away from his face and relaxed mine as well. But I was still reeling from my thoughts, not ready to face him quite yet. I closed my eyes again and collected myself, taking in one last deep breath.

He could see I was still in a daze and wrapped his arms around me. "You, okay? I am here for you, whatever you need. I'm all yours." What did he mean, he was all mine? I wanted to be all his so badly, but this wasn't real. I could feel his presence and wanted so much more. And yet, I knew I couldn't.

I felt so unsteady, so unsure of myself. I was in turmoil and constantly questioning myself. It had taken me a year to start to piece my life together. Was Marcelo going to make it better or worse?

I looked up at him, unable to reply. I replied, hesitant to ask him what he meant, in case I wasn't prepared for the answer.

Montreal was haunting me. I had waited all my life to experience something so intense. That night, in that outfit, with that man, dancing in his arms, feeling his entire body press up against me and devour me with his eyes—I had never felt so desirable. My soul had longed to be touched like that by an attentive man. It had been powerful, moving, arousing. I didn't need to sleep with Marcelo to feel that way. Him being there with me was enough. Wasn't it? Then why could I not ignore that nagging insatiable feeling?

"You already have," I lied. I couldn't face the possibility of him or me wanting more.

Marcelo said, "You have changed me somehow, opened my eyes to new possibilities this past year. I want you to know how much I appreciate your outlook." What was he talking about? I just texted him every once in a while. Maybe I had affected him the way he had affected me. Maybe we were rescuing each other.

Marcelo held my hand and led me back towards the hotel. I collapsed on the bed and Marcelo sat beside me. My thoughts were still drifting. The exhaustion got the best of me, and I passed out momentarily on Marcelo's shoulder. When I came to, my head was resting on his chest and he was napping, so I decided to enjoy the moment. It was surprisingly therapeutic. It scared me a little to realize how much I liked it. The drive, the distance, the scenery, the company, the experiences. Even my racing thoughts, doubts, and questions.

"What's the plan this evening?" Marcelo asked when he woke up.

"I have a great evening planned. I booked us a luxury three-hour sailing tour with the Okanagan Yacht Tours. It includes a lovely dinner, a two-person tube ride, and maybe some swimming," I replied, smiling with anticipation.

There was only person that could've made this trip better, Carmen. I was so missing Carmen. We had worked so hard to plan this perfect trip for us. This was supposed to be our bonding time. To reconnect and figure out how to fix our messed-up lives. I would make it up to her, but I couldn't deny, I was glad I came.

I grabbed my more scandalous bikini (you only live once, right) and put it on. As I slipped it on and checked myself out in the mirror, I was pretty happy with the reflection. Being the old maid that I was, my body marked by the experiences of my life, it took me a moment to really look at myself. I touched my breasts to make sure they were really there. That may sound strange, but for most women, their breasts are a physical thing. They exist, they are real. Not for me, and no, not for vanity's sake. Don't get me wrong, women should do whatever they want to their bodies to make them feel good. It wasn't so much of a choice for me.

As part of my journey in that last year, I had undergone extensive plastic surgery to get a mastectomy, expander, implant, belly flap, reconstruction, and nipple tattooing to make my breasts look like real breasts again.

That was because ten years prior, I had been diagnosed with an aggressive form of Stage III invasive ductal carcinoma. I had breast cancer. My babies were so little when I was diagnosed. I had surgery, chemotherapy, and radiation therapy, all the while trying to be a wife, mother, sister, daughter and friend. It was one of the darkest times in my life. And yet, it was one of my finest—to be that strong, that determined, that focused, that willing, to not break, to not be weak, to not die. I had to. Fight. Battle. Conquer. Survive. And I did. And now I was here, with my fake breasts, scars and implants, but I was here.

When we arrived at the dock to board the yacht, I was in awe. I didn't get to do much "lake" living and definitely not on a gorgeous sailboat like the vessel presented before me. The 36-foot sailing yacht had stark white sails set against the clear skies and calming blue waters; it was incredible. We boarded and as the yacht moved along the aquamarine waters, it would shift and glide as we made our way to a more isolated area. The breeze was blowing through my hair and the sun gleamed down, brightening everything it touched.

Now, I was here with Marcelo, feeling a little flustered and confused Should I feel ashamed that I was wrestling more with the idea of experiencing another man than breaking the bonds of my marriage? No, because I was accepting that I was broken, imperfect, vulnerable and in need of something more. It was easier said than done.

We were going to be boating and tubing and I would just focus on that. "You're going to have to take this off before we can get into the tube you know," Marcelo said, pointing to my cover up. I wasn't sure I had the courage to take it off, having felt a lot bolder in the bathroom earlier. We were the only ones on the boat and I told myself that I didn't look that bad. It was my confidence that was stopping me. I was determined to have some fun on this trip, so I went for it. I decided to slip it off slowly to the rhythm of the music playing in the background, pretending to be in one of my pole dancing classes. The captain on the boat whistled, in an encouraging way, no disrespect. As much as I loved dancing and Marcelo couldn't stop looking at me, it started to get a little embarrassing, so I hopped over to the tube and put a stop to the silliness.

Tubing was exhilarating. We did large circles and figure eights through the crisp, clear waters. I gripped Marcelo's arm and the tube for dear life at moments and got splashed more than I wanted to. I was laughing, screaming and everything in between! But riding the waves and being in the open water felt amazing.

We hopped back on the boat and huddled in some large fluffy towels to dry off and warm up. The sun hadn't quite set and it felt nice on my skin. I was feeling a little more comfortable in my suit as well, so when Marcelo snapped a few photos, I didn't totally flinch. We enjoyed a light dinner and Marcelo enjoyed a bottle of wine and drinks the captain served up. I could tell he was relaxed from the dorky smile on his face.

As we sat and stared out at the water, he squeezed my hand gently and said, "Did you know that when humans touch, even the simple act of holding hands, they release the hormone oxytocin? Some call it the feel-good hormone. It triggers feelings of compassion and trust. Our bodies hunger for it, touch. It calms you and deepens your connection while heightening your awareness." I felt myself squeezing his hand back, wanting to feel more. He was talking about neurotransmitters and I was getting turned on. I wasn't sure how much more "feel good" I could handle. But he did feel good, really good.

Sitting along one edge, our feet dangling against the rail, cuddled next to each other, we looked out at the vast lake. When the boat rocked, I lost my balance and fell into Marcelo, pressing my body up against his. I was terrified he might be able to tell my breasts were not real, not that it mattered, but every once in a while, I would feel like it did. As I regained my balance, my bikini top was exposing a scar. I saw him looking at it. When he didn't ask, I chose not to talk about it.

He wrapped his arms around me, holding me in place so I couldn't fall over. I could feel the warmth from his shirtless body against my exposed midriff, skin on skin, with nothing between us. It felt too good to be real and I tried to shift out of his embrace, but he wasn't ready to let me go. He had his black rimmed Ray Bans on, so I couldn't really see or read his eyes.

He whispered ever so softly in my ear, "You know, you are the best thing that ever happened to me in Montreal. And I don't regret any of it."

The constant feeling of guilt, confusion, and being intensely aroused was getting painful. The fresh air, the warm sun, the gentle sway of the boat, the music playing, it was too much for me to handle. I was feeling so liberated and helpless all at once. The longer he held me, the more my body wanted to let go of the control. I felt unguarded because I was supported.

Marcelo brushed the windblown hair from my face and caressed my cheek. He reached around my waist and held me. I wanted to feel his body against mine. His hand slowly moved down to my chin and although I wanted to hide, he tilted my chin up. And then, without warning, he kissed me. I was so caught up in the moment, away from all the chaos of my life, that I had forgotten for a split second that I was a mom and a wife. I was just here, with a man who was giving me what I needed.

I pulled back just enough to break the kiss, but not the lingering feeling of our bodies touching.

I tried to look through those darn sunglasses to see his eyes, but he was sheltering them from me. "I told you that night in Montreal that when I asked you about an open marriage, I wasn't just being curious, I was making you an offer. And I told you earlier, I am here with you because this is what I want—I want you. I don't know where we will be in a few days, but right now, I want this." And he kissed me again. This time I didn't pull away as I wrapped my arms around his neck. I wanted this too. I needed it. I wasn't sure what would happen in a few days either, but right there, right then, it made sense.

We made it back to the hotel, barely able to contain ourselves. Yet, once the door shut behind us and we were alone in the room, he slowly led me towards the foot of the bed. He took his time when he gently slipped my dress off, slowly pulling at the shoulder straps and allowing them to fall down my arms. Then gently tugging at the waist as the dress slid down the length of my body and into a pile by my feet. I was feeling self-conscious as he stood there looking at me, holding my hands in his allowing him to see all of me. His fingers slowly trailed up my arms to my shoulders where he slipped the straps of my bikini down. He reached behind me and untied the bikini strings. He let the top fall to the floor. As his fingers traced my body, he got down on his knees and allowed his fingers to rest on my waist before he undid the strings of my bikini bottom as he continued to caress my hips. He let those fall to the floor as well. As he slowly stood up, inhaling deeply, his lips close enough to touch my skin, his eyes indulged on my naked body. I was terrified, not of him, but of the exposure. He did not let me cover myself but instead pulled his shirt off while guiding my hands to those sexy swim shorts. I hooked my thumbs onto the waistband and slowly slid them down his long legs. I could barely breathe. He walked me to the bed and as he pulled the covers back, he guided me onto it. He lay down beside me, taking his time but wouldn't let me cover myself in the sheets, not yet.

For ten years, I had felt like a freak, with only one breast, uneven and marred. The large, ugly, jagged mark across my chest where my breast used to be. To no fault of his own, it impacted my husband. It wasn't about perfection or beauty. He had tried to accept me, but to see his wife disfigured was hard. It was a reminder of what I had been through. Years went by before he could find the courage to touch the scar. From then on, the intimacy was different; he avoided touching me and I felt he didn't really see me as a woman anymore.

Although I had made the decision on my own for reconstruction, he had confessed that he wanted me to have two breasts. I wasn't upset or judging, I understood. It was difficult for me to look at myself in the mirror and a struggle to use an artificial prosthesis. Silicone was too heavy and painful. Foam was too light and didn't sit right. Reconstruction was not easy, simple, or a perfect solution. It came with challenges and risks. But now that the surgery was done, having two breasts made me feel more like me, for me.

As Marcelo's finger gently traced each and every one of the scars along my body, I felt so vulnerable. No one had seen me like that. Each scar had a story to tell, its own history and emotional attachment. Some came with painful memories, others joy. The scar above my left breast was from my chemotherapy port. The scar under my right arm was from the lymph nodes that had been removed. The scars under my now smaller breasts were from each step in my treatment, recovery and reconstruction. The smaller scars along my abdomen had been from a hysterectomy I desperately needed due to complications. The scar close to my belly button was from my flap for my breast reconstruction. And the long "smile" scar above my pelvic bone was from my c-section. His hand rested there for some time, taking it all in, all the things I had already been through. Although I didn't say anything, it's like the scars told their own stories and he understood. I had designed a symbol for being a survivor that also encompassed all the important events in my life and had gotten a tattoo of the symbol. He eventually found that too.

He kissed me gently. I hesitated and pulled back and then tried to cover up the hesitation. He immediately noticed and stopped. We had this way of communicating without saying anything to each other. I felt when we had a physical connection, we didn't need to really say a lot. I lay my head on his bare chest and closed my eyes. He finally broke the silence and said, "We don't have to if you're not ready. This is a lot."

I inhaled slowly and deliberately, breathing in his essence. I did want this. I just couldn't allow myself to indulge in such a kind man who was so willing to please me. I arched my back, pressing my body deeper into his and yet I felt confused.

"I can tell your body wants it Karina, is aching for it, but when I look into your eyes, I see doubt," he said. "You are important to me and I don't want to ruin what we share. I will be okay with whatever you want."

I was trying to think but my heart was pounding, my body was aching and my mind was fuzzy and racing.

In an instant, I could destroy everything (if I hadn't already). I had been loved by the same man for twenty years. I had shared his bed, his life, been by his side as his wife. We had a family together. He was all I knew.

I had been dutiful, even obedient, but he had never loved me, been passionate or charismatic or gentle. And I did not love my husband, I was not happy. I hated admitting it. I felt ashamed and guilty and yet I felt hurt and betrayed and I couldn't deny it anymore.

I had only met Marcelo once before this trip. We had connected on a level I had never expected. And this past year through our communications, he understood me, supported me and offered me the only thing I had asked for, kindness and friendship. That kindness and friendship had turned into fondness and independence, things that were lacking and I craved. This man beside me was no longer a stranger. Maybe we were coincidental soulmates if you believed in that sort of thing. I had to have met him for a reason. Could I be wrong about him? No, for the first time in my life, he felt right. He saw me to be the woman I had been longing to be for so long.

He was the kind of man I would've fallen in love with, if I had been allowed. I could be myself when I was with him.

I felt this urgency, this passion, this hunger. I had tried so hard to fight the desire. It was then that I realized I needed it, to feel alive. This was about me. I was done being broken and unhappy. This wasn't just about the sex. It was the whole experience. Giving into my feelings and being wanted and desired. I knew it couldn't last, but I did know I could have it now. I didn't want to feel the regret that lingered and frequented my thoughts from Montreal.

He kissed me again and this time I did not hesitate to kiss him back. The longing in his embrace made me realize he needed this as much as I did. He was all mine and I was all his. I stared deeply into those kind yet driven eyes.

I don't know why I said it, but I did, "I don't want to be friends anymore, I need to be ravaged, I want you to—" I didn't need to finish my sentence because I could see a need in his eyes, he knew what I needed. And he needed it too. The look in his eyes had changed; he was yearning and longing.

He was as hungry as I was and he didn't hesitate to taste, touch, caress and linger. He did things to my body I had only fantasized about. When he called my name, I moaned, and when I moaned, he groaned.

My body ached for more, and when it wasn't his mouth, it was his hands and when it wasn't his hands, it was his body. I dared to dominate and he was forceful and playful all at once, pushing back, pressing, testing, tasting, stroking and satisfying. He wasn't afraid to hold me, position me and take me as he pleased. And I wasn't holding back from pleasuring or satisfying him.

Our bodies were inseparable. It was intense, passionate, unpredictable and powerful. Limbs intertwined, lips kissed, tongues desired, fingers roamed and yearning penetrated over and over again as the night slipped away.

I didn't know I could feel so violated and respected at the same time. Dirty and spent, I fell asleep in his arms and slept more peacefully than I could ever remember.

Chapter 9

Run Away with Me

Right on schedule, my alarm went off at 6:00 a.m. Without waking Marcelo, I carefully rolled out of his embrace and turned off my alarm. I looked over at Marcelo and thought, *there isn't going to be any romantic cuddling this morning.*

I crawled out of bed and looked at myself in the mirror, thinking I would see shame reflected back at me, but I did not. I couldn't recognize this girl and the calm and tranquil vibe I saw., And I couldn't seem to wipe the fulfilled grin off my face. I felt so satisfied, oh so satisfied. But it wasn't just my body. My mind, spirit; my whole self felt it too. It didn't make sense, I should have felt guilt, I had been so naughty but the feeling of pleasure trumped any sense of wrong. I felt free.

I stepped under the hot stream of water from the raindrop showerhead and allowed the almost scalding liquid to cleanse my skin. I closed my eyes, holding onto the feelings of the night before. I slowly moved my hands over my own body, recalling every inch that had been touched by him. Some spots were tender, some maybe even a little raw. I bit my lower lip, tasting a little blood.

Was this really happening? When I washed my body, I imagined it was his hands touching me as they had the night before. I lathered up the soap. No matter how much I used, I couldn't remove his smell or his touch from my body and I didn't want to.

One night. One incredible and memorable night. Now, I had to move on. The song lyric, "I'm not in love, it's just a thing we make..." played in my mind, what did it mean? As the endless stream rinsed me, I kept my eyes closed, craning my neck from side to side and reminiscing every moment from the night before. Reluctantly I turned the water off and with that the memories of the night before.

I slipped into a fitted pink and gray tank top that said, "My running style is described as: Seductively Awkward" and a pair of black running shorts. Although the spreadsheet was on the nightstand, I didn't need to look at it to know what the plan was for that day. It was race day!

I had been training with my girls Rebecca, Tess and Carmen for this day for the past three months and it was very important to me. I hated running when I was younger and chubbier. As I got older, I still wasn't much of a runner for the sport, but for the therapy and the high from the endorphins after a hard day. And although not as effective, it was cheaper than seeing a therapist.

"Rise and shine sleepy head!" I called out to Marcelo who was still passed out in bed. We had to be on schedule. I knew this trip was going to be busy. I wanted to make the most of every moment so I had packed a lot in.

I heard a moan. I looked over at Marcelo who was still in bed. He had no intention of getting up. He had no idea what was going on. I had failed to mention earlier in the trip that Carmen and I had signed up for the Kelowna Wine Country Half Marathon Run and he had failed to read the entire itinerary in the coffee shop. That seemed so long ago, although we had been sitting there just 48 hours ago.

"Wakey, wakey, enough beauty sleep, it's time to have some fun!" I mocked as I threw his running shorts, t-shirt, and a running bib with Carmen's name on it at him.

"What is going on, Karina?" he asked. He rubbed his eyes and as he focused, he read the name of the race on the bib. His expression changed from one of excitement to agony. Marcelo was five years younger than me and his legs were probably twice as long. Even if he hadn't trained, he could fake his way through this. I am sure he had mentioned running in previous texts. At least that's what I told myself.

My body was designed to work out, dance and do yoga. It was curvy and petite, not built like a runner at all. But I loved to run; I loved the adrenaline, clearing my mind and taking my frustrations out on the pavement. If I could do this, so could he. My goal was to complete it, not set a record. The opportunity to run through wine country, take in the sites and just pound the trails for two and a half hours was driving me.

"There is no way I am getting up and running a half marathon today. I think I'm a little hungover. I can't run this. Besides, you worked my body pretty hard last night." He tried to hide his smirk. "I'm not even sure my legs are going to function. Why didn't you mention this earlier?" He was groggy and trying to sound angry, but it came out adorable. I climbed onto the bed and straddled him over the sheets, pinning him down by his arms. Even if he claimed his legs were not functioning, other parts of his manhood clearly were. He made me very aware of that.

I tried to stay focused and looked straight into those gorgeous gray-green eyes. I could drown in those eyes, mesmerized by his smile.

"Look mister," I said, sounding as serious as I could while being distracted by his gorgeous body writhing underneath mine, "you chose to invite yourself on this trip, so you are going to do as required. Besides, it's good for you, and I have booked us luxurious massages after the race." As he continued to squirm, I thought if he had pinned me down and had his way with me just then, I'm not sure I would've made the race. My body was hungry for it, to tease and taste him, feel the hardness of his abs and softness of his lips, trapped by his body while his hands played with my body like it belonged to him. Instead, his body relaxed and a good thing too because I wasn't sure I could hold him down much longer.

It was important to me to complete the race. In the past, I probably would have given into the idea of not signing up or going to Kelowna because my husband would've convinced me that running around in a circle was not only useless but meaningless. But not this time, I needed to do this for myself. Even if Marcelo didn't do it with me, I would do it alone.

My phone buzzed and there was a text from Carmen. "Good luck with the race today, girl! Miss you so much! Wish I was with you. Stay on pace and get your personal best! All the love..."

My heart ached a little. She was going through so much and I wasn't there to be with her. But I couldn't let myself feel guilty. I had promised I would find a way to make it up to her, and I had a race to finish.

I texted back, "Miss you more, beautiful. I'm running this for both of us. Stay strong and know I am here for you."

There was a text from my Arjan, wishing me luck. "Ma, you got this, I know you will rock it. Can't wait to see the finisher's medal." He had remembered. He wasn't embarrassed of his chubby, old mom on race day. I smiled, not sure who was prouder of who.

"Wait! I almost forgot! I need lipstick!" I cried.

Marcelo looked at me like I was crazy and said, "Are you nuts? Why would you need lipstick?"

I told him, "I needed something small to make me feel good every day and that something just happened to be lipstick." It's strange how a tube of coloured wax could boost my outlook on life, but it worked. I applied the bright, matte, fuchsia colour and smiled at myself in the mirror. I was ready!

I dragged Marcelo out of bed, got some food into him and we got to the race with about twenty minutes to spare. That turned out to be twenty minutes too many. As we stood waiting to start, I recognized a familiar face and immediately turned in the other direction. The presence of a particular someone was upsetting my aura.

Marcelo looked at me puzzled and asked, "What's wrong, don't feel like running anymore? I'm good to go back to the hotel or hang out at the beach today!"

I rolled my eyes at him and said, "Don't look over, but here comes trouble." Before I could explain, there was a tap on my shoulder. I turned around very slowly, deliberately taking my time before making eye contact. There he was, standing there, looking me up and down like he owned me.

"Hello, hello, Karina! What a coincidence, you signed up for the Wine Country Half as well? That's great!"

This was not a coincidence but a setup. It was Brad and he knew that I had signed up. I just hadn't expected to see him. We had run together in the past, but that was the past.

He wrapped his arms around me and gave me a big squeeze. I just stood there, arms at my side, shuddering a little.

"Oh, come on, no hug for an old friend?" he said with this attitude that made Marcelo look uneasy.

I glared at him. "Brad, this is Marcelo, Marcelo, this is Brad." They nodded at each other, not bothering to shake hands; each probably wondering what was going on. I could feel some tension between them. In a lot of ways, Marcelo and Brad were alike. Tall, dark hair, extremely intelligent, successful, powerful and oddly charming. But Marcelo was younger, hotter, sweeter and kinder.

Carmen always joked that I had my type, "You and your thing for Italian boys with a weird sense of humour, I don't get it! And why you agreed to a loveless marriage to a brown guy who is so not right for you, I will never know." She made it sound like I had a choice.

Brad and I had met on the very first day of high school. He was nerdier than any guy I had ever met. Nervous, timid, and lost. No social skills or fashion sense; I'm talking stained button-down shirts with a skinny tie, flood pants, and he carried a briefcase for a while. When your parents put you in an academically driven program, the pickings are slim.

High school can be an awkward time, but I was lucky to find a group of friends who had the same geeky outlook while I brought the fun. Studying, movies, parties and more studying. The boys were immature as hell, sometimes more of a nuisance than fun, but we eventually figured things out. Brad was cute in a geeky kind of way. We were two quirky teens trying to survive the adolescent jungle. We were study buddies, then friends, then best friends. I loved being with him, but I didn't love him. I didn't believe in love and all its nonsense. Who had time for that?

He was usually crushing on one of my friends, even tried dating a few of them, but he failed miserably. I would laugh and help him survive his relationship disasters. He pretended to help me with homework just so he could talk about girls. We looked out for each other, took care of each other and it brought us closer together.

Eventually, we went our separate ways, I stayed in Calgary to complete my degree, he went off to Waterloo or McGill University. He was so smart and destined for big things. He was one of the few guys I knew who was up for the challenge of getting his MD and his Ph.D. He still tried dating and failed miserably. When he would come back to town, we always made it a point to see each other over a late dinner, dancing, or a quick coffee.

The summer before I got married, we spent as much time as we could together. He had grown out of his nerdy phase and had matured into a cute, well-mannered, intelligent and well-dressed man. He'd lost his baby fat and started running, putting on lean muscle. One evening, we planned a night of food, drinks, dancing, and nonsense with friends.

"You're wearing a dress!" he said when I picked him up. I guess I didn't do that very often. He was ogling my body in the tight, short, cleavage-baring, hip-hugging, red dress I wore that showed off all my curves—a dress I had hidden from my mother as I left the house.

"Yes, why?" I answered, almost embarrassed I had dressed up.

"I can have way more fun with you when you wear something that hot!" he said while flashing his cocky smile. I just rolled my eyes; it's not like he owned me, even though he acted like he did.

The dancing and drinking had triggered something in him that night. I was pretty sure he was dating one of my friends at the time. He told me they had broken up, but I'm not sure I believed him. While on the dance floor, he drunkenly pulled me aside and said, "Let's play carpenter, first we'll get hammered and then I'll nail you! Baby, I'm here all night and I want you." It was the worst pick up line I had ever heard. I mean, seriously.

As I drove him home that night, he couldn't keep his hands off me. I walked him to the door of his friend's condo and he kissed me. He really wanted me. He had never asked me out, never shared his intentions. We flirted but I didn't take him seriously. He opened the door and wrapped his arms around me as he invited me in. We snuck into the spare bedroom. I don't know what I was thinking, but he kept coming up with one corny line after another. And, well, being young and stupid and curious, one thing led to another. It was the most ridiculous twenty seconds of my life.

It was strictly physical, there was nothing but lust driving his needs; the thrill of being able to get in my 'pants'. It didn't mean anything. I didn't want him like that. I thought I would've felt more towards him but it wasn't intimate at all.

Immaturity and inexperience fueled it. I wasn't angry or upset. I was glad it happened. It helped me realize how I felt about him.

It was obvious we were way better friends than we would ever be lovers. Even the whole friends with benefits thing wasn't appealing. I was just hoping he got it out of his system. Over time, his lust had turned into misdirected love, but he couldn't be there for me. I could not offer more than friendship. When he realized I was getting married, he accepted he had to move on. If he wanted to be in my life, he would have to remain my best friend. And he gave me that for a very long time. Throughout our lives, we made it a point to make time for each other, good, bad, or ugly. We managed to stay friends for almost twenty-five years.

Unfortunately, once his wife had read our intimate exchanges and strained our friendship, it had ruined us. He hadn't been able to fix it. His wife was always suspicious that he was cheating and I was suspicious that she was reading all our exchanges.

Everything changed. I knew he had been unhappy in his marriage. He wanted an out. I would've been so convenient for him, the reason for divorcing his wife, giving him the excuse he needed, the "affair" his wife had accused us of. He couldn't do that to me.

As things got worse in their marriage, his behaviour towards me was damaging, although he didn't realize how much he hurt me. He would whisk into town, expecting me to "sneak" around with him, showing up at the house unannounced or expecting me to pick up the bill if we went out in case his wife found out. He was being selfish and disrespectful. I had trusted him and now it was lost.

I wouldn't be his wife and I didn't want to be his mistress. That only left room for friendship, but he destroyed that. If he had to let me go for his marriage, I would have respected that. It was clear, he couldn't let me go. I also wasn't ready to let him go.

This went on until finally I couldn't do it anymore It was unhealthy, the drama, the pretending, the mind games, the worry. He had been my rock. Now he was not. We left things unfinished, I couldn't face him.

Feeling Marcelo's hand tap my shoulder snapped me out of the uncomfortable memory. Brad was still standing in front of me, a smirk on his face. Now I had no choice, he was here.

"Will I see you at the finish line or the after party?" he asked.

"I hope not," I replied, walking away. I was done with him. I heard him wish me luck.

Marcelo reached his arm around me and held me close as he asked, "Are you okay? Who was that guy? Do you want to talk about it?"

"One of the reasons I have issues trusting myself when it comes to relationships is because of that man. I'm sick of being betrayed," I responded, eager to escape and start the race.

Marcelo looked at me with his kind eyes and sweet expression, "Sounds to me like one of those situations that was out of your control—be it with your parents, your husband, or whoever that was. But watching you shake him off, it looks like you're finally being true to what you really want. Keep focusing on what your heart desires and go after it."

I smiled at him, maybe he was right. And right now, what I wanted was to complete this race.

The announcer at the Wine Country Half was hyping up the crowd with loud music and crazy warm up moves. The crowd was electric. I felt like the air was vibrating. Pure energy was pulsing through the crowd. There were so many people running, volunteering, cheering and celebrating. When the buzzer went, the crowd moved in unison. We advanced across the start line and began our 21.1 km trek for the day.

About ten minutes into the run, Marcelo looked down at his bib and said, "Since I'm going to be Carmen for the race, tell me more about her. What's she like? It should keep me distracted from my throbbing calves for at least a few kilometers."

I laughed warmly—if he was already complaining about his calves, this should be an interesting race. "You would like Carmen. She's tall, slim, strong and stunningly gorgeous. She loves holistic learning and teaching. She's a yoga teacher but is learning about other natural healing and therapies. She can move like no one I have ever met. She's the one that got me into yoga. I'd say she's about five years younger than you. She's a free spirit; she's had a tough life."

"Karina, it sounds like you're trying to set me up with her! I'm happy right here—except for the running part," he said, trying to laugh at his own joke while breathing hard.

"Well, if she wasn't married, living in Calgary and going through the biggest crisis of her life, I totally would've set you two up," I replied. "I could see you two clicking and being happy. She has been through a lot in life and could use a kind soul like you to take care of her." I said it so matter of factly, it was strange.

"Well, if she's anything like you, I am sure I will like her. You two are quite the team. I hope I get to meet her someday. How did you meet?" he asked, wincing a little, but still keeping pace.

"I met her when we were both pregnant. She's a lot younger than me. I can still picture her scared face when she walked into that baby class. She had met a guy who was almost twenty years older than her who had wooed her. When they found out she was pregnant, they got married. It was a big mistake; they weren't meant to be. And worse, she lost the baby. She couldn't make him happy. She thought if she could give him a child, it would get better," I explained.

"After she lost the first baby, they tried again. She lost that one too. They kept trying, but she kept losing them. Although they were both healthy, somehow, they weren't compatible. Each failed pregnancy broke her a little more and he started to resent her. He lost interest in her, but she stayed with him because she didn't know how to leave," I continued.

"In some ways, I saved her when she was at her worst. She loves my boys like her own and I love her in my own way. She helped me and we have always been there for each other. She also got me through my worst times. Whether it was physical, mental, or something in between," I finished, breathing a little heavily myself.

"What did she get you through?" he asked, although he already knew the answer. I hesitated. I looked at him out of the corner of my eye. His expression was sweet and his gaze was kind and receptive. I knew I should've told him before but I wasn't ready. It felt right now. I began to tell him about how Carmen had been by my side during each pregnancy and hospital visit. How she had come with me to the doctor when I had been diagnosed with Stage III Breast Cancer weeks after delivering. She had cried at my bed side when the first surgery hadn't gone as planned and I was in pain from not being able to breastfeed. She had been there after my mastectomy, my treatments, when I lost my hair, when I got a wig.

She was there for my surgeries as my body continued to betray me and I had to find ways to repair it. I would've been broken without her support. My husband, although supportive, was quite squeamish and couldn't handle hospitals, and it was difficult for him to watch his wife go through it. I had heard of marriages falling apart because of things like that. I knew my husband wouldn't leave me, but something had changed between us. I was now weak, broken, disfigured, more afraid of the outside world and even more shaken.

"When I say Carmen and I not only found each other, but that we saved each other, I mean it. I would not have survived without her. I'm not really sure either of us would be here today if it hadn't been for the other. I was by her side during her darkest time and she was by mine through my toughest. We managed to find joy, excitement and a way to live in the moment despite it all. Now, I feel like I'm ready to keep going; to keep on living life.

"She helped me rebuild and supported me when others couldn't. My parents had a really hard time with it. Allergies aren't even a real thing amongst Indian parents, let alone a disease. My mom couldn't wrap her head around why this had happened to me. She blamed karma and my sins from a past life because she felt there was no other explanation. and needed to point the blame somewhere. She also couldn't face the reality of it all, that this could happen to her baby—she denied it at first and then all she would do is pray. Pray to every Hindu god, go to temple, worship at people's homes, bring back all sorts of blessings, symbols and omens from India in case modern medicine wasn't enough.

"Last year marked my ten years as a cancer survivor. I had a party with my close friends and family and yet, I struggled to call it a celebration. I'm relieved that I *cheated* death; I had to look it in the eye and then stand up to it to fight. But I worry that I brought three babies into the world when my body was full of disease. I hate the destruction it's done to my body. I'm exhausted by the strength I required to fight to make it. That part of my life happened long ago, it's one I advocated for and talked much about when I was going through it. Now, my scars are reminders of those times. But I want to continue, I don't want to live in that pain anymore. I'm done reliving it. I want to keep moving."

He understood. Not that I needed him too. I realized, as the blood pumped through my veins and I focused on my breathing, that I didn't need anyone to understand my life or my choices. I just had to live, for me. I deserved it.

I plugged my music in and decided to focus on my pace. I did want a personal best and although I felt secure talking to Marcelo, I needed to run. Marcelo was breathing hard and needed to focus on moving his legs. I smiled pointing at my headphones, signaling I could no longer hear him. I zoned in on what needed to be done and blocked everything else out. This was for me and I needed to concentrate on me.

I felt the ground under my feet as I took each stride, pounding to the rhythm of the tunes. I felt the air on my skin as my body started to perspire from the effort it was putting into the run.

I increased my pace and started breathing more deeply. My arms moved in sync with my legs, pushing me further. The cloudless blue skies were so soothing, the sun just starting to warm up the air. The beauty of Lake Okanagan, the Rocky Mountains dominating the skyline and the delicate flowering fruit trees lining the orchard fields.

As I continued to focus on my run, the world started to fall away. It was just me. It was like a sci-fi movie; everything behind me was fading or falling away vanishing pixels as I pushed forward. The sensation of the wind on my face and the fragrance in the air was like Mother Nature's perfume welcoming me. My body felt lighter, like it was willing itself to run. I passed a few hydration stations, sipping on water and electrolytes to keep my body fueled. As other runners passed me, I encouraged them on and they high fived me. The endorphins were being released and, the adrenaline was pumping. I could feel Carmen's presence there beside me, encouraging me to continue.

My body was telling me I was nearing kilometer 18, my weakness. I don't know why; it wasn't that my legs felt sore or that I couldn't breathe, but I would have a mental block, a wall that would go up and stop me from wanting to continue. I wasn't going to let it stop me today. I found my nineties, electric house, dance music jam *Sandstorm* and pumped up the volume. I cranked my neck from side to side, relaxing my muscles. I closed my eyes momentarily to focus on my goal ahead. And I simply ran. There were moments where my mind was telling me to stop, where my feet slowed and my ribs ached, but I ignored it and pushed through.

As I neared closer to the finish, I could taste a little blood as I continued to breathe, but I knew I had done it. My body wasn't going to give up on me now. I had not only finished but accomplished my personal best. The sweat had been dripping down my face and had dried and now I had white saline streaks down my face. Some of my lipstick had rubbed off onto my teeth and I am pretty sure my eyes were a little red from the sunscreen dripping into them. Perhaps not my best look, but I didn't care! I used some water to splash on my face and the edge of my shirt to wipe away the sweat marks. The photos they took at the finish line were more comic relief than achievement, but I didn't care. This was my moment.

As the volunteer awarded me with my finisher's medal, placing it around my neck, I felt a sense of accomplishment that I had done this for myself. It felt so good. My kiddos would be so proud. My girls, who had been training with me, would want to celebrate. I knew my husband would still think it was a waste of time and money. But I didn't care about that. I did it on my terms, my pace and I finished.

It was strange, but I had forgotten about Marcelo. It wasn't until I had grabbed an apple and a protein bar that I noticed him standing in a greenspace nearby. I was happy to see that he was still breathing, wavering a little, but still breathing. He was happy to be done, but also happy to have completed it. He was busy hydrating and munching on snacks. He walked over to me and hugged me.

"I am so glad to be done with that. I survived, but you crushed it. I am so proud of you. I can see why your boys call you a 'Rockstar' mom. You just keep on surprising and amazing me." He had this smile on his face and what he said was so heartfelt, that I started tearing up.

It wasn't fair for him to make me feel so good, I knew I couldn't keep him. I kept reminding myself he wasn't real. I didn't want to ruin the moment with my tears, so I choked them back, put on a smile and hugged him tight.

“For the record, you aren’t so bad yourself, I didn’t talk to you that night just for your good looks! You’re amazing too!”

We took a sweaty selfie and clinked our medals, like we would beer glasses. It was a proud moment.

Chapter 10

The Spaaahhh...

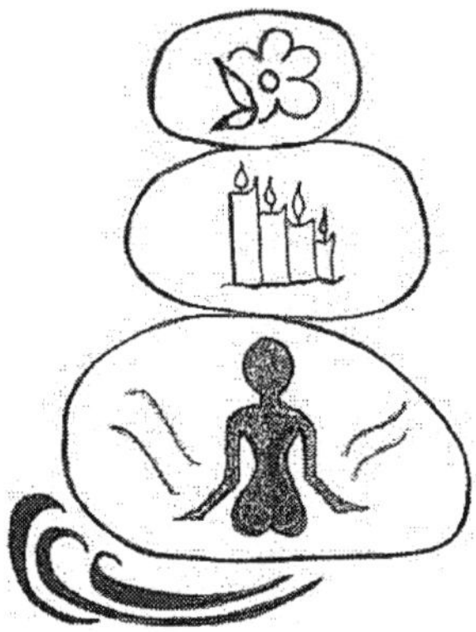

Congratulating, thanking and saying our goodbyes to the many runners we had met, we headed for the spa. I couldn't wait to indulge in the foot rub, body wrap and massage waiting for us. I needed to relax my muscles. And I wanted to see how Marcelo would fare; hopefully he wasn't a squirmer on the table.

Massage is something I spoil myself with, although I use the word "spoil" lightly. My body has been through so much trauma that without regular therapeutic treatments, I would not have survived. There is very little relaxing and a lot of pain involved. And Jenna is the best person I have found to inflict this pain on me.

Jenna was one of my besties from yoga. The sweetest, purest, toughest and oldest soul I had ever met for being all of 28. She led a life full of hardship and tragedy, but she was always smiling and ready to face the world. She was slim and had shoulders that looked like they had been chiseled out and carved. Gorgeous lashes waved over her baby blues and her super short acid blonde hair was always perfect.

She was a complete contradiction with her delicate manner but powerful techniques, her tattooed body and simple outlook, but with so much depth and knowledge. She was much more than just my therapist, she was my confidant, my soul searcher and most definitely my friend.

Once I had become a regular, Jenna would come to my house to let herself in to my house, as I always kept the front door unlocked for her. She would set up her table in the living room. Smiling her brilliant smile, she would say, “How are we doing today?” as she wrapped her arms around me warmly. This was her way of easing me into what I knew was to come.

She was merciless and determined to work out any knots, using her thumbs, elbows and suction cups. While she worked, we chatted about life, men, yoga and the philosophies of the world. I didn’t mind talking to her while she rubbed my naked body still focusing on my trouble spots. I think it helped ease my mind. Of course, when she was done pounding, stretching, and pushing, I could barely breathe, not even sure I was supposed to feel that way. She would apologize for what she had done to my body and I would apologize for making her work so hard. The problem with having a broken body is that it always needs fixing. But with each treatment, she made it better. She was a true gem. I'm not sure others would have put up with me and my strange requests, but she cared. I joked that it was a good thing I liked a little pain for pleasure, otherwise I wouldn't be able to tolerate it.

Now, here we were in the luxurious spa reception awaiting to be pampered. I am a simple person until I find an indulgence in life. I don't have many, but the ones I do have, I thoroughly enjoy. Reflexology is one of them. Having someone rub my feet for 45 minutes, using different aromatherapy oils, hot stones, releasing pressure points and relaxing the nerves, was better than sex. The sweet Latino lady who was my therapist that day not only had strong hands but a magical touch. She knew exactly which pressure points to trigger and how to release them. I didn't know I could have so many knots in the bottom of my feet, but as she worked each one, I moaned a little and I felt a little more relief. Then she rubbed the tops of my feet, ankles and calves with hot stones. She continued to manipulate my toes, the arches and the heels of my feet. The pleasure, pain and pressure were immense, intense and extremely fulfilling. I was lost in the sensation and hoped no one else could hear me moan softly while I took it all in.

After the reflexology foot massage, we were given hot herbal tea and fresh, homemade, granola snacks dipped in dark chocolate. It's like they were reading my mind; I was feeling pure bliss.

We were led to a changing room where we were given fluffy terry cloth robes and fuzzy slippers. We then headed to a sauna style heated room with two oversized massage tables with a curtain dividing them. We had to slip out of our robes and slip under the provided sheets.

I was lost to the world in my own zone. It started with a gentle "warm up" massage, followed by a black soap wash where they held handheld rain drop showers to cleanse our bodies on a separate table.

The black soap wash was followed by a body exfoliation made with coconut oil and walnut seeds used with a scrub glove. After another rinse, the esthetician applied a purifying mask all over my body and face which was made from mango, mandarins, honey, and ghassoul clay. After allowing the mask to sit on the skin for fifteen minutes, it was gently rubbed off and our bodies were rinsed again. We were patted dry and for the final segment of the treatment, our bodies were hydrated with argon oil through a relaxing massage technique. We even received a special scalp massage. It was pure pampering. My body and mind were completely satisfied.

When they had finished, I couldn't move and I didn't want to. The sensations of the foot rub, scrub, mask, oil, and massage were intermingling and lingering on my skin. I was so relaxed. I think I heard Marcelo snore. Of course, we couldn't stay there forever, so eventually we made our way out of the spa, delighted and somewhat exhausted by the experience.

Leaving the spa, I realized I needed caffeine. I saw a coffee shop nearby. I grabbed Marcelo by the arm and we made our way over to it and I collapsed in the nearest chair on the patio. I stood up again to make it into the shop and almost squealed.

"Are you okay, ma'am?" the not even twenty-year-old barista behind the counter asked, looking at me with a strange look on her face. Did she just call me ma'am, for real? A certain episode of Seinfeld popped up into my mind. I was so tired, I decided to let it go. I probably looked worse for wear given the long day I had, but still, I did not like that term.

I smiled as politely as I could, "I'm just excited to see you have the nitro flash brew on your menu. It's one of my favourites. Could I please get one with a shot of your dark chocolate syrup?"

She looked at me puzzled, nitro flash brews were known for their higher caffeine content and I was adding chocolate to it. Trying to sound impressive and looking over at Marcelo, giving him a flirty smile, she replied, "Well, I know a lot of the older customers like the nitro, gives you an extra boost of energy so you can stay awake past 8:00 p.m. It looks like you could use the extra shot of chocolate."

I forced a smiled and must've lunged a little because I felt Marcelo pull me back. Was this pretty little thing seriously calling me old and making a move on Marcelo? I may not be twenty anymore, but please, this was ridiculous.

"Karina, sweetheart," Marcelo said, "why don't you grab us a table on the patio and I'll get our drinks?"

I dismissed the waitress and walked away, somewhat relieved to be able to sit down. I pulled out my phone to take a look at myself. I had to admit, with no makeup and my hair a mess from the oils and the treatments, I did look a little rundown, but my skin was glowing and when I touched my arm, it was smoother than butter. The exfoliation, scrub and argon oil had made me feel so soft. I didn't care about the barista, I wanted to enjoy my coffee, take in the scenery from the patio and chill out. Although I did put my hair up and applied some fresh lipstick.

Marcelo brought over my nitro brew and a shot glass with a pinkish liquid in it. "A peace offering. I told the barista how much you enjoy Kombucha and she gave you a sample. They make it in house and have it on tap."

"You sure she didn't spit in it?" I asked. "Or did you have to give her your number in exchange for the shot."

"Hey, you know it's not like that," he said, mocking me. I rolled my eyes and looked away. I needed a minute to myself. It annoyed me that I let people affect my mood. I know I couldn't take it personally. It was nice to have Marcelo there, taking care of me. I wasn't going to let this silly girl ruin it. I decided to take his advice and enjoyed the coffee.

"Have you traveled with friends a lot?" Marcelo asked, changing the subject.

"I've travelled with my family, but I was never allowed to with friends. My mom wouldn't let me go and worried about my safety and virginity. My husband doesn't like travelling and definitely not with other people, says it's too much work and a waste of money." I rolled my eyes. "I definitely feel like I missed out on a lot," I explained.

"Like what?" Marcelo asked, a troubled expression on his face.

"I had planned a ski trip," I replied, "we were going to spend the weekend at a lovely hotel nestled in the beauty of the Rocky Mountains. My husband wasn't too keen, between the cost, the physical exertion of skiing, and being outside in the cold, but I wanted my boys to try it, so I signed them up for ski lessons so my husband wouldn't have to do anything.

"That sounds great," he replied. "I've skied the Rockies before, many years ago, but last season, I went for skiing locally for three days along with some après ski afterwards, got a fair bit of snow too. Took a bit to recover."

"Well, nothing compares to skiing in the Rockies," I said. "I've never heard of 'après ski' though, sounds fancy, what does that involve?"

"It's...uh...not as fancy as it sounds," he smiled and looked sheepish.

"Come on—tell me. Just so you know, you are the biggest tease I have ever met. Never have I met a man who talks as little about himself as you do." I said, trying to coax him.

"It's nothing, really," he said teasing me.

"Fine, I'll look it up," I laughed. I grabbed my phone and searched it up. I read aloud, "According to the urban dictionary, après ski—When you have just awoken from a nap after shredding all day and your main intention is to get hammered, dance naked on tables and look for ski bunnies."

He laughed. Of course, it was just a pretentious way for him to say he was getting drunk after a hard day on the hill. I teased him, "I'm guessing you avoided the nakedness on tabletops by showing off the wicked dance moves you picked up from me!" I knew he was far too serious to get involved with anything that had to do with tabletops.

"Ha! Well, there was certainly a lot of tabletop dancing in the vicinity!"

"And what were you doing while that was occurring?" I asked, although I already knew the answer.

"We were chilling at a table—but lots of people were dancing on top of the bar," he said, defending himself.

"I would have to think about who I would want to party with, you or the people at the bar!" I teased him even more.

"And did you après ski on your trip?" he asked.

I looked down, embarrassed. "I was hoping we could try some après ski. There was a great lounge attached to the hotel. But before we left, my husband looked up the hotel and said it was a complete waste of money and that I should look for a cheaper one. He also questioned whether the boys even needed ski lessons. So that was the end of that."

He tried to cheer me up, "Well, how about you try again? Organise a trip with friends?"

"I would love to do a friends trip someday. Rebecca and I almost coordinated a family vacation to Costa Rica, but unfortunately things fell through and we ended up cancelling. My husband was relieved. I was bummed." I replied.

Marcelo sympathized, "That's too bad about Costa Rica. It sounds like it would've been fun; it's always a little more work with kids but still a cool adventure. I love traveling with friends. A few friends and friends of friends had planned a trip to Rio one year. We were there for New Year's Eve, so it was a festive time. It was eye opening. It totally helped that we knew someone who was local and spoke Portuguese. We were surrounded by beaches and hills, and the food and the atmosphere were incredible. It was such a fascinating spot to visit. We were in Paraty and Ilha Grande. And then we checked out the

Iguazu Falls—so much to see." His eyes twinkled as he reminisced about his trip. His enthusiasm was always refreshing.

I said, smiling, as I didn't want to dampen the mood, "I do love traveling and hope to do more of it. I did book a trip to Los Cabos last year because I got an amazing deal." That was the only way I was going to convince my husband.

"Right, I think you told me. I think I told you I did a very last-minute trip around the same time to Playa del Carmen for a friend's birthday, which was great!" he said.

"I remember. Playa del Carmen. You didn't invite me!" I pretended to be hurt. "Kidding! It sounded amazing."

"Next time—we will have to plan something," he said sincerely.

"It would be fun if we did a trip together," I said, non-committedly. "I'll keep it in mind now that I know you book last minute! One day, we will book a friends trip."

"For sure! Did you book any tours?" he asked.

"I did. I booked a snorkeling boat excursion. I wanted to take the boys for scuba but they aren't old enough, but we should." I said.

"Nice! That sounds great. I love snorkelling—we were supposed to do the cenotes in Playa."

"Hold on, I need to look up cenotes," I said as I googled it on my phone. It was a natural underground swimming pool hidden by caves and bedrock. It seemed surreal. "Wow! Looks like an amazing adventure!"

"We ended up drinking instead, did a mezcal tasting," he said. It was his turn to look guilty. I looked at him, questioning what mezcal was, having to look it up on my phone again.

"Tasting sounds fun, I could probably handle a sip! But I think I would prefer the cenotes." I laughed, wishing we could go on a trip to Mexico together.

"You don't need to drink too much of it, it's pretty strong." He smiled back at me.

"Well, what I didn't tell you was that I had a serious mommy fail which was totally out of control on the snorkel tour. There were four scantily clad chicks smacking each other's bums and dancing to seriously inappropriate lyrics right in front of my boys. I picked a family friendly tour! It was a challenge!" I was still embarrassed by the incident.

He hesitated, but said, "Haha! Well, remember our friend from Montreal, he ended up going home with two women, while my trip was followed promptly with some version of Mexican flu! Haha!" We both started laughing.

"Wow! A threesome! Impressive! Sounds way better than any flu. Sorry to hear it. You should've booked a massage. I had one on the beach. Guessing you never booked one for yourself."

He said, "I should have but I keep putting it off...one day I will."

I decided to have a little fun with it, and asked trying not to giggle too much, “What are we talking about? The threesome, the scuba or the massage?”

To which he wittily remarked, while blushing, “All of the above!” while laughing out loud.

I couldn’t resist, it was fun to flirt with him, so I said, “Well, I have done two out of three!”

When I didn’t get a response from him right away, I said, “Aren’t you even a little bit curious as to which two?” He was definitely blushing now hiding an embarrassing smile.

He simply replied, “No comment.” I liked making him smile.

Sitting on the patio of the local coffee shop, sipping my nitro brew, soaking in the sun and having a relaxing conversation with this gorgeous man felt so good. The run, the spa, all of it made the day perfect. Giving myself permission to look after myself was satisfying. Marcelo continued, “You don’t always have to travel abroad to have a great time. I am sure you can do lots with the boys around where you live.”

“I guess so, it’s just not the same. I took my boys for a hike last week, it was supposed to be relaxing.”

“Hiking is always fun. I had this golf thing last weekend, you should get your boys to try it,” he said.

“Golf?” I questioned. “Are you any good at it? Do you like it or was it for clients?” I asked.

“No clients, thankfully. I play just for fun once in a while. I played competitively when I was a junior,” he said laughing slightly, "but I hardly play now. How was the hike? Was it relaxing?"

"It turned out to be challenging—the boys, not the hike. I had to bribe them with milkshakes. But when I get back home, I'll sign the boys up for a tee time—could be fun or could be a disaster!"

"It'll be fun – I know you would be great with your boys." He encouraged me.

"And you, you played for fun? For a guy who used to play competitively? Yah, right! Although I don't know why I'm not surprised. Remind me never to play with you. Although I think you would make a great teacher! But how's your patience?" I joked.

"First game of the year, seriously, it was just for fun, had a few beers after to relax," he laughed, trying to sound casual.

"First game or not, fun or not, beers or not, did you win?"

"Yep," he admitted, kinda shy about it.

"Ah, so you're competitive, smart and sweet...I totally knew it." I complimented.

I wanted to ask him something more serious, but I didn't know how to approach it. I decided to dive right in. "I hope you don't mind me asking, but how are you so perfect and not married? How do you deal with being alone? Do you get lonely or do you like doing your own thing?"

He looked a little taken aback at the change of questioning. He didn't answer right away. Finally, he said,

"I do like being on my own; it gives me the freedom and the ability to do what I want to with my life. But at the same time, I don't have anyone to share it with. Sometimes it's nice, to not have to worry about others, and I am starting to find my rhythm. I'm a little set in my ways too, I'm not sure I would want someone else to interfere with that. Maybe I haven't found the right person to share it with yet."

I don't know why I said it, but it slipped out, "I know it's not the same and I know I may never belong to you, but that doesn't mean that we can't enjoy what we have together now."

He looked at me with this unforgettable look and reached for my hand across the table. He squeezed as he lifted it, indicating I should stand, which I did. He maneuvered my hand so I would follow it around the table towards him. When I got close enough, he turned me slowly and let me sink onto his lap. He squeezed me tight and kissed me. His silence told me enough.

Chapter 11

Take My Breath Away

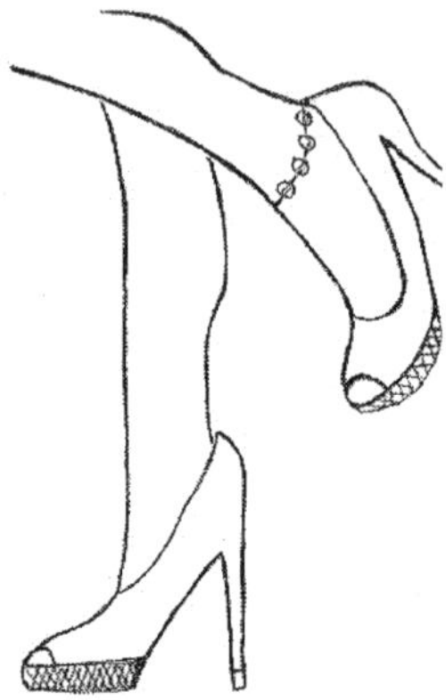

Looking through my things, I found the dress Carmen had picked for me the last time we were out shopping. It was tighter and shorter than I would've picked out for myself, but Carmen had great taste and knew what I could get away with. The dark gray, faux leather dress accentuated my breasts and hugged my waist and rested just below my glutes. The front of the dress "laced" up with a thin black string with silver eyelets on either side of the dress, pulling it together. From underneath peaked out a black bra with red lace, which just showed through the tie-ups—a little teaser! I had slipped on the matching black panties. I surprised myself with my alluring wardrobe.

I saw Marcelo watching me as I applied my favourite shade of Cherry Blossom lipstick. He admired the dress from afar and then walked up behind me and slowly traced his fingers over my shoulders, now incredibly silky and soft after the spa treatment that afternoon. He bent his head down, nuzzling his face into my neck, kissing me gently. He drew his breath in deeply—the combination of my perfume, body lotion, and hair product intermingling to create a stimulating scent.

He pressed his lips to my earlobe, I could feel his warm breath exciting my senses as he whispered, "You are incredible." No man had ever treated me or touched me or made me feel the way Marcelo did. I didn't know a man could arouse, please and take of me like he did. I didn't know a man like him could exist.

"You are too kind." I winked, looked him over and smiled. He was wearing a deep blue, long sleeve, button down dress shirt that was a tiny bit big for him. It made him look hot and adorable at the same time. Dark faded denim jeans and navy socks. I didn't know a man could own so many shades of blue.

He allowed his hands to roam all over my body. He felt so comfortable but unfamiliar, it was intoxicating. His touch awoke sensations I had felt the day before. A kind of pleasure that I had longed for, ached for. Marcelo knew how to caress, linger, embrace, stimulate. I let myself enjoy his roaming hands but escaped before we got too carried away. I enjoyed this man, but I needed a night of dancing.

Marcelo had found a fabulous restaurant that came highly recommended, and we decided to check it out. The restaurant was a little Italian Asian fusion place that served unique plates all accented with delicious delicacies and garnishes. They had a fabulous seafood selection, some tapas style starters, and incredible entrees. Just reading the menu was making me salivate. I loved menus: chef's creations, masterpieces with little embellishing touches of aioli, oils, cheeses and sauces, which were all so mouth-watering.

Only problem was, I couldn't eat. Don't get me wrong, I love to eat, I just find it challenging sometimes. I have always had issues with food. I battled an unhealthy relationship with emotional binging and was always trying to count calories or trying to pop pills to feel less bloated or uncomfortable. I had tried every diet ever written – fasting, cutting out food groups, liquids, proteins, but I just couldn't do it. When it wasn't a fad diet, it was stress, anxiety and intolerances to all kinds of foods. I have learned now to accept it—to cultivate a more loving relationship with myself and with food.

The fitted dress was not designed for a hearty meal. I didn't want to eat anything rich that might upset my stomach, and I didn't want to eat too much before a night of dancing. I decided on a light seafood starter, something I could rarely order because of Aryan's shellfish allergy. When he wasn't around, I felt less guilty ordering it. The restaurant had a medley of shrimp, mussels, clams and scallops in a light white wine, lemon, garlic, olive oil and vegetable broth, which I ordered with a tantalizing Asian-inspired salad with watercress, sesame dressing and lightly seared Hamachi (yellowtail). Marcelo ordered a fusion-style bruschetta, a paesana salad and the Ossobuco and paired it with wines to his liking. It was all so delicious. For dessert, we shared an Amaretto infused cheesecake. Good thing Marcelo ate most of it. Looking out of the large bay windows onto the calm, dark lake as evening slowly turned to nightfall and the sun set gracefully over the horizon, it was turning out to be a wonderful evening.

The organizers from the Wine Country Half had planned an after party. There were two-night clubs in town, one called the Sapphire and the other Liquid Zoo. Both sounded interesting. The organizers had decided on Sapphire.

The club was just starting to get busy when we arrived. I recognized many people from the race earlier that day. People greeted us with warm smiles, high fives, hugs and some of them were even wearing their finisher's medals. The disco lights were flashing, the décor was hip and the beats were pumping. One wall was adorned with a huge, creative art piece—it said "Dolce Vita" in large, hollow steel letters and inside each letter were rows of old-fashioned incandescent bulbs, highlighting the letters and illuminating the wall and mirrors around it. The vibe of the place just got you into the mood. There was a young, very talented DJ in a white jumpsuit, swaying her head to the music through her headphones, her long blonde hair catching the light from a disco ball in the centre of the room.

There was a small balcony above the dance floor where a go-go girl wearing a J-Lo inspired, gold, sparkling, low navel cut jumpsuit and high heels was swaying her hips. In another corner, a large, golden bird cage showcased a gorgeous, black cage dancer. He was in tight, bright pink, spandex shorts and was gyrating like nothing I had seen. I loved go-go dancing and dancers. They were the perfect balance of powerful and sensual.

As we settled in at the bar, Marcelo looked a little uneasy. “You good?” I asked him.

“Of course,” he replied. “It’s been quite the day and my nerves are a little shot. I hope you don’t mind, but I’m going to sit for a bit and maybe grab a drink,” he said, plunking himself down on a bar stool.

Poor thing, he probably isn’t used to so much action, I thought. Probably the predictable business travel schedule and conferences were as exciting as it got. My idea of non-stop and his were very different. I was used to juggling many requirements, living off very little sleep and trying to get the most out of life whether I was out or stuck at home. I always joked when my mother told me I was doing too much, “I will rest when I am dead.” I guess for him, all his time was his time; in my world, very little of my time was actually for me.

Before grabbing a stool next to him, I decided to check out the lounge and chat with some of the fellow runners. Just as I was about to return to him, I was cut off. It was Brad. He stood in front of me, checking me out, very obviously objectifying me. I rolled my eyes.

"Hey babe, looking good tonight," he started.

"Nice to see you too," I said sarcastically. "What do you want?" I asked, trying to be as cold as I could.

"I would say a dance—" he started, but I cut him off.

"I'm not dancing with you. You've done enough damage to ruin both our relationship and your marriage."

He tried to explain, "You're being an idiot, it doesn't have to be this way."

I rolled my eyes. "When you decide to man up and stand up for our friendship, you know where to find me."

"Will you give me 30 seconds?" he asked so frantically and desperately that I stopped mid-turn, falling for his needs as I always did. Before I could change my mind, he grabbed me around the waist and pulled me aside, behind a large column. At first, he just hugged me and held me. Then he grabbed my ass. I tried to push his hand away but wouldn't allow it. Why did he think he owned me? He pinned me against the column so I couldn't escape. He held me and slowly moved his hips against mine. I felt so uncomfortable.

He moved his hands to grab for mine and pinned them above my head as he pushed his body into mine. He confessed, "We have been friends for over 25 years. You have had to have figured this out by now. Can you really be this oblivious? I have been in love with you since the first day we met!" I wanted to remind him that he was never in love with me, he only wanted to sleep with me.

When I didn't say anything, he continued getting a little upset, pressing into me harder, hurting my wrists a little, "What would you have me do? I accepted the friendship, hoping I could change your mind. But you're tainted by your marriage, damaged and don't even believe in love."

I couldn't comprehend what he was saying. I still didn't know what to say.

He wasn't finished and was getting more worked up, "I got married when I knew I couldn't have you and have been trapped since. If you had wanted me, I would've been yours. You must have a really good reason for pushing me away. Please help me understand so I can stop being pissed." I was numb and couldn't breathe.

He brought his head down low, close to mine and whispered although his voice still sounded angry, "I never meant to hurt you and I know what a difficult position I have put you in," he grinded his hips into me implying the innuendo. "I care about you and I miss you. I know I messed up, but I want you back," and as he said it, he spun me around, pinning me against the wall so my back was to him. I felt sick. He was playing his usual selfish and manipulative games. I don't know if he was drunk or desperate, but I hated the way he was overpowering me. I could feel him pulsating against me. I had to find a way to escape.

"Karina," he continued. "I want to take you away, just the two of us. Give me what I need, be a real woman. A woman that will pleasure and satisfy, get down on her knees." This time he thrust and reached for my breasts and squeezed. I wasn't good with that.

I pushed back, trying to escape, but he took it as an invitation. I tried to push harder but I couldn't compete with his overbearing strength.

I said as forcefully as I could, "I was always there for you but I don't need you, I need to move on. You don't get to be a part of my life anymore. And you hurt me and I don't want anything to do with you, ever! I am done!"

He laughed, knowing that he had the upper hand and was enjoying himself way too much. I felt disgusted and needed a way out. I couldn't breathe. I felt like I was suffocating.

Just then, Marcelo found us. The flushed, angry, panicked expression on my face must've been obvious because Marcelo pulled Brad off me, got in his face and said, "I don't know what your problem is buddy, but get out of here before there's real trouble and stay away from her, for good." Then, he grabbed my hand and freed me from the situation. I felt this strange feeling in the pit of my stomach, an ache, it was like nothing I had ever felt before. It was incredible, I had never felt so relieved and vulnerable as I did at that moment. Marcelo had "rescued" me. It felt so surreal to have someone protect me, someone take care of me so I didn't have to do it on my own. Maybe it was my nerves, but I was so glad he was there. I let out an audible sigh of relief. As much as I didn't want someone to lean on, it was nice to have someone else's support and have him take care of me. He led me to the dance floor.

I was breathless, and all I could say was "Thank you..."

He squeezed me tight and laughed, "Don't get your hopes up, I wouldn't make a very intimidating bouncer."

I looked up at him, relieved to have him close to me and said, "I know you wouldn't be intimidating. Your gorgeous face and kind eyes, they would devour you. And by they, I mean all the women. But you did rescue me when I needed you most." Marcelo was blushing.

"Did I make you blush or are you getting used to me?" I asked.

"I am getting used to you...in a teasing kind of way," he said as he squeezed me tight.

The timing couldn't have been better, because a throwback old school 112 song called *Peaches and Cream* came on as we reached the dance floor. He put his arms around me and said, "I might not be as good as a dancer as some of your other partners..."

He wrapped his arms tighter around me as he pulled me in, bent his knees slightly and pressed his body to mine so I could feel how good he felt to have me in his arms. I wrapped my arms around his neck and allowed myself to feel secure and safe.

"I don't care about that, and you know it. I love dancing with you." I reassured him, not that he needed it. We danced, intertwined in each other's arms, not caring about anyone else. I think he had been practicing because he was more confident moving me around on the floor. Maybe he was just more comfortable and enjoyed dancing with me.

"You're remarkable," I whispered to him, confessing how much he meant to me. I cared about this man. "Thank you, for rescuing me. I don't know what I would've done. I know I can be a lot to handle. You are genuinely too much of a good thing."

He smiled his adorable, dorky smile.

We had danced for a little while when he said, "I adore you and I know you love to dance, but my feet hurt, I might need a little break. Meet me at the bar in five, I have to use the restroom."

I obliged and headed over to find a place to sit. He joined me a few minutes later and ordered a craft beer. I wanted to make sure he was okay, but before I could say anything, he hugged me close and whispered, "I got you. If you want to tell me or talk about it, I am here for you. If you don't or aren't ready, I am good as long as you are good. I am sorry, I've tried to be here for you. I've seen so much of your sadness. I'm not sure I am being the man you need me to be."

My heart ached, I didn't deserve him, he was such a good man. "Don't apologize. You've been kind, amazing, and supportive. I wish I could do more for you. I don't expect anything, and you are the sweetest thing to be here for me."

I wanted to lighten up the mood, so I looked around the club, intentionally checking people out. He raised an eyebrow at me while taking a long chug of his beer. I smiled and asked playfully, "Let's play a game." I scanned the room again and asked, "If you could take anyone home tonight, who would it be?" I wanted to see what he was into, what he liked. He looked surprised, but he scanned the room and his eyes started to follow one of the bartenders. She was somewhat tall, fair skinned, dark hair, big eyes, perky breasts, fit and looked sweet.

"Her?" I asked as I followed his gaze. He looked away, feeling guilty for checking out someone else. There was no need. I had asked him after all.

"I can see that," I continued, "she's very pretty, and she's talented at the bar. Good choice. But would you be willing to share?" I don't think he was expecting that question as he choked on the sip he had just taken, but then his face changed, like he was visualizing it.

He recovered by asking, "Enough about me, who would you take home?"

I scanned the room again. There was a pretty, petite, brunette woman standing in the far corner, swaying her hips to the music like she knew how to move. She was in a tight, gray halter top wearing light makeup and dangly earrings. "Her, for sure." This time he spit some of his beer slightly covering his mouth with his hand to avoid attention. This was all in fun, besides, I enjoyed keeping Marcelo on his toes! I smiled and gave his arm a little squeeze.

I heard the DJ come onto the mic. "Let's put our hands together for Karina! We have our very own debut go-go dancer in the house tonight. Please come to the stage and take your place on the speaker!"

Had I heard that right? I wasn't sure what to do, and then I saw Marcelo grinning away. I might've mentioned that I wanted to try it, but I never thought he would take me seriously. I am fairly sure he was falling over laughing when I had told him about the pole dancing. He pulled me up and led me to the DJ speaker.

I was so embarrassed and excited at the same time! I didn't want to disappoint, but I had never done it. Go-go dancing and performing in a club was mesmerizing. I felt the rhythm pounding through my body, the hypnotic tunes moving me automatically to the beat, people grooving and watching—it was surreal.

I was so high from the experience; I wasn't sure anything could beat that rush. When I thought my legs were going to fall off, I called to Marcelo. He came over and I placed my hands on his shoulders and let him grab me around my thighs. I slowly slid my body against his as he brought me to the floor. My toes barely touched the ground and he kissed me gently, I felt slightly elevated, floating and bent one leg before completing touching down to feel the ground under me, as "Cry to Me" by Seal started to play. I felt like Jennifer Grey must have in Dirty Dancing when Patrick Swayze swept her off her feet. Even though I wasn't sure I had much left in me, I let the bass pump through my body as Marcelo held me tightly in his arms for one last dance. My hips gyrated, my hands roamed and my body bounced, circling him, moving, grinding up and down. I wrapped my arms around him, beads of sweat starting to form on my pounding chest from all the activity. Our bodies were warming up to each other, finding their own rhythm, moving in unison.

As the song finished, my legs were jelly and I was ready to go. I stepped outside the club, taking in the fresh air and not paying attention, almost tripping on my heels. My feet were sore from all the activities of the day, but I knew I had to make it to the car. It wasn't going to happen, so I slipped them off, opting to walk in bare feet. Marcelo smiled, probably remembering Montreal.

As we were driving back from the nightclub, I was more intoxicated by Marcelo's presence than any alcohol could affect me. I couldn't keep my hands off him even though I was driving. He had protected me. He had danced with me. He was attracted to me. He paid attention to my needs. He was exactly what I needed. Like a thought bubble, the quote "The art of seduction is getting drunk on lust" popped into my head—and I was definitely feeling it.

I must've missed our turn to get back to the hotel, because the road got awfully dark and narrow. We drove into a secluded area by a lake. There were no people and the only light was from the moon glistening on the water. I stopped the car and parked. I checked the GPS—it had led us there. I knew we weren't at the hotel, but the moon, water and the night sky looked so inviting.

We stepped out of the car. Marcelo took my hand, led me out a way and told me to look up. The sky without any interference from the city lights was amazing. Millions of twinkling lights in the form of stars were shining down on us. The constellations could be observed and the super bright stars or planets could be seen with the naked eye. It was a warm night and the night air felt comforting. There were tall trees in the distance and the moonlight was just bright enough to illuminate the sky in a silverish glow. We walked to the edge of the lake and I dared to dip my feet in the cool lake water. It felt so good, numbing and healing all at once.

There was a picnic table nearby and Marcelo disappeared towards the car, coming back with blankets, towels and robes. I looked at him, wondering when he had the time to pack them. He had purposely changed the GPS in the car as we were heading back from the club so that we would end up there. Staring at the water, I felt his presence behind me. It felt like that night on his rooftop. We stood there, silently taking it all in, the cool water on my toes, the warm breeze on my skin, the smell of fresh flowers and rich pine surrounding us. He let his hands rest on my shoulders as he gently kissed the back of my neck. As he continued to kiss me, I felt him undo my dress, unclip my bra and carefully pull at my panties. He kissed my shoulders, this time sucking and biting slightly. I knew it would leave a mark, but I didn't care. He reached for my hand and squeezed our palms together, then continued to draw circles in my palm with his thumb. I was so lost in his touch that when he grabbed my hand and abruptly, without hesitation or warning, pulled me into the lake, I instinctively screamed. He quickly covered my mouth with his to mute the cries. It had felt good on my toes, but when my body hit the water, it was torture. The movies made skinny dipping look so romantic and exciting, but I was paralyzed as the chilly water washed over my naked body.

"Take a deep breath and relax. Let your body adjust and give into it. Feel the water all around your body and in the meantime, I will keep you warm." His deep comforting voice whispered, the only warmth I felt was his breath on my neck.

He lifted my body so that I could wrap my legs around his waist, his arms slipping up my back. I clenched my legs tighter around him as I wrapped my arms around his neck. The thin layer of water between our naked bodies began to warm up and he held me tight, pressing his body into mine while holding me up. The sensation of the cold water, his warm body and the feelings rising inside me were all too much. He pushed my hair back and kissed me. He held the kiss for a long time until I completely gave into him. He knew I wanted him and not just physically, it wasn't just lust driving me. Having a man take me in a lake in the middle of the night made me feel so free and wicked, allowing this man to do these things to my body in public. He gave me intimacy, security and satisfied my desires. He was so strong, holding me in the water while satisfying me. I whispered, "You take my breath away every time I am with you." as nothing but pleasure washed over me.

Even though I wanted Marcelo to hold me forever, my toes were going numb. I couldn't stay in the water much longer so I kissed him and reluctantly slipped out of his embrace. I ran out as quickly as I could, trying to recover and grabbed a towel. Marcelo couldn't stop laughing as he followed.

Wrapping ourselves in our robes, he lay a blanket down on the picnic table and lay down on top of it, looking up at the stars. He patted his hand beside him indicating that I should join him. He crossed one long leg over the other and crossed his hands behind his head. I snuggled up against him, trying to warm up. Lifting my head to look at him, he seemed so perfect. Like he knew what he wanted, he went after it and he got it. He had never struggled in his life.

My life was the exact opposite. I struggled all the time. Trying to prove myself, to feel better, to not deal with other people's problems. If things hadn't started to turn around that past year, I wasn't sure what I would've done with myself. Life had been hard. I had faced a lot of challenges, overcome a lot of obstacles, and learned to redefine myself. To stand up for myself. It must've been nice to not have to worry about any of that.

"It's not that simple," he said, like he was reading my mind.

"What are you talking about?" I asked.

"I see you, judging me. Yes, I might be single, but that doesn't mean my life is simple. Karina, sometimes you complain about how tough your life is, in your delightful two-storey house with your three handsome, healthy, smart boys, your husband who goes to work every day to support you, with your demands, whims, car, clothes, vacation and everything else and I can't help but think that you don't realise how good you have it. You're debt free, hassle free, stress free... and still you are not happy!" He trailed off.

I was shocked. I didn't know what to say. I understood where he was coming from. From the outside, I'm sure my life did seem pretty good. And I did appreciate all of it, my boys, my husband, all the hard work that went into building our lives, the money, but I also felt I had to sacrifice a lot to make that happen. But he had no idea how sad and vulnerable and devastating my life had been, and how many things had felt like they were out of my control or that I hadn't had a choice in the decisions that were made for me. I was stuck with tradition, always doing the right thing and never feeling or being me. And above all, I had a right to be entitled to my feelings without his judgement.

"Well, who are you to judge?" I replied. "In a day or two, you'll go back to your perfect life: your amazing well-respected job, travelling every other week to a conference in a different city, hanging out with friends, taking girls out, and you'll look out of your conveniently located condo with the stunning view of the Saint Lawrence River. My life has never been on my own terms. When I should've been focusing on studying and my career, I was busy raising a family. Do you know, that while you were busy working on your Ph.D., I had had three kids? I could've had a life like yours. I envy it. I never had a chance to follow my success. I knew I couldn't do it all, and even if I tried, I wouldn't be able to do it well. So, I focused on being a mom. I don't regret it and I am grateful everyday for what my life has given me; sometimes I wonder what could've been different. You got to be in control of your life."

"But you have no idea how good you have it," he countered. "Your husband might be stable and mundane, but that makes him reliable and supportive. And besides, in a day or two, you will go back to your loving family, your yoga studio where you have a hundred people who adore you, your precious Carmen, your coffee girls, your mom buddies, your dancing partners."

He was...what was he saying? He was upset because he was lonely? He was upset that I would go back to a life filled with people and none of them would be him? And he would go back to no one? But he had Daryl, his colleagues, and his mom. As I thought about it, I understood—maybe that wasn't enough. If there had been nothing else in my life, there had been people I called mine. I loved them all dearly, cared about them and how they had touched my life. And I would do anything for them. He had no one. But he did have me.

"After this trip, you'll send me a text about the party you are stressed out about planning, what such and such said about such and such at the studio, how you're planning a trip with your amazing boys, or how no matter how annoyed you are with your husband, you will be sharing a bed with him at night," he continued and then trailed off again. I felt that this was the first time since I met him that I had had a real conversation with him.

There I was, thinking he wouldn't miss me at all because there was no room in his life for my mess, full of drama and chaos, but maybe it was something he was looking for and missing in his own life. Maybe he was tired of the adventure and travel and wanted to settle down. But he was a very eligible bachelor, why hadn't he?

"What do you want?" I asked him. "Why are you still single?"

There was a silence.

"There was a girl...once..." he said slowly, almost like he didn't want to confide in me. He had built up some serious walls and, in some ways, I guess I barely knew him. It had been clear from his reservation in conversations that he had serious trust issues. I waited. I didn't want to pry or rush him. When he was ready to tell me, he would. He eventually continued, "There was this girl once, we were really close. I was in love with her. She meant the world to me. I even proposed. I really thought she was the one..." He was killing me, but I knew I had to be patient. "And then, one day, I found out the truth. It destroyed me. She wasn't who she said she was. She had been using me for my money and I had been too naïve to see it. She had a boyfriend, a completely separate life. I don't know how I didn't know. She maxed out multiple credit cards of mine, stole from me and didn't even return the engagement ring, not that I wanted it. But the one thing she did steal from me that still bothers me was my father's antique pocket watch. It was special to me, engraved and all. I hate that..." he stopped himself and took a breath before continuing. "I haven't been able to let anyone in since her. I can't trust anyone." He looked me straight in the eyes. "You are the first person I've told, even my mom doesn't know the truth."

I was touched.

"You can trust me..." I tried to console him as I stroked his hair. He looked vulnerable now, looking to me to comfort him.

What he said next shocked me, "Karina, I know it's only been a few days, but I have never experienced anything so intense in my life. You really are an incredible person, and you are special to me. I may not always be able to express myself and I know I can be distant over text; I guess I'm not really used to the attention. What we shared in Montreal was unexpected and unfinished. I haven't been able to get you out of my thoughts since that night."

I wasn't expecting that. I mean, I had thought about him a lot since that night. He had awakened senses and feelings in me that no other man had been able to. He was the first man who made me feel loved, he actually cared for me.

I couldn't speak.

He wrapped his strong arms around me tightly, pressing my cheek against his chest. I placed my head in the crook of his neck before he continued, "What if you didn't go back? I mean, to him. I know you care about him, but I know you don't love him. You have to go back to your kids, but if you are truly that unhappy, why stay with him when you can have me? I could be that man for you, take care of you." He paused. "I think I might be falling for you."

My world started spinning. What was he saying? What was he asking? This was too much. I wasn't ready for love, another relationship, even though this man felt so good. I couldn't speak, I couldn't find the words.

Finally, I said, "I'm not ready to let you go. I just found you and you make me feel things I have never felt before. This last year has been so difficult for me and your friendship has meant the world to me. Knowing I could count on you, talk to you, no matter what was going on.

You have always been there for me, despite the fact that you barely knew me...I love what we share, but...I'm not ready for another relationship. i need time and you'd miss your independence. Besides you need someone who can give you all the things I can't." I looked at him, placing the back of my hand gently on his cheek. "I don't know what the future holds, but right now, my heart belongs to you. I am forever grateful."

He smiled his outrageously charming smile. "If you're happy here, right now, with me, that's enough."

He kissed me; slowly at first and then more passionately. Maybe it was the night air, the dress I had been wearing, the red lace bra, or that we admitted to falling for each other— whatever the case, as we laid on that picnic table under the stars it wasn't long before he became charged, fiery, and deliberate.

We were fueled by passion. Staring up at the night sky with all the twinkling lights was hypnotic as our bodies moved in a natural rhythm with the sound of the water behind us. In some ways I felt like I was in a fairy tale, in the enchanted forest with prince charming who had just rescued me, yet there was nothing childish about what we were doing. Marcelo had managed to allow me to forget any hesitations I might have felt and ravished my body.

After the yearning had subsided just slightly, and the desire had been somewhat satisfied, we lay there, taking it all in. Of course, I wanted more, but along with the paranoia of being in a public place and being spotted,

I was worried about creepy crawly bugs, so we grabbed our things and head back to the room.

It was a good thing we were only about ten minutes from the hotel, because we couldn't wait to get into bed. The girl behind the desk at the front lobby gave us a shameful and excited grin when we walked in arms linked with only our robes on.

I wanted to get back to the room so he could satisfy that burning desire I could feel in the pit of my stomach, one I couldn't turn off. I needed to be his in as many ways as possible. As we stepped into the room, I slipped the "Do Not Disturb" sign on the outside of the door. When I turned to make my way back, I found Marcelo in bed, his robe long gone.

Chapter 12

Om Shanti Om

Sounds of birds chirping outside the hotel room window woke me. It was early, but I had slept soundly. I felt good. Sore, but good. I was pleasantly surprised to find myself in bed with Marcelo, his arm wrapped around me, his body pressed up against my back. It felt so natural. I could smell the mix of scents from the spa, the club and the picnic spot. It was so reminiscent of the day before. Had all that happened just yesterday? It felt like a year ago. And yet, here I was in his arms for one more day before we would have to head back. I pulled his arms tighter against my body, gently kissing his knuckles and closing my eyes, trying hard to capture the feeling, the smell, the touch so I could always remember it. I held on for as long as I could and then he rolled over and just like that, he was gone; a harsh reality of what was yet to come.

I knew I needed to get out of bed but I wasn't quite ready. Just as I was about to sneak out, I felt a familiar hand on my back, fingers drawing circles over my shoulders. They worked their way over my curves. Tiny kisses covered my neck and I was pulled into his arms.

"Good morning sexy," Marcelo's morning voice made something inside me stir; I couldn't leave now.

"Good morning handsome," I said and the smile he returned confirmed he was very happy to have me beside him. I had never been with a younger man and his stamina was incredible.

As he pinned me to the bed and climbed on top, teasing me with his tongue, his hands and his hard body, I allowed him to roam and play. He lifted my leg above his shoulder and nibbled kisses all the way up my leg, making circles with his tongue across my belly.

"You have no idea the affect your HHC has on me, do you, gorgeous?" I moaned as I felt the weight of his body pressing into me.

"My what?" he asked, puzzled.

"It's too naughty for me to say out loud, but the PG version is your hands, hips and chest," I teased.

"Here I thought you were talking about my huge hippocampus and cranium," he smirked. I loved it when he talked geeky.

"Well, it's definitely huge! And very hard!" I giggled and tried to escape but he wouldn't have it.

"I'm not going to let you get away that easily. You need to experience the full effect of my HHC!" he said and smothered me with a kiss. He flipped me onto my tummy and had me rest on my hands and knees while his hands pressed along the length of my back. He held me by my hips, in full control of my body. I didn't know it was possible to feel this much pleasure from every position he put me in.

Afterwards, I really needed a cleansing shower. When I stepped under the hot spray, I felt like he was somehow slipping away with the water going down the drain and there was no way for me to hold on. I had all these thoughts pouring over me, but now, even though life was still messy, it was a happy mess. I felt more rounded in my chaos. I was so lost in thought, I didn't even hear Marcelo until he joined me in the shower. I didn't know a man could worship a woman's body the way he did—the things he did to me. He was so bold and thorough and satisfying. And all while standing, kneeling or bending me over. I was definitely going to be walking funny today and it had nothing to do with getting a massage.

We had a bit of a drive if we were going to make it in time for the morning greeting at the Yasodhara Ashram. I wanted to continue deepening my yoga practice and the natural path would be spending some time at an ashram. I had heard about the infamous structure and the teaching of the yogis at Yasodhara. Given we were so far from India, this was the next best thing.

I was excited to be able to connect in a place other than my regular studio. My studio had proven to be my safe haven more than once; it was a special place. I had discovered it on a quiet spring morning when I was dropping the kids off at school. A sign outside had read, "Grand Opening, New Yoga Studio, Try a Free Class". I had never given much thought to yoga before that. I liked to work out at the gym, run on my treadmill, or pedal on my bike through the park; I wasn't sure where to fit yoga in. I guess I thought it was too easy and too hard all at once. I was never one to stretch, so the thought of a class where all I would be doing is stretching was overwhelming. Plus, I was a cardio junkie, which meant that sitting still was pretty much impossible.

"Welcome to the studio!" A cheery petite girl with way too much energy had greeted me. I almost stepped back out of the studio for fear I wouldn't be able to do it. "Follow me, I will show you where to set up!"

Before I knew it, this girl in her perfectly matched pink yoga pants and criss-crossed sports bra, showing off her tiny waist and Buddha and Om tattoos, was grabbing my yoga mat and leading me into the studio.

I had never experienced anything like it. It was dimly lit; there was soft, calming music playing in the background and the room was hot. Not a muggy, humid, can't breathe kind of hot, but a warm, inviting, under the sun, infrared radiant heat. The room looked full to me, at least thirty bodies all lined up in rows, their mats laid out, feet outstretched towards the front of the room. I tried to follow as best I could without stepping on anyone, worried I would drop my water bottle on someone's head. The instructor led me straight up to the front of the room, where there was a full-size mirror in front of me and another one to the right of me. I froze. I couldn't be there, not right at the front.

I didn't even know what a yoga pose was let alone a sequence and she wanted me in the front of the room with these big mirrors showing off every lump, bump and jiggle. No way! She unrolled my mat on the floor and grabbed my water bottle. She was so friendly that somehow, I couldn't be annoyed with her. She gave me a big smile and a little hug giving me a false sense of belonging before stating, "I think we have found you the perfect spot." I looked in the mirror, and the more I looked, the more mortified I was. I wasn't young, flexible or brave enough to be here and I could not do yoga.

I started talking myself out of it. Then, I took a breath and decided to try again, saying to myself, "Since I am here, I might as well try it. If I make a fool out of myself, I don't ever have to show up again. I probably won't even like yoga. Too much staying still, breathing, and focusing."

Everyone around me was tiny. I hated being the biggest girl in the room. I hated being so unsure of myself. I hated being the worst person in the room. I hated that feeling like this. I lay down and stared up the ceiling tiles, hoping they would provide me with some answers. They didn't. I waited anxiously for the instructor.

Just then a calm and inviting voice began the class. "Good morning everyone. Let's start by taking some deep breaths, in and out the nose, ujjayi breath, focusing on our breathing. We will be working through some sequences tonight and I promise you will feel calm and relaxed. Take the time to set an intention and by the end of class, you will feel more like yourself."

More like myself? I had no clue what she was talking about. I still had thoughts from the day—my to-do list, the kids and what I would make for dinner that evening. I decided to listen to this soothing voice telling me to breathe. My mind drifted and I started letting go of my thoughts.

Breathing was a great tool for the challenging poses to come. It kept me centered and allowed me to focus on each movement. I was so afraid I was going to fall over on my face—I don't know how I didn't. The more I thought about the movement and the breath the less I thought about my day and all the stress I had walked in with. I was dripping with sweat, but each pose felt good. Pretty soon, all my anxiety started to melt away. I even glanced at myself in the mirror and when I did, I looked myself right in the eye and gave myself a smile. My skin was glistening with sweat; my cheeks had a healthy colour to them and this lighting was very forgiving. It was as if I was the only person in the room, and no one else mattered.

By the time we had to get into savasana (corpse pose to close the class), I was so ready to just lie down and let go. I was so surprised at how easily I was able to close my eyes; my mind was no longer wandering and I didn't care about the ceiling tiles or what had been stressing me out about the day. I felt a strange calm. When we let out our audible "Om" sound, vibrating from the base of our navel, I felt comfort like no other. When the class was over, I knew I was going to come back for more.

I deepened my practice, coming back day after day, sometimes even twice a day. I pushed myself and realized that even if I was bigger, I was stronger, more capable and always willing to try harder. And that was enough for me.

I created a bucket list for myself, first it was just poses and then it was alignment, breathing techniques and focus. My frustrations after the initial few weeks started to fade when I realized that this was a practice of patience. The weeks turned into months and months into years. Every few months, I would surprise myself with my flexibility, strength or balance. I also realized that my practice wasn't just about the poses, it was about my mentality.

I started making friends at the studio. We shared our stories and our troubles. Whenever I was having an off day, having to deal with crazy family, demanding kids, or had a fight with hubby, I could always breathe and clear my mind in the studio. We quickly became a community of "warriors" as we called ourselves. Who knew a word could make you feel so powerful? The girls were supportive and the more we shared and bonded, I knew I had made the right choice.

I hadn't thrown myself into a project in a long time and it felt amazing. The stronger I got, the more I wanted to do it. Not only did I push my practice, but I devoured all the knowledge I could from every teacher, every class, learning about the principles and fundamentals of yoga. I took every challenge to the edge, beating my past records and craving more. The more I understood, the more I connected. Every chance I got, Carmen and I would learn more, do more, practice more. She introduced me to new styles and transitions that tested my coordination, balance and memory all at once. Now I understood why yoga was so important to her and how it helped her get through the pain and difficulty of her life.

My grandparents had introduced me to the very basics of yoga when I was young, but the daily practice in a hot studio was altogether different. I know poses don't matter in the big picture of yoga, but the day I did my first unassisted headstand was quite the accomplishment. It was thrilling, to press my legs into the air and hold myself up. It was like when the world was upside down, the blood rushing to my head, maintaining the pose, the world made more sense.

One day after class, Jenna told me, "Girl, I love your confidence, the way you always set your mat up in the front of the room—you don't care about anyone and you are so strong! You could power through any class, no matter what they threw at you. You are pure motivation!" I was shocked. I didn't actually believe her at first, remembering the fear I had felt when I first started. It was nice that she recognized what had taken me a long time to find. This woman, who I idolized in the studio, who I looked up to and wanted to be like, wanted to be like me. We were so different and yet we had this connection that made us stronger. We weren't competing with each other or comparing, we were bringing each other up. It was refreshing and empowering.

She told me about her loser ex-husband and I told her about my uninteresting one. She told me her crazy family problems and I complained about the in-laws. She told me about her boob job and I knew I could ask her advice for mine. We were open, honest, and even harsh when we needed to be.

She was too young and had got involved with a very unstable man. It was a rocky "relationship" at best with her "husband", a guy who had cheated on her even before they were married and continued to into the marriage. At least she didn't have any kids to complicate things. He couldn't hold his liquor, had a gambling problem, and had no idea what responsibility was. She was navigating the world of relationships and trying to find her happy.

Once she realized her husband was unfaithful and unreliable, she got a boyfriend who was not only a great listener but great in bed, who she met up with every few months. She needed this until she could figure out how to get out of the marriage. I supported her for finding what worked for her, no judgement.

Jenna was curious the first time I told her about Marcelo.

"So, who's the guy you met in Montreal, Karina? Let me see his picture." Like I would have a picture. At least, not one that I would admit to. And he would never send me a selfie, not that I had asked. I did a quick Google search and found a random picture that I pulled up for her, as we only had five minutes before class was about to start.

"Ooohh, he's fine, I love his eyes. You should do it; you should go for him," she said, gawking over the picture.

"You could use a side piece like that, get the blood pumping and the juices flowing, too bad he's not here, but that's all the more reason for you to travel a little more. You said he travels for work, meet up with him at one of those conferences he attends," she nudged me as she grinned. I had dismissed it completely, shaking my head and calling her crazy.

Then I admitted, "Well, I have read a few of his published papers. It would be exciting to watch him present at a conference. And he did say the conferences were non-stop, making it difficult to get any rest! I am sure I could find a way to occupy the time."

She rolled her eyes at me, "Only you would think a guy presenting a technical paper is exciting, I would be enjoying the free wine, the parties and the wild sex! What would that make you, a geeky groupie?" We both laughed as she gave me a warm hug. I guess she knew me better than I knew myself.

As we checked out, Marcelo headed over to the breakfast area and reached for a muffin, I stopped him. "Today starts with fasting," I told him. He looked at me like I was speaking a foreign language.

"With what?" he asked.

"Look, today is another bucket list kinda important day for me. We are going to drive down to Kootenay where the Yasodhara Ashram is. It's going to be a day of fasting, meditation, silence and yoga." I was so excited I could barely contain myself. He was shaking his head now. He was processing the idea of someone getting excited over not eating, not speaking and putting their body through torturous contortions all day.

"I get that fasting is important to you. But after all you put my body through this morning, if I don't eat something, I am going to go hypoglycemic and pass out. I need some energy to keep up with you!" He playfully spanked my bottom while taking a bite of his muffin.

"Fine, I need you ready to go and can't have you passing out on me, so eat up!" I replied. I watched him devour the rest of the muffin while grabbing some fruit and a cup of coffee. "Thank you for being a part of this," I said.

He looked up at me. "Thank you for including me. I think it's fantastic you want to do this. And I want you to do what makes you happy, but next time, can we do scuba lessons?" He was playing with me, but it was clear he would have preferred anything to yoga.

"I didn't schedule it, but it's on my list of things to do. If we don't get to it, we will just have to plan another trip." I said even though I knew I was being silly or optimistic for even thinking it. It was something to add to our "maybe someday" list which seemed to keep growing.

He wrapped his arms around me, giving me an affectionate and reassuring hug. I hated how good he felt. I mean, I loved how good he felt, but I knew it couldn't last. Tomorrow was our last day on this trip and then I would be home, with my husband, my kids, my house, my commitments. I held my breath and squeezed harder, hoping the hug would keep me from facing the world I would have to go back to. Unfortunately, it didn't work. I knew the ashram would be great for clearing my head space and hopefully let me meditate on my disposition.

I think Marcelo was a little uneasy about going to the ashram and all it entailed. He definitely wasn't much of a yogi and he was pretty sore from the half marathon I had put him through. I think some people would consider my idea of a holiday torture, but I couldn't help myself, it's what I loved to do. Jenna would've loved it and Carmen was a yogi master. She was so flexible and strong. She practiced every day and her strength, balance, and endurance were mind-blowing. She always pushed me. I wished so much she could be there with me. I tried texting her but got no answer. She was probably still at the hospital.

The picturesque drive from Kelowna to Kootenay through the mountain range was gorgeous. The winding roads through the peaks and valleys made for quite the drive. The highway snaked alongside the Kokanee Creek—the water the colour of emerald, brilliant turquoise and aquamarine when the sun caught its surface. The summer season brought all the lush greenery to life with flowers of all shapes, sizes and colours. It was a little sanctuary of Canada's homegrown natural world.

The Yasodhara Ashram was breathtaking. The Temple of Light was infamous for its shape. The enormous, stark white, luminous building was built on the edge of a cliff overlooking the Kootenay River. The shape of the building from an aerial view was that of a lotus flower.

If it had been up to me, ! would've stayed a month at the ashram. I really wanted to visit an ashram in Rishikesh, India. Getting completely absorbed in the simplicity of the life is something I craved. I had embraced all that yoga had to offer, but I knew at this point there would be no way I could get away from my kids for a month, so I was going to take it one step at a time. And today, I was going to indulge in the ashram experience completely.

When we got to the registration, I stopped so quickly that Marcelo slammed into me. Before he could ask me what was wrong, I screamed, a little scream, but I screamed. Standing in the gift shop, with a singing bowl in her hands, was none other than my sweet friend Carmen. I couldn't believe it. I had to pinch her to make sure she was real.

She wrapped her arms around me, kissed me, and spoke softly in her mousy voice, trembling as she confessed, "I left him, I just couldn't do it anymore, I had to leave…" Tears were rolling down her face as she hugged me tighter. "Can you believe it, his mistress showed up at the hospital! She was this big breasted, dark haired, strikingly gorgeous woman. She was well put together and looked smart and accomplished even though she was young. And…and…and she was, she was pregnant!" She was shaking visibly. I held her tight, wiped her tears and kissed her cheeks, holding her again trying to comfort her with my embrace.

I was shocked. I was devastated for Carmen. How could something so cruel be happening to such a sweet soul. How could her husband punish her like this? My heart ached at the thought of another woman causing her so much pain. The thought of this woman being pregnant was more painful than the adultery.

"It's going to be okay, we are going to get through this together. I am here for you, I have always been here for you." I clutched her tightly. "I am so glad you came. The ashram, yoga and meditation will be good for you. We can spend the day on the grounds, reconnecting. You need this. And after, we can do something stupid to celebrate. And then we will deal with your husband together. Wait, how did you get here?"

She explained how she had taken the bus and figured I could get her home. Of course, I could get her home. I was so glad she was there, and we were going to have a great time and put a plan together for how to piece her life back together when we got back. I could feel her pain as I recalled what it must've been like for her to be sitting at the hospital, to not only have her husband's mistress show up but show up pregnant. She didn't deserve this. She had been through so much already.

Looking over my shoulder, Carmen said, "Uhhh, there is this kinda sweet but dorky white guy standing behind you, staring awkwardly at us like he doesn't know what to do. Any chance you know him?" I looked over my shoulder and there was Marcelo, shrugging his shoulders and looking sheepish. Oh my, how was I going to explain this to Carmen?

"It's a long story, but Carmen, this is Marcelo and Marcelo, this is Carmen." I looked at Carmen. From her expression it was clear she had made the connection that this was the same Marcelo I had met in Montreal. I tried not to make a big deal out of it. I had told her all about him but now it seemed complex somehow.

"I promise, I will explain everything," I whispered to her as I spun round, "but right now, we have a hatha yoga class to get to..." and with that I headed to the registration desk leaving the two of them to stand there uncomfortably. I made sure we were all registered, paid for the singing bowl and then we headed to the Temple of Light for our class.

The unique structure was just as magnificent on the inside as it was from the outside. The lotus shaped building had so much natural light as each "petal" was a solid glass wall or door. The construction was so mindful of its purpose; everything had a meaning, a place.

Yoga mats had already been laid out in rows, each with a towel and a water bottle. There were props available as well including blocks, straps, bolsters and even wheels. We each grabbed a few blocks and a strap and found mats side by side. I placed my blocks and strap beside me, sat down cross legged and took a deep breath. I could smell the gentle scent of rose, sandalwood and jasmine in the air. I lay on my back gently and before closing my eyes, I indicated to Marcelo that he should do what I was doing. Then I closed my eyes and took another deep breath. In yoga, you always breathe through the nose. In and out, using your abdomen to fill with air and expunge everything with every exhale. Your breath helps to control your thoughts and if you can control your thoughts, you can control your universe.

I could feel my body on my mat, my stress releasing and my awareness of the universe deepening. I was feeling a form of consciousness that only solid concentration brings. Suddenly, there was a loud crashing sound and I jolted back to reality. Marcelo had dropped his water bottle on the floor. I glared at him as he shrugged his shoulders. I hoped he would survive the class, but I decided to close my eyes and block him out of my thoughts. If I could focus on my breathing, everything else would fall away. It took a few minutes, but soon I was only in my mind.

As I connected to the hatha yoga class, the power of breathing, the link between the poses and my mind, I felt a strength from within. Each inhale was to embrace, each exhale was to let go. Every once in a while, I did sneak a peek at Marcelo to see him struggling to sit in butterfly pose, his knees high in the air, not being able to bend, reach, or touch. He did his best to follow the instructor, but by the end, the only pose that really worked for him was savasana, he needed to just lie down and not move.

After the ninety-minute yoga class, he was rubbing his joints, already feeling the aches from the beating of the hard floor and the difficult moves. I was feeling calm, relaxed and rejuvenated. The long holds allowed my muscles to stretch, the balancing allowed my body to focus on my stability and the vinyasa and standing poses allowed me to work on my strength. Carmen looked more refreshed as well.

We had lunch planned at the ashram. All meals are taken in silence. Although Carmen and I had a lot to talk about, the silence allowed us to reflect and take a moment to communicate without talking. Marcelo was physically uncomfortable, trying to sit on the floor while eating lentils, rice, cauliflower and eggplant with his hands. I did my best not to laugh out loud, mostly making eye contact with Carmen or just focusing on the amazing practice I had completed. And of course, enjoying the delightful Indian inspired vegetarian meal.

The meditation session was unique in that there were a few elements to the practice. It was referred to as a Satsang (being with the truth). It included chanting, singing, meditating and breathing to connect. The first time Carmen had invited me to a Satsang and told me I would have to try and sit still for 75 minutes meditating, I thought I was going to die. I couldn't keep my body or my mind still for thirty seconds. Since then, I had come a long way and I appreciated the calm that meditation brought to the soul.

We decided to check out the grounds after the meditation was over. I think Marcelo sensed Carmen and I wanted some time to talk, or his knees were desperately killing him, because he said he was headed to the gift shop to find some Voltaren before hobbling off.

Carmen and I walked hand in hand along the scenic pathways and made our way over to a gazebo structure overlooking the river. We sat down and took in the view. It was breathtaking.

As we sat down on a bench, she broke down, "I don't know what I'm going to do." She was crying uncontrollably, weeping so hard I thought her heart was going to pop out of her chest.

"You are going to do what you always do. You're going to cry, you are going to breathe and you are going to get through this. Your soul is finally free and you can allow yourself to bring your spirit out in full force and use your strengths and skills to be who you need to be. You were always destined for more; he has been holding you back on the false hope of children. You need to let him go and let your heart guide you to a stronger you." I cradled her in my arms as I spoke.

I held her and held her and held her. I didn't know how else to comfort her. I guess the yoga and meditation session had allowed a lot of emotions to surface and she had just let go.

She started talking about her husband, the mistress, the mistress' pregnancy, about each and every one of her own failed pregnancies and how each one was more painful than the last. She said that going to the hospital had brought back painful memories and she didn't want to do it anymore. It triggered something in me too, all those difficult memories we hold on to and don't want to face. I took a deep breath before I said, "I gave up a pregnancy once."

She looked over at me, shocked, "What, when? How come you never told me?"

I looked at her, unsure whether I should continue. "It never seemed like the right time, you were always hurting and I didn't want to add to it. It was a painful and difficult choice I had to make before we met. And after everything you had gone through and had no control over, I wasn't sure how to tell you."

"What happened?" she asked.

As the tears rolled down my face, I confessed, "It was a long time ago, the summer before I got married. I was trying to figure myself out. I made one stupid decision, not thinking it would lead to anything. I went home with him when I shouldn't have. It was foolish and unprotected. And I got pregnant. I was young and unsure of how to bring a baby into this world out of wedlock. If my parents had ever found out, it would kill them or they would kill me. I didn't know how to approach them. And the wheels were already in motion for me to get married. The world would know the baby wasn't my husband's and he would never have it. I couldn't tell the father because I thought I could trust him to protect me and take responsibility but realized he never would take care of me. It was a huge mistake and I had to deal with it all alone. So, I made the only decision I could." I couldn't speak anymore.

Carmen was taking it all in, what I had just confessed. I couldn't tell what she was feeling, she was expressionless. She was deep in thought. "Oh my God! Who's was it?"

"It was a one-night stand." I told her, knowing it wasn't true. This was hard to talk about and I wasn't sure I was ready to reveal more.

"You don't believe in one-night stands. It was his, wasn't it? Brad's! This makes so much sense now. The insane relationship the two of you have had for twenty some odd years. He was the mistake you made, wasn't he? And you were trapped. You didn't tell him?" Carmen started piecing it together in disbelief.

"Stop! I did tell him. He didn't believe me. Then he said he loved me. Do you think I believed him or trusted him? Things would be different somehow? It wouldn't. It doesn't matter. He's no longer in my life. No one else knows. Please." I pleaded.

"And instead of being true to yourself, you decided to go the safe route and became committed to a marriage you didn't want. Become the traditional Indian housewife to cover up the guilt and tainted persona of you even though it wasn't your fault. Your confidence started to falter. You were just going from one mistake to another because you were too afraid and buried it all this time." She shook her head in disbelief.

"I don't deserve to be loved or cared for…" I trailed off.

"Oh, Karina…don't ever say that. You are signing up for therapy when we get back, you need to talk to someone. And I am always here for you. Always, no matter what." Carmen understood; there was so much sadness.

We were both sobbing, free flowing tears streaming down our faces. We sat there and held each other. I wanted to protect her and comfort her and make all her pain go away. Despite the sad memories we were sharing, I felt supported by her presence and consoling her was healing. I knew that although what Carmen had been through was difficult, she was going to be okay—we both were. We had survived, we were strong and we were moving in the right direction, as tough as it was. It felt right, to be in the ashram with each other.

I had missed her so much on the trip and I was so glad we were going to be able to spend this much needed time together. I took a couple of deep breaths and told her to do the same. We were still locked in each other's arms when Marcelo showed up, "Are you two okay? I leave you for thirty minutes and you both fall apart! You should've told me to buy tissues from the gift shop!" He made us smile as we both shrugged and wiped our tears. As he approached, Carmen moved over slightly and patted the bench, hinting he should squeeze in between us. She had warmed to him quickly; her kind soul welcoming and connecting, especially with another kind soul. I could see an instant bond between them, like they would be really good at taking care of each other. He smiled at her understandingly and gently put an arm around her.

He reached around and put his other arm around me. It was soothing to have him there, between us, holding us together. We each put our heads on his shoulders and sat there, enjoying the view, the calm, the peace for a few moments.

Chapter 13

Righting the Wrong

Visiting the ashram was therapeutic and cleansing. The toxins my body had been holding onto were releasing; my mind felt clearer and my soul felt lighter. If I could have found a way, Carmen and I would've spent a month there, but a day would have to do for now.

As we walked to the car, through the lush gardens, Marcelo pulled me aside and said, "Karina, you told me so much about Carmen. You were right, she's absolutely delightful. I can see why she's your best friend."

I had a feeling he would like her. I was happy he had got a chance to meet her. This trip was turning out to be better than expected.

We had booked a room at a hotel that overlooked the lake. It had beach access and gorgeous views. We walked into a spacious room with a small dining area, a large couch and a lovely four-post king-sized bed.

Carmen dropped her things on the couch and looked over at Marcelo; she smiled and said, “Well, this will work for Karina and myself, where do you plan on sleeping?”

He looked so confused and out of place and uttered, “Maybe I should look into booking my own room.”

I grinned, giving Marcelo this look like I was tormenting him and said, “You will probably have to sleep on the couch, as cruel as that is.”

Carmen chuckled and walked over to Marcelo, gently tracing a finger over his chest. She was even more comfortable with people than I was, her training as a yoga teacher and as a pole instructor had brought out a stunning confident side of her that put people at ease. Marcelo was enjoying the attention.

“Marcelo, I think that maybe we could come up with some kind of arrangement,” Carmen said, winking at me as she spoke, “if we got creative. Any ideas?”

Marcelo was blushing and so out of his element, “I think that maybe...we could...well, you know...” he trailed off.

I decided to let him off the hook, "Let's get ready for a fun afternoon first and then we can worry about the sleeping arrangements. Besides, I want some quality time with my girlfriend."

I still couldn't believe Carmen was here. What made things even better was how well Carmen and Marcelo were hitting it off. I was thrilled to see how well they got along.

Carmen slipped into a gorgeous, black, high-cut bikini bottom with a lavender strapless tube top with ruffles that folded over each other. She put on a wide-brimmed sun hat and large lensed sunglasses. She looked delightful. Even her flip flops had sequencing and slight wedges. I could not compete with Carmen's glamour or beauty, but I didn't have to. I was happy to have my lovely best friend with me. I found a bright fuchsia bikini to slip into, nothing fancy, but cute. I slipped some flip flops with daisies on them on and my large pearl rimmed sunglasses. I saw Carmen check out Marcelo in his trunks—not that I could blame her. And although he tried not to be obvious, he may have glanced over and checked her out too. I smiled, enjoying these wonderful people in my life.

We headed down towards the beach as the sun's rays warmed our skin while playing delightfully over the waves of the lake. The hotel had inflatable tubes for guests to use, so Carmen and I decided to grab a few and head onto the water while Marcelo decided to rent a paddleboard. As we dipped our toes and placed the tubes in the water, the initial shock of the cold water touching our sun-kissed skin awakened our senses. We adjusted to the cool temperatures and soft sand oozing between our toes as we ventured to walk further into the lake. It wasn't actually cold, we just had to allow ourselves to surrender to the feeling. We carefully lay our bodies in the tubes, and with a delicate push, we were off. I could feel the sensation of weightlessness overcome all of my other senses as the tube floated along and carried me over the soft waves while the warm sun beat down on my skin. I exhaled and began to relax. Floating in the middle of nowhere under a cloudless sky was like Mother Nature's therapy.

When we were far enough away from earshot, Carmen dived into conversation, clearly delighted to have some time to quiz me about the last few days. "So, that is Marcelo? The infamous Marcelo! He is so much cuter in real life. I can see why you were so into him in Montreal. Those eyes are definitely worth staring into for hours on end. And he is so into you—the way he looks at you, I can feel your connection, you two have a definite vibe. So, did you sleep with him?" Before I could answer, she said quickly, "Actually, don't tell me—I'm not sure I want to know. Okay, I do, but best we save that for later."

Without directly answering, I said, "Carmen, I've never felt so alive. He is remarkable!" I flopped my head back in the ring and stared at the sky, smiling from ear to ear.

She knew I wasn't ready to open up, so in her quirky way to find out more, she asked, "Describe him to me like you would your favourite recipe?" I looked at her quizzically.

Carmen poked my arm, waiting for me to reply. I did love to bake, but how was I going to compare this man to something I would mix up in a bowl and put in the oven was a mystery to me. I thought for a few minutes.

"Fine," I stated deciding to play along. "He is like my favourite oatmeal chocolate chip cookie. He is a fine Italian boy like pastry flour, a smart choice like oats, sweet, kind and real like brown sugar, meaningful and subtle like vanilla, rich and smooth like butter, slightly beaten up by his past like the eggs and strong and intriguing like the dark chocolate! He satisfies the indulgence of temptation! He the perfect balance of sensible, sweet and scrumptious!" I had to get creative with my analogy.

"You always did have a way with your words and your recipes!" Carmen said as she continued to laugh and splashed me gently with the cold water. She paused and what she asked next surprised me. "Are you going to keep him?" She looked serious.

I looked at her stunned. I choked up a little when I replied, "Darling, he was never mine to keep."

"But however, are you going to let him go?" she wondered. "You can deny it all you want, but you have fallen for him. You might not realize it, but I can see he has stolen your heart."

"I may have given my heart to him, but it's not like that. I wanted to be wanted and that's what he gave me.

I don't fall for anyone, not even him, although he is as close to perfect as I have ever met. I need to take up drinking so I could blame it on the wine." I tried to avoid her accusation.

"No amount of drinking or denial will make that feeling go away. You are so into him you can't control it. Look, if you know he's not yours to keep, you will have to let him go eventually. But right now, this is something your husband was never able to give to you, this love and attention you have been craving all your life. Cherish it and enjoy the moment."

I hated how right she was.

"I know and I am." I decided to be honest about my thoughts about her and Marcelo. "Don't take this the wrong way—I know it might sound weird to say right now—but I think he would be great for you. He's so affectionate and caring, and I think he would look after you. I know, right now, everything is a mess, so this is not the time, but trust me," I turned to look at her, she was staring back at me, surprised but not alarmed by what I was saying, "he's good for the soul."

She shook her head softly but reached over to hold my hand. "I missed you so much Karina. Seriously though, I don't think either of us can think about men and relationships right now. Let's just have some fun and let loose. Marcelo seems like a great guy to do that with. And I'm so glad I get to be with you," she replied.

"It's so lovely having you here too!" I said to her, reaching back, clasping her hand in mine.

Eventually, we drifted back to shore and the three of us decided to walk along the beach over to some large boulders. We took in the view of the lake and the cloudless sky—the serene tranquility of it all.

We made it back to the room and Carmen slipped into the shower.

Marcelo came over to me and whispered, "Hey Karina, what were the two of you talking about?" He gestured for me to sit with him on the king-sized bed.

I sat on the edge and placed a hand on his thigh. As I worked my hand up his leg, I kissed him and whispered back, "It's none of your business." and winked.

But what I said next surprised both of us, "Actually, I was saying that I think you and Carmen would be really great together. She has a lot going on right now, but she is amazing. You are incredible and have given me something I have needed for so long, but we both know my life is too complicated for anything..." I trailed off without finishing my sentence, it was too painful and I was protecting my heart.

"What if I want to see you again, I know there is more to our story, whatever that looks like." He said longingly.

"I think there is to, but I don't know how we would ever make this work. After tomorrow, I will probably never see you again. I think Carmen could use a fresh start. And I think you need to start trusting again and letting someone in. Whatever this is, what we are, will hopefully reveal itself in time, but for now, I don't know how our paths will cross." I said, my heart feeling a little heavy.

Carmen stepped out of the bathroom in a smashing, royal blue dress that she had "borrowed" from me and apparently never returned, probably because it was one of those dresses I bought two sizes too small, hoping to fit into someday. It fit her body snug, with mesh lining all the way (yes, all the way) down the front so that you could see from her cleavage to her navel, revealing her breasts just enough to leave you breathless. Her more petite breasts made it easy for her to not wear a bra, which made the back of the dress even more stunning, as it was also made entirely of mesh. The bottom of the dress rested high on her thighs revealing her long, strong legs. Her long straight black hair lay gently on her sleeveless shoulders. Paired with 4" stilettos, she was stunning. Marcelo looked her up and down, he couldn't keep his eyes off her. And she was such a sweetheart, she charmed people without even realizing it. Her flirtatious yet innocent nature.

I quickly showered and dressed. I had also picked out blue dress for tonight (no, we had not planned it). It wasn't as revealing but it was flattering and fun. It had a rippled scrunchy effect with wide shoulder straps and rested above the knees. I wore heels that made me 3" taller. Marcelo escorted us out of the hotel, putting an arm around each of us. The restaurant was close by so we had decided to walk.

As we headed down the main street, we came across an outdoor local market and music festival. We decided to check it out. Some people were drumming and singing. Different stalls had fresh produce and jewelry for sale. Some people were painting and selling their artwork, others were selling honey and jam. I could feel the positive energy and it warmed my heart to see a group of people gathered around having a great time. I loved shopping and supporting local, so I wanted to look around and purchase a little of everything from as many stalls as I could. I grabbed Carmen by the hand, ditching Marcelo and headed over to the honey stall.

"Does this take you back to your youth? That brief period when you had all those eye-opening experiences before you got married?" Carmen asked. I looked at her puzzled. She continued, "When you were young and had a great job, an abundance of friends and a positive outlook on life? Wild friends who would always talk you into the next adventure: backpacking, sky diving, or road tripping. All those stories you used to tell me about going to the markets in Europe, Vancouver and Mexico, pretending to travel for work. And the elaborate shopping sprees, birthday gifts for every friend, always picking up the bill, the ones your parents didn't know about. You had a pretty sweet car with the overpriced sound system. You were so free and motivated. Where did that girl go?"

I had forgotten how much I enjoyed living life, the freedom. It had been so brief and everything had changed so drastically. "That ship has sailed," I said, automatically mimicking what my husband had engrained into me over the last fifteen years and quickly covered my mouth in surprise. How was it that I had allowed myself to lose so much of my identity? Had my parents quashed it, had hubby created that hold over me or had I just given up on myself to no longer be that person? Little by little, I lost who I was and wanted to be.

"What are you talking about Karina?" Carmen scolded. "That ship has most definitely not sailed. It might have detoured for a while, when you were busy raising your kids, fighting cancer, taking care of me and not working, but it's still there, a part of you. You just need to pick up your sails and set your course, find the wind and get back on track. It's still your ship to sail."

"What does that have to do with this?" I asked, confused.

She held my hand and led me to a table and picked up the most darling silver charm I had seen, a small Kermode (spirit) bear. She placed it in my hand.

"When I first met you, you had the most dazzling bracelet on. It was a simple silver chain, but it had 40 or 50 charms attached to it. Each one represented something important in your life. All the cities you had traveled to in your twenties, the people in your life, your car, your degrees, birthdays, experiences. It defined who you were; how fierce, determined and motivated. I have seen glimpses of that warrior, it is time for her to shine again." She kissed me on the cheek.

"No one is holding you back but you. You can make all the excuses in the world that your life isn't good enough, your husband is controlling, your kids are too much work, you don't have the energy to make money, you suffer from emotional binge eating. I get it, these things have suffocated you for fifteen years. That might sound harsh and mean, but if this trip and the last year has shown you anything, it's that anything is possible, so it's time to put the excuses away and be that compassionate and courageous woman I met in that baby group who helped me become who I am today." She had this look in her eye, I couldn't place it, but it looked like compassion and pride and excitement.

"Please don't make me cry. I hate it when you're right and you know I love you for your honesty. You are pretty bad ass yourself, which is why we make a brilliant team. I think I needed to hear that." I gave her a big hug.

Carmen hugged me back and then walked over to Marcelo, grabbing him by the arm and leading him to a booth that was selling jewelry. Perhaps she was going to get him to buy her something. I smiled as I watched them walk away. They looked adorable together.

I turned, and as I did something caught my eye. There was a stall selling antique watches and trinkets, so I headed over to it. It was like it was fate, because as soon as I approached, I saw exactly what I was looking for, placed on a red, crushed velvet tablecloth. It was a beautifully crafted antique pocket watch, gold-plated frame with a black background displaying the face. The watch itself had roman numerals with a skeleton display, which meant you could see all the intricate details of the wheels, springs and cogs. It also had a chain which you could attach to your belt if you chose to. I had to have it.

Marcelo had lost his to that awful woman. It seemed fitting to remind him of this trip and what he meant to me. I picked it up, feeling the weight of it, rolling it around in my palm. It truly was a well-designed little thing. I didn't really care what it cost, I wanted something for Marcelo to remember me by. The only thing was, I wanted to get it engraved, personalize it, which would have to wait until we got back to Calgary. Hopefully I would find an opportunity to get it to him, or I could surprise him by mailing it. I paid for it and hid it in my purse.

Carmen had a strange expression on her face when we met up again. Like she was hiding a secret. She whispered quickly, "He bought you something!" and that was it. She could be so mysterious at times although I noticed a shiny new anklet on her, which I guessed he had bought for her. He was thoughtful and generous.

The restaurant was lovely although I wasn't sure how much Carmen wanted to say in front of Marcelo. Marcelo was also being cautious as he didn't know what to say in front of Carmen.

Food was always an easy topic to talk about, so I perused through the menu delighted by all the amazing dishes. I figured I could find something to talk about.

I began, "This menu is so inspiring, all the sauces, preparations and pairings. I love being in the kitchen. I can't wait to experiment with the boys when I get back home."

Carmen added, "Her true passion is baking." Which it was.

"It's true. The smell of fresh baked bread or the way a chocolate chip muffin crumbles in in your mouth while the chocolate lingers on your tongue. These days, it's getting to the point where the boys are challenging my skills. But I love it. Marcelo, how about you, do you bake?" I asked casually knowing he didn't spend a lot of time in the kitchen.

"Not enough, but I have a few staples I can whip up if I have to." He tried to sound like he knew what he was doing, but I couldn't help but giggle.

"Have you ever made tiramisu?" I asked as our server brought over one for Carmen and myself to share. Marcelo had ordered the dark chocolate ganache cake.

"Haha, have not had tiramisu in ages" he said as he stole a bite from our plate, "But, I've had quite a few cinnamon rolls and brioche buns, none of which I made." He smiled.

I teased, "Well, something for us to try, making tiramisu, someday. I made a brown butter cream cheese icing for the cinnarolls I made with the boys the other day, so good!"

"Seems like you are operating a bakery at your house." He complimented.

"Like I said, love to bake! When we do get around to it, you can dazzle me with your intellect and I can dazzle you with my baking." I smiled, thinking about the chocolate sauce he had fantasized about drizzling on my body. Something to leave for another day.

As we finished, Carmen was still feeling anxious and wanted to leave. It was still very pleasant out, as we walked back in the warm night air, although none of us spoke a word.

I could see Carmen still had a lot on her mind, so when we got back to the room, I asked Marcelo to run out and pick up some wine and to take his time. Carmen and I changed into our swimsuits, grabbed robes, put our hair up, and made our way over to the outdoor hot tub. It had a decorative gazebo sheltering it from the rest of the hotel on three sides but it still provided a lovely view of the lake. As we approached, we were relieved to see we were the only ones there. The night sky provided a tranquil starlight ambience. Even in the darkness, we could see ripples forming in the lake. I dipped a toe into the hot water and sighed, it was so delightful. We both slid into the bubbling water and found some jets to rest against. As the massaging streams, warmth and night air took over, I heard Carmen sigh heavily.

"Talk to me, tell me what's going on. How are you really holding up?" I asked her, genuinely concerned for her wellbeing. I could feel her reach her feet towards me so that our toes touched. I stroked her calf with my heel while our legs tangled together.

She looked so sad and worn down, like she was holding a lifetime of problems on her shoulders. "I just thought I could fix things. When we met, I was so young, so foolish. I wanted it to work. I do love him. I wanted to give him a child..." She stopped herself. "I feel so helpless," she sobbed.

It broke my heart to see her sitting there crying. "You have to stop focusing on him. You've been through so much and have found a way to be so much better than the pain and the hardship. I am so proud of you for being so strong," I said.

I felt helpless as well, I wanted to help her but I didn't know how. I reached over to her across the tub so that I could hold her hand.

I tried to comfort her. "You found the strength to come out here and when we go back, we will do it together. You are not a victim, you are not weak. You saw the ugly truth, the darkness and you were able to rise above it. You think you love him, you have just not known anything else for so long. You will find someone who really loves you and will take care of you." I pulled her over to me so she could sit beside me and I wrapped my arms around her.

"I hope so." Carmen wasn't convinced. "I don't know what to do." She looked at me with her big, brown eyes, her usual fiery self now timid and scared.

"The first step is to make the decision, which I think you already have. And the rest will come together, one step at a time." I could see she needed something, but I wasn't sure what.

She looked me deep in my eyes. "How about you? I think you've surprised yourself. You are definitely on a journey of self-discovery..." I saw a tiny smile. I figured she was thinking about Marcelo and me.

"I've decided that I can't make any more excuses. I need to find my own path. Marcelo was just the push I needed to finally say enough is enough. It's almost embarrassing when others point out things about me, I have refused to see about myself for so long. But that's okay because I have to recognize them in my own time. I've also realized that the people who aren't helping me to stand up are also not helping me to become stronger. We both need to get rid of the negative and toxic people in our lives. I can't hide anymore. We can't allow ourselves to take crap from others. If you are going to poke the bear, you better be ready to dance, because I am not going to allow people to put me down anymore. And neither are you!"

"Poke the bear?" Carmen laughed giving me a comical look, even though her face was marked with tears. "I definitely won't mess with you—not anymore!"

I laughed along with her. "Thanks for the talk earlier. It was nice to be honest. I can see things more clearly now," I continued. "I don't want to play by anyone else's rules. I want to help others. My nuttiness has helped me raise my boys into young men I am proud of and protect fiercely. I want to be completely myself and help others see who they really are as well, without judgement. I'm getting stronger. Things feel better." I looked at Carmen. She was staring at me, her huge eyes filled with longing. "Please Carmen, what can I do to help you? You look so sad."

"I'm so lucky to have you, to call you mine," she whispered. She paused; she looked unsure of how to continue. Finally, she pulled at my waist, indicating for me to slide closer to her.

I slid over closer until I was only inches away from her and gently pulled her into my arms. I looked into her eyes. I held her face in my warm hands and wiped away the tears that had streaked her face. I looked into her beautiful eyes, longing to be loved, to feel better. I reached over and kissed her on her cheek, reassuring her that everything would be okay. I wrapped my arms around her and pressed my warm body to hers.

I pulled back and looked at her, holding her face again and kissed her other cheek. I wanted to comfort her and make her feel good, make all her troubles go away and see her happy. I wasn't sure what she needed but I wanted to be there for her. Her mind seemed so far away, like she was thinking of something but wouldn't let me in. I felt so helpless because she couldn't tell me what she wanted.

She kept looking at me with those deep brown eyes. She didn't blink as she reached behind her. She undid her bikini top, but it still rested on her breasts. She put her hand on mine and slowly slid it down her throat and chest. She let it rest on her breast and squeezed my hand. This was the last thing I expected, I was a little stunned by her gesture. What was she doing? I looked into her eyes, trying to read them. She stared back, like she was trying to reach into my soul. I felt a connection of yearning.

She said, "Do you know how long it's been since I've been touched, really touched by someone who loves me and needs me? My husband hasn't been intimate with me in months. And even then, it wasn't intimate, it was automatic."

I didn't remove my hand. Instead, I obeyed what her body was telling me. I leaned over and kissed her, but this time, I enveloped her mouth, my lips encountering hers. She welcomed my kiss with her tongue. She continued to kiss me, needing me more and more. Her arms went around my neck, holding on tight.

I was surprised by what we were doing, but I was also curious and excited. We had been friends for so long and had been through so much together. We had always been close. I loved her on such a deep level because of all the pain we had endured—it was like we were bonded by our tragic pasts. We trusted, supported and comforted each other. What we were doing felt so natural, like a continuation of our friendship. She needed me on that level and I wanted to be there for her, make her feel whole again. I would do anything for her. And I needed her too. It was emotional, intimate and sensual—all the things we had both been lacking in our lives. Even though it was unexpected, it wasn't a mistake. This was part of her healing. And she was helping me to heal too.

She slipped her bikini top off, revealing herself to me. She was so beautiful. I had seen her in her workout bras and pole shorts, but this was so different. In class, she was strong; now, she was vulnerable and exposed. I pulled her closer to me, so I could feel her body against mine in the salty waters of the hot tub. As I continued to explore her body, she gave more and more of herself to me.

I had thought about what it would be like, being with a woman? I had never experienced it before. She was so delicate and tender. My tongue explored her neck, ears, mouth and her touch was so gentle yet deliberate. She knew from her own experience what to do, where and how to touch me.

As we continued to explore, we didn't have to say anything to each other. Once, I heard her whisper under her breath, "I want this. I need this. I want to share this with you."

I was alarmed as I could hear someone approaching. When I looked up, there was Marcelo, standing on the edge of the hot tub and that wasn't the only thing standing up. His eyes were glued to our bodies, so much so that even when I was staring at him, he didn't register it right away. When we finally did make eye contact, the expression on his face told me he was torn. As much as he wanted to join us, he didn't want to interrupt what he was witnessing. I also wasn't sure what to do. Carmen turned around to see what I was looking at.

When she saw Marcelo, she smiled. She slowly turned around on my lap, exposing her body to him. She used my hands and slowly maneuvered them over her body, seeing how Marcelo would react. He swallowed, hard. She wanted to entice him, but she wanted me.

I leaned down until my lips grazed her ear and whispered, "What do you think? Should we let him join us?"

As she pulled away to face me again, she smiled at me, shook her head, and whispered back, "Only if you are okay to share."

"I think you already know the answer to that, anything for you and I would love to share him with you." I replied.

She turned to Marcelo and gestured for him to join us. He was still in shock. He nervously pulled off his shirt.

He looked so unsure and didn't approach us right away. I am sure he was curious and wanted to please us, but this was very unexpected for all of us. I didn't know what I was doing either. I reached my hand out to him and pulled him towards us.

He slipped in behind Carmen, sandwiching her between us. He gently bent his head towards mine and kissed Carmen on the neck before kissing me on the mouth, pressing himself into her and her into me. Carmen welcomed what was happening. Instinctively, she reached behind her and wrapped her arms around Marcelo's neck, exposing more of her body to the both of us. She was very aware of the man behind her; his hard body pressing into her, his strong legs hugging her hips. She looked at me and smiled. I held her waist and smiled back, reassuring her that I wanted this as much as she did. Mixed emotions of hurt, healing, pain, lust, desire, aching and love were intermingling between us, fueling us.

She felt Marcelo's hands cup her breasts and let her hands slide down his body, taking in his chest, abs, thighs. She embraced what was happening. And she liked it. I wasn't expecting Marcelo to be so bold, Carmen to be so receptive and myself to be so open, but I was accepting of the bond between us. He continued to kiss me while he pleasured her.

"This is going to be so much better than scuba diving," I heard Marcelo say under his breath. I couldn't help but grin.

"You sure you're up for the challenge, big boy?" I teased, although I wasn't even sure I was up for the challenge. This was going to be something new for all of us. I felt like we were all craving it, even if we were unsure about it.

Things were getting very heated in the pool and it wasn't because of the temperature of the water. We needed to get out of public view, it was getting a little too risky.

Our bodies separated long enough to find our robes and make our way back to the hotel room.

"Marcelo, you didn't really think I was going to make you sleep on the couch tonight, did you?" I said jokingly, as our half-wet, half-naked bodies made our way to the king-sized bed.

"I thought you weren't going to satisfy my erotic fantasies on this trip," he was referring to my comment when we first drove out here. He was paying attention.

"Marcelo, who said anything about satisfying your fantasies..." I trailed off very aware that we were all going to satisfy each other.

Chapter 14

Perceptions

Never had I thought I would I wake up the next morning to find Carmen cuddled in bed between Marcelo and myself. It felt so natural to have her there. She looked so lovely and peaceful, sleeping away without a worry in the world. It was like it was meant to be. We had shared this unexpected night together, and as inexplicable as the events of the road trip had turned out to be, it made sense to me.

I could hear my phone buzzing. It was probably my kids or my husband. This time I didn't jump to answer it right away. I knew they would be good for an hour without my immediate attention. They were probably checking in or playing a joke. I hadn't really worried about them much over the last few days, I knew they could take care of themselves. Of course, I always thought about them, but now I felt more reassured and less panicked. I was able to let go a little and it felt nice.

When Marcelo stepped out of the room, Carmen cuddled up against me and asked, "Karina, you look happy, happier anyway, are you?" I paused, I had to think about that one. I hadn't thought about being happy for so long, I had forgotten what it felt like. That unbearable sensation of pressure on my chest not allowing me to breathe or think had been lifted. I had enjoyed the independence I had allowed myself these past five days. I didn't feel as scared to face the world. I felt clarity, in tune with my thoughts. And I felt more confident. I was finally being honest with myself.

I replied, affirming to myself as much as answering Carmen, "Yes, I guess I am happier. Things are moving in a direction that I can foresee and I am ready to do me again too. Looks like you are feeling better too. We will get through this together."

"It's because of you that I am finding the strength to get through this. I know it's going to be tough, but I know what I need to do. I forgot what it felt like to be loved. I see the flaws and lies I was surrounded by. But I also see a future where things will be good again." Carmen said.

I didn't want to go home, but I knew I had to. The experience had been mesmerizing only because it existed in a moment in time. If it continued, it would be tarnished by reality. We couldn't continue like this. At least I couldn't. I had a life to sort out first. I knew that in a few short hours, it would all vanish and I would be back to being a housewife and a mother.

Honestly, even if I wanted it, I wouldn't even know where to begin to try and make any kind of relationship work. I would go from making one kind of sacrifice to another. I had made enough sacrifices already and I would still have many more to make for my kids. All of us were in such different and difficult places in our lives. I didn't want or need more complications.

When I started this trip, I wasn't looking for love, but I realized how much I missed being desired and allowing others in. I wasn't looking for admiration, but I recognized how much I craved being adored and appreciated. I wasn't looking for permission, but respect and believing in myself. I had planned this trip to strengthen my friendship with my best friend; then I was prepared to do it alone. Instead, I found companionship, kindness and a sense of healing.

As for Marcelo, I knew I wasn't in love with him; I was in love with the idea of him. I didn't want to need him, at least, not just him, to depend on one man for the outcome of my life. He represented something that I had wanted for a long time: freedom, independence, support, and attention. And Carmen, I wasn't in love with her either. She had needed to be taken care of and loved in her moment of need. I would always be there for her and support her. And I needed my best friend, always by my side, no matter what.

Marcelo had also satisfied a very carnal desire for me. Yet I knew we couldn't be anything more than what we had shared. It wouldn't be fair to either of us. I was done being tied down, could not give him kids and I was ready to do something else with my life. Marcelo, on the other hand, needed to be with a loving and caring woman, one that was available to him. I was not. I figured, as independent as he was, he still wanted to settle down and start a family. I couldn't give that to him. Carmen needed someone to take care of her and treat her with the love she deserved. I could not give that to her. But Marcelo and Carmen could give to each other what I was void of.

For the first time in a long time, I was in love, with myself. Or at least I was learning to love myself again. I haven't allowed myself to think about who I was or what I wanted in so long, I had forgotten. And more so, how important it was. I wasn't being narcissistic or selfish, I just knew that I needed to focus on myself more than any other man, woman, husband, child, or person in my life. And I was going to allow myself to put myself first once in a while, not because I deserved it, but because I needed it.

In the meantime, I had a few precious hours left with my beautiful friends and I was going to make the most of it. We had a very lazy morning that involved delicious breakfast food, playful conversation and meaningful distractions from the fact that our trip was coming to an end.

I did manage to sneak out for a few minutes to give Arjan a call, I wanted to make sure the boys were okay, even though I knew they were. I also needed some strength as I wasn't sure what I would be coming home to. When the phone rang three times and I was about to hang up, Arjan answered, "Hi Ma, my brothers and I were just talking about you, how are you?"

"You probably had nothing good to say, I am guessing," I replied, worry setting in.

"Of course not, we were just saying how awesome you were to pack for us and make us this delish food while planning your own running and yoga thing. We are proud of you. And believe it or, we look up to you." Arjan knew just what to say. I could feel the tears welling up.

Before getting too emotional, I replied, "I have missed you boys so much and I can't wait to hug you. I am sure the trip has been a blast for you boys. This has been an amazing trip for me too and someday I will tell you all about it, but for now, know that I am a stronger and a better person because of it." I felt like I was confiding in him somehow.

"Mom, you are always strong and know what to do. And whatever it is, we got you. Now go have fun and we'll see you when we get back. Miss you!" Arjan laughed but I could hear in his voice that he was being serious. I found it odd and comforting that neither of us brought up their dad.

"Give your brothers hugs from me. Love you. See you soon." I whispered before hanging up.

My boys were getting older and turning into mature young men. They were needing me less and less. Sometimes I felt like I dependent on them more and looked for their approval. All those years I invested and sacrificed to feed, bathe and clothe them were so that they could become incredible, intelligent and independent creatures. The urgent need for mommy was no longer as real. I know the energy I had put into raising them wasn't wasted, but I was becoming somewhat insignificant to them. I could barely keep up with their energy, technology and terminology, so the reality that I needed to focus more on myself was even more evident.

And later that day, I would be returning home to them. My family, but more so my boys. How drastically my life had changed since I last saw them. My outlook on life was different now and I could no longer escape from reality. I would have to face it as I had a lot to sort out. I decided I wasn't ready to tell my husband about all the details of the trip, at least not right away. I had to figure things out for myself first and there was a lot to process. I understood I was committed to my family, but maybe I could find a better version of myself. I cared for my husband, he was a smart, stable, capable. He was the parent approved decision, the man my parents chose. But it was complicated, the duty, expectations and sacrifice. This journey had showed me that things had to change.

Carmen, Marcelo and I reluctantly packed our things and eventually headed to the car. Driving down the highway, we looked out at the gorgeous scenery. I could feel fear rumbling inside me as I knew I would have to face tough situations when I got home and I wasn't sure I was going to be able to.

Carmen called out, distracting me, "Can you take the next exit? We need to make one more stop before heading back home." I looked over to the large billboard on the side of the highway indicating that there was a stop coming up and turned onto the exit.

One last insatiable desire that needed to be filled. We were headed to the Rocky Mountain Chocolate Factory. We drove up to the little chalet of a factory and the rich smell of chocolate was emanating from the building. As soon as I walked through the doors and saw the decadent displays, I wanted to buy one of everything; every dark chocolate bar, bonbon and truffle to take back to the boys.

The boys. I know I tried not to think about them but sometimes they just crept into my thoughts, they were a part of my heart. The boys, no matter what, how angry or frustrated or done I was, they somehow brought a smile to my face. And lately, they understood that even though Mama was the one taking care of them, I sometimes needed them too, some taking care of.

They would do something to surprise me and I would ache. If they were hurt or in pain, I would crumble, because I was getting to a point where I couldn't always help them. They had big boy problems that were emotional and social and I couldn't just kiss it better. At least they would let me cuddle or hug them and I could still take care of them or talk to them and that meant the world to me. I was close to them, I felt they could tell me anything. I hoped someday I would be able to tell them about the choices I had made and the difficulties in my life. To teach them, raise them to be better and to help them understand that life includes all kinds of challenges.

I had no idea what kind of adventures, heartaches, accomplishments and disappointments they had in store for their lives, but I was so glad I brought them into this world. My philosophy, as bizarre as it was, was that if anyone was going to make mistakes raising my kids, it was going to be me. Being a stay-at-home mom, allowed me to raise them in my own way. It wasn't always perfect, but deep down, I knew what they needed, each of them, in their own way. They were going to shine and become incredible human beings. And so far, I think I hadn't screwed things up too much; for them or myself.

Thinking back to what Arjan had said to me on the phone about being there for each other tugged at my heart. I could sense new paths ahead even if I was afraid.

The smell of chocolate brought me back to the factory. I was being drawn in by the powerful smell of cocoa. We got to sample the darkest of chocolate barks, with the highest cocoa content. I held it on your tongue and sucked on it gently, and it sent sensations of bliss through my body. Carmen brought me back to reality when she reminded me that we needed to get going. Of course, I bought way more chocolate than I needed to and as we headed out from the lovely chocolate factory, I squeezed Carmen tightly, thanking her for pointing out this little piece of paradise. And for being my best friend.

We had a long drive home but I was in no rush, I enjoyed the serenity of it all. In a matter of hours, we could be crossing provincial borders and I would be sharing the same highway my husband and boys would be driving on to find their way home from their camping adventures. We would be reuniting.

The drive home was quiet. What conversation we did have was light. Perhaps each of us was contemplating about our future or reminiscing about our adventure from the past few days. Regardless, there was an ominous yet optimistic sense in the air. I chose to focus on the optimism as much as I could.

I dropped Carmen off first, she wanted to get home to get things in order before her husband got home from the hospital. She needed to get a divorce lawyer and sort out her life. I was going to be there for her every step of the way, like she had been for me so many times. I hugged her tight and kissed her goodbye. Marcelo grabbed her bags and helped her inside. I had a good feeling about those two.

We pulled away from Carmen's and decided to drive to a Second Cup and grab one last latte before saying our goodbyes. Five days prior, I had picked Marcelo up from the airport and we had started at a similar destination. We sat at a table hidden in the back and I held his hand in mine. It felt warm and reassuring. I looked into his dreamy, gray-green eyes, not knowing when I would see them again, if ever. I didn't know how to say goodbye, mostly because I wasn't ready to. I knew that he was only a text away if I needed him, but somehow, it seemed more final than that.

He looked at me with that goofy, charming look on his face and said "Karina, you look so sad, I can see it in your eyes. Don't do that to me, not now. What's bothering you?"

"Can I ask you something?" I said, hesitant although I felt so comfortable with him.

"Of course," he replied. "You can ask me anything." He gave my hand a little squeeze.

"How did you know...how did you know you were in love?" It sounded so stupid when I said it out loud, but I needed to know.

Slightly confused, he took a few seconds to think about his answer. "Well...you just know. You feel deeply for the other person. You connect with them. You want to make each other happy. You want to share everything and be with them. Just seeing them makes your heart flutter. Why? How did you know you were in love?"

I looked down. I wasn't sure I could answer the question. I wasn't sure I had been in love before. Lust, passion, intimacy...sure, but love, I couldn't be certain.

"I mean...I love my husband—I have a duty to him. I'm committed to our relationship. We're partners and we've been together forever." I rationalized. I wasn't sure what I was admitting to but I decided to continue, "A part of me thinks I've learned to love him more than falling in love with him. Maybe that's a part of being married, it needs to be practical and functional, love is optional." I thought about what I had just said. Did I really believe that or had I been convinced into believing it, been taken for granted? "I do know that I love my children unconditionally; they are my everything."

"But that's not what we're talking about," he said gently. "How about head over heels in love—love at first sight?" he asked.

"But that's not love. That's infatuation, obsession, desire. It's your brain and your hormones playing tricks on you," I countered.

"You know, they say you don't choose who you fall in love with. You have no control. It's complicated, but it's beautiful and something everyone should experience."

"But I'd never been allowed to date, to figure out what I wanted in a relationship or who I was compatible with. If I ever did have an opportunity, it was more curiosity or an opportunity to experiment. It had always been hidden as it was forbidden or wrong." I thought about how Brad had been manipulating and cruel. Daryl had been charming, but out of my reach because he was a gentleman. My husband had been my professor, so much older and somehow always my superior and controlling. "Other times it was out of convenience or I was trying to keep up with expectations of those around me."

"Are you saying you married out of convenience? Or because it was expected of you?" He asked, looking puzzled.

"I know my parents wanted me to get married as soon as possible, so that they wouldn't have to worry about me, which is why they set up the marriage. They needed this to work so badly that it almost felt forced. Traditionally, daughters were burdens in the Indian culture. I know they didn't believe in relationships and pre-marital sex. I know they wanted me to settle down and be a good wife." I looked into his eyes trying to see if he understood.

I thought about it some more and how I was always so busy trying to please everyone else, "I give my heart to everyone. I guess that's in my nature. I am passionate and flirty and blind and misguided and caring and always looking to feel the kindness and affection I express. My heart allows everyone in, so in a way, I feel very intensely for all my friends. I feel every person plays a role, has a special purpose to be in my life. It's hard for me to only let a few people in. I don't operate that way. In a way, I love all those around me and yet I don't have love in my heart."

"I can see that about you. You're very good at giving your heart to everyone. You're an endless possibilities kind of girl. And never ask for anything in return." He looked down and brushed his thumb lightly against the back of my hand.

He looked sad when he asked, "So, you've never felt your heart skip a beat or had that feeling in the pit of your stomach whenever you think of someone?"

I was doubting myself; I felt a strange feeling in the pit of my stomach when he rescued me at the club. But that wasn't love, was it? And I couldn't admit it to him, could I? I was too guarded to allow myself to love, to give myself to someone completely. But in the last few days I had let my guard down, given my heart to him. I had let Marcelo into my heart and felt an undeniable bond. He had not been a part of my chaos I normally considered my existence. I think I had allowed myself a little luxury to experience that thing called love. But I did know I couldn't love him forever, not right now.

"Would you let me love you a little? My heart skipped a beat when I got your text message from the airport, does that count?" I took the risk of admitting my feelings towards him while trying to rationalize my thoughts and not sound silly.

He smiled, the kindness returning to his eyes. "Of course, I will let you love me a little. You need to stop asking permission for everything, it's your heart, your free will."

"Thank you for this journey, I couldn't have done it without you. I don't know what will happen after you leave, but I will treasure these last five days forever. I just hope that no matter how things turn out we can remain in each other's lives. I didn't know I could give myself to someone so completely and still hold onto so much of who I am. Thank you for allowing me to be me and for giving yourself to me. The life I want now, is not with you and not without you, but because of you." I trailed off, not knowing what else to say.

Marcelo stretched his other hand over the table so both our hands were intertwined. He looked deep into my eyes. "I took a chance and came out here in hopes of meeting up with you again. And I am so glad I did and even more glad you decided to share this trip with me. This was life changing. And I also don't know what will happen after this but know that I am always going to be here for you, for whatever you need, I will try to give you what you are looking for." He was being so sincere.

I whispered for fear I had given away too much of my heart, "I am so lucky to have you looking out for me. And, you have given me so much. All I could ask for is kindness and friendship. What more could a girl want?"

"As you wish," he said tenderly as he held my gaze and squeezed my hand. I finally understood.

We both smiled at each other, knowing how painful our parting was going to be.

Chapter 15

Back Home

Home. I pulled up to the garage door and felt the finality of it all. I was back home. I opened the garage door and there was an empty spot where the minivan would go. Beside it was my husband's midnight jade SUV and beside that I parked my Audi RS5. The house was empty. Somehow, I had managed to get home before the rest of the family. I unloaded my things and headed inside. I paused momentarily at the door, allowing the sun to shine into the garage before closing it.

It was quiet. It was so quiet. No complaining kids, no demanding husband, no barking dog. It felt foreign to me. Instinctively, I felt like I should call out their names, but I knew they were not there. I didn't know what to do with myself, I felt out of place. And then, I don't know why, but without control or reason, I screamed, loudly and passionately so that my voice resonated throughout the entire house, echoing and hollow. I took a deep breath in while I listened to the silence. I screamed again, my throat feeling scratchy and raw. I slid my body down the door until I was supported by the floor. There I was. I was home. And it was the last place in the world I wanted to be. And yet, somehow, I was comforted that I was back in the security of my house. For an instant, I thought about what it would be like if it had really been just me—no complaining kids, no demanding husband, no barking dog. It wasn't always like that and I couldn't, it felt like a betrayal. And it's not what I wanted, not really.

Thinking back, to when I had come home from the trip to Montreal, I was broken, falling apart and had been in a really bad place. It had taken me this last year to realize that I could no longer recognize myself and that something needed to change. And I was proud of myself that I had started making those changes. Although things were not perfect, I was on my own path. I knew I was no longer broken, but I was not yet whole either. I would be building my life into something I needed it to be, figuring out how the fragments fit to create something new. I had hurt for a long time, now, I was healing. That void of unfulfillment was starting to diminish.

I knew I couldn't run away, I had nowhere to go. Even if I wanted to go to Carmen or Marcelo, I couldn't. They were both important to me, they had shared so much and given me their love, but they were not going to fix me. Only I could do that. I couldn't abandon my children—they were a part of me and I still needed to be in their lives. I knew I would be a better mother if I could be a positive, powerhouse influence and not a weak, broken woman. I needed to be the person I always knew I had the potential to be, and I had to do it on my own terms.

My phone buzzed. It was my husband, texting me to let me know they were on their way home, but that they would be at least four hours. They were going to grab a bite to eat on the road so I didn't have to worry about making dinner. That was considerate of him, letting me know I didn't need to make their dinner. I would find something for myself in the kitchen, I was sure. Before, it would've bothered me. Now, I was happy to know he was taking care of them and no one worried about me.

I pulled myself together and went up to the master bedroom. I needed to strip out of my clothes. As I did so, I did not hide my body. I stood in front of the full-length mirror and admired. I saw a few bruises and marks from the days before. I accepted my scars as battle wounds. I liked my stretch marks, my love handles, and even my belly. I started the water, filling the tub, adding aromatherapy Epsom salts and decided to soak for a few moments, enjoying the silence and calm before the family came home.

I opened my suitcase and pulled out the blue dress that had the scent of both Marcelo and Carmen and inhaled deeply. When I closed my eyes, it was like I was right there with them. I wasn't ready to wash that dress quite yet. I almost texted Marcelo, thinking I wanted him to come over to be with me. Then I realized I couldn't. I was home and I would have to accept that he was gone. He could no longer be mine.

I slipped into the tub and as the water washed over me, it brought me right back to the events of the last few days. The sights of beauty, nature and friendship, the feel of the pavement under my feet when I ran the race, the sound of my ujjayi breath when I connected with the poses in yoga, the crisp smell of the luscious vineyards, the touch of a man and a woman that satisfied me in every way. I could feel the sensations of the hot springs, spa and hot tub, all of it.

This journey had been about myself and I had finally stopped thinking about others long enough to think about me. This trip had turned on a switch and now I couldn't turn it off. It felt good. I felt insatiable and like I needed more from life. A life I had been ignoring for too long.

Lingering on memories and thoughts, I enjoyed a long soak in the tub. After, I grabbed some of the cheese and fruit we had picked from the orchard, put on some music, and looked at my phone. There was a message from Marcelo. I hesitated. I had just left him and I felt empty. This message was more torment than a tease right now. I couldn't read it, not right away. It didn't feel right. And I wanted to save it for later, when I wanted to escape from the chaos. I cuddled on the couch with a warm fuzzy blanket and lay my head back while I waited for the boys to arrive.

Somehow, I'm lying in bed instead of the couch. I'm under the covers and not wearing any clothes. I reach down to find I only have one breast; the other one gone, only a long scar remains. I look over and lying beside me is my husband. I can't tell if I want him to be there or not. He reaches over and climbs on top of me with a strange smile on his face. I am confused and a little mortified as I hear my own voice calling out and I can't stop myself, uncontrollably repeating, "Marcelo, Marcelo!"

I jolted awake, sweaty and disorientated. My heart was pounding and I was having troubles focusing. I was having a nightmare. I needed to snap out of it. I took a breath. I was still on the couch, the house was still quiet. I realized I was alone. It was just a dream and no one had heard me calling out Marcelo's name. I was horrified by the incident. I felt icky. I decided to lay on the couch with my eyes closed a little longer, hoping the feeling would go away.

An hour later, the storm arrived: the thudding of the boys' feet walking through the house, the gear and luggage being strewn across the hallway, the familiar sound of the boys voices as their loud conversation arguing a moot point and oodles of excitement filled the air. Immediately, the music changed to whatever it was the boys wanted to listen to and the chaos surrounded me. I sat up and ran over to my boys, pulling Arjan, Aryan and Arjev tightly to my body, giving each of them big hugs and kisses. I had missed them so much. Looking them over, I said, "And you have most definitely grown since I last saw you five days ago. You look so mature and strong."

Arjev thought he was being sweet when he replied, "And Ma, you look older too." I couldn't help but smile and gave him another hug. It's strange how my body ached for them. A mother can never stop loving her children.

They were so excited to tell me all about their adventure. Arjan had pictures, Arjev souvenirs and Aryan war wounds. They couldn't stop talking, so much so, that I didn't even get a chance to say hi to hubby. Eventually he made his way over to me, barely giving me a hug. He looked beat and exhausted. They had had a good time and that's all that mattered.

The boys gathered around the table while I pulled out some cheese, fruit and chocolate from the trip. Aryan grabbed some ice cream from the freezer so they could make sundaes.

"Ma, this chocolate is decadent! I can't wait to experiment with it." Aryan said as he shaved a bar over his sundae and fruit.

Hubby reluctantly joined us at the table but he was too tired to listen to stories the boys had to tell and after a few bites, decided to take a nap. He had a headache and to sleep in a real bed would be luxurious after camping. He got up and headed towards the bedroom.

Just then, my phone buzzed indicating I had a message. Arjev grabbed it before I had a chance to. He figured he had free reign on my phone and for the most part he did. Except this time.

"Mom!" he exclaimed, "Why is there a picture of a half-naked man on your phone? He only has white underwear on. I can see everything!" My heart stopped. Marcelo would've sent a picture like that. Maybe it was spam? I quickly grabbed the phone and looked at the image. I only needed to look for a split second to know who it was.

It wasn't Marcelo, he would never—too serious and not a selfie kind of guy. It was Daryl, trying to be funny. Of all the times for him to send me an unsuitable text, it had to be right now. He had joked about it over a year ago—never did I think he would actually do it. Luckily it wasn't anything too inappropriate and you couldn't see his face. In a panic I accidently deleted the text from Marcelo without even reading it. I was still recovering from the shock of the dream and now this. My nerves were not going to hold up.

My husband raised an eyebrow and I dismissed it quickly, telling him it was a joke and we could talk about it later. I gave him a sympathetic smile and a kiss on the cheek and he went upstairs to nap. Hopefully he wouldn't be too tired or grumpy when I would have to explain things to him later.

That night, after the kids had gone to bed, my husband and I had a fairly heated conversation about where things were going in our lives.

He accused me, "You had an affair with Daryl. I knew it, in Montreal, I shouldn't have trusted him!"

I denied it stating, "This has nothing to do with Daryl. He's a good man." And that was the truth. I continued, "I feel suffocated in this relationship and in order for me to be a better version of myself, I need to make more changes in my life."

I played the argument out in my mind: *Why couldn't I be happy with him? Because I wanted more than obedience and duty. Why couldn't I accept him? Because he didn't see me for what I was worth. Why couldn't I love him? Because I had outgrown him and his ways.* I could see this now. I had become accepting, tolerant and forgiving because I thought it was the only choice I had.

Instead of listening to me, he was still focused on Daryl, "I want to know the meaning of the photograph and what was going on!"

I told him "Nothing! Nothing is going on with Daryl! He's just a friend trying to be funny. He's a single guy and way more millennial than most men I know. And besides, everybody posts half naked pictures more openly on social media platforms these days."

He accused me, "Have you been sending photos of myself?" Of course, I hadn't. I would never do such a thing, even if I wanted to.

I told him, "No, I know you wouldn't approve. Besides, the photo isn't the issue and it was honestly nothing but a silly joke," which it was. The prior five days, I wasn't so sure about. But I needed time to figure things out. I couldn't tell him about Marcelo or what had happened with Carmen, things were already messy enough. I needed to know what I wanted before I could talk to him about it.

Our argument progressed and became more heated. "I think we should cancel our trip for the stupid triathlon that YOU planned!" he started. "I didn't like the idea in the first place—it's too much work, it costs too much money and who really thought that running in a circle would be a good idea anyway? You spend too much of your energy trying to keep the kids entertained. They don't need this and they can find things to do around the house to keep busy. And why bother going so far for a silly sport, at least pick something local."

I could feel the frustration surfacing. I couldn't do this anymore. I could not give into the things that were important to me. I said calmly, "I think it's a great idea for you not to go. But I have already planned this and don't want to disappoint them. I will be going with the kids as I want to have some bonding time with them. You went on the camping trip, now it's my turn."

“Sometimes I can’t believe we have been married this long, you can be so irrational sometimes. Borderline psychopath! This is such a stupid idea. Sometimes you need to just listen to me, take my side and understand where I am coming from. Be a good wife,” he said dismissing me.

I said, trying to be strong, even though I was feeling shaken and upset by his words, “I don’t want to put you in a position you don’t want to be in. And I think you could use some time to think about it and stay home. Catch up on your accounts at work. Do what makes you happy. Figure out what you want.” I made up my mind that it was okay that he didn’t support me. And I was going to pay no attention to his “good wife” comment.

It didn’t feel right, the whole situation, everything had changed so quickly. There was no understanding, let alone support. I know it was coming from a place of frustration and insecurity, but it still hurt. I don’t think he had even missed me. He didn’t ask me about my trip. Maybe he wanted me to feel guilty about it, that I had ditched them for five days. I was feeling manipulated and controlled. Nothing about my life mattered to him. And I was “back on duty”.

I wasn’t angry with him. I didn’t blame him. I just wanted different things. I needed space. I had put up with him for so many years and it wasn’t what I was looking for anymore.

Exhausted, I went upstairs and fell into bed unable to process anymore. I knew I wasn’t perfect, but I didn’t deserve this either. When he joined me in bed, I know it he wasn't in the mood for affection but he didn't seem as irritated. He touched my shoulder and for a split second I thought he would whisper in my ear "I am sorry darling, forgive me..." or "Come here beautiful, let me hold you;" I thought, maybe, it would be different, he would be intimate, something I had longed for from him for years. But I realized, it was me that had changed, not him.

Instead, he said, "I am feeling a little tired tonight, but's it's been a few days, so let's get this over with quick..." and before I realized it, he decided to have his way with me. This was not unusual in our marriage, for me to satisfy him and provide when he needed it.

There was no intimacy or connection. I don't know if he was punishing me for not being on the camping trip or reminding me that I belonged to him. Maybe this was his way of making up for us arguing or perhaps it was what he was used to and expecting. After my trip, it was the last thing I wanted yet I could feel myself falling back into routine. I wasn't ready, because things were so different for me, but I couldn't share anything with him. I allowed him to do what he wanted because this is what we did, as man and wife. He didn't kiss me or look at me. It didn't feel right to be touched by my husband, not like this with no sensuality or pleasure involved. He climbed on top of me. He was more physical than usual. There was nothing tender or loving about it; it was very mechanical. After he was done, he rolled over and went to sleep. There was no gentleness or emotion. I curled into a ball, tears rolling down my face, but I made sure not to make a sound. He didn't like it when I cried.

This was not the man I wanted to spend the rest of my life with, not like this. What had happened to us? He felt like a stranger. I ached to have Marcelo hold me or Carmen hug me, but there was no one. I felt so alone and unloved; I could barely breathe. That was it. This was no way to live. I couldn't be scared anymore. It had been so long since I stood up for myself. I cried myself to sleep, promising that things would have to change.

The next day, I took the boys to the mall, as they needed hoodies and were craving cinnamon buns. Although our homemade cinnarolls were better, I needed to get out of the house. When we got there, I popped into the specialty engraving shop and pulled out the pocket watch I had bought at the outdoor night market a few days ago. I wanted to get something engraved on it for Marcelo, something special. I had thought about it since I had found the watch and had come up with a few ideas.

The first one was "Carpe Diem" because that's what the trip had been, but it seemed cliché. I thought something sappy like, "My Marcelo" or maybe sassy like "boy toy". Then I thought maybe something unique like "SCAR", which was ironically more fitting than I realized. All my scars, it somehow connected me to him. SCAR also was an acronym for Spa, Club, Ashram, Run. It seemed too raw. In the end, I went with "Enjoy every minute...K"

We were heading over to the food court when a familiar voice from across the crowd said, “Hey there stranger, fancy seeing your pretty self here…”

It was Marcelo. There I was, standing in the mall with my three boys and he was standing right in front of me. I froze. So many memories and emotions came flooding back, I felt the force of it push me back and almost lost my footing. I clutched my son’s arm for support. What was he doing here? Why was he talking to me? I was no longer the girl from a few days ago, I was back to being a mother of three. There was no way I was going to let Marcelo meet my boys. I wasn’t ready to let him into this part of my life.

I looked at him questioningly. “You must be mistaken. Sorry.” Looking away, embarrassed by my behaviour. As I walked past him, our arms brushed and I could feel that rush and intensity, almost painful, I had felt just a day ago. I dismissed it, focused on my boys and led them over to the cinnamon buns.

“Come on boys, let’s go see if we can get a free sample,” I said, trying my best to distract them.

“Who was that man?” my youngest, Arjev asked. He was always asking questions.

“No one, dear, he’s nobody, let’s go get some cinnamon buns.” I turned around to see Marcelo still standing there with his hands in his pockets staring at me as he heard my response. I cringed at my own words, knowing it wasn’t true but I felt hopeless. He shrugged. He understood. He smiled, he turned and he left.

His departure seemed so sudden and permanent, like I would never see him again. It felt rushed, like that night on his rooftop. My heart ached and I was caught up in the moment as I realized I would never experience that intensity again and that he would be gone. I looked at my phone and found his contact. I hesitated. Then I texted, "Wait..." At least I knew that in a few short hours, he would be back in Montreal and out of my life. But I still ached. Five minutes later, I settled the boys at a table and told them I had to go to the bathroom. I could barely see Marcelo standing behind a massive pillar, looking at his phone. For a split second I thought to myself, what would happen if I ran away with him right now? Would he treat me well and take care of me? Would he commit, love me and be emotionally supportive? An illusion. I wasn't ready. And I could never abandon my boys. I dismissed it.

As I approached him, I grabbed him by the arm and led him to a quiet corner in the mall. I kissed him instinctively. I held the kiss as he wrapped his arms around me. The warmth of his body comforted me. I felt his arms go around my neck and he slipped something around it. I looked down and saw a silver, Greek key chain necklace with a pendant on it. The pendant was of the Tree of Life set in a deep pink—my favourite colour. Framing the circular pendant was an ornate crescent moon.

"Something to remember me by. Carmen helped me pick it out that night at the market. She said it was exactly who you were. I can see that too." He flipped it over on his thumb resting his hand on my chest so I could see the back. He had engraved the back with three simple letters, KCM, for Karina, Carmen and Marcelo. It was perfect.

I held onto him for one more minute before slipping the pocket watch in his hand. “I know it won’t replace the one you lost,” I said, “but this is something to remember me by…” He smiled warmly. “Wow. Thank you, but you really didn’t have to, I wasn’t planning on forgetting you…ever.” he said. “It’s perfect.” I could see it meant a lot to him.

To lighten the mood I said, “Life is too short to be serious, so be charming.”

I hugged him, squeezing him more tightly, breathing him in deeply, closing my eyes and doing my best to hold onto him. We locked eyes as I released his embrace. And then, I let his hand go and walked away. I couldn’t look back, the aching feeling too painful.

I looked down at my phone and for a second, I thought I should delete his contact, but as I was about to, I received a text. It was from him. “Your secret is safe with me.” I smiled. He always knew what to say and when to say it. Having a friend wasn’t a bad thing and honestly, I wasn’t ready to let him go completely. I put the phone away and went back to my kids who were halfway through their cinnamon buns.

As soon as Arjev saw me he asked, “Ma, where did you get that pretty necklace around your neck?” I couldn’t get anything past this guy!

Even though life went back to normal for a while, it didn't feel normal. Now that I had allowed myself to see, be and feel this other side of me, I wanted more of it. I tried to distract myself with more work, more yoga and creating more journals, but it just wasn't enough.

The triathlon was coming up in a few weeks and in between training, accommodations, gear and prep, I knew I would have a lot to do. Suddenly, panic set in, what if I couldn't do this myself without my husband. I know I had told my husband I could, but I wasn't sure. Why was I so weak and insecure? Had my trip taught me nothing? I could do this. I had to do this, for me and for my kids.

As the day approached, I felt better about going. We were going a road trip for a triathlon, which was exciting. I felt anxious—I didn't want to disappoint them. When I asked the boys to step up and help, I was very surprised. Arjan hauled the bikes, checked the tire pressures, packed gear and made sure we all had our helmets. Aryan busied himself in the kitchen baking muffins and savoury snacks for the road trip and energy balls for the race. Arjev did the laundry and packed the cooler. I couldn't believe it. I was so impressed and proud. It gave me the confidence to know we would be okay.

"Hey Ma, we are almost packed. I can't wait, I'm so pumped for this race. I can't wait to see you at the finish line, for both when I finish and you finish!" Arjan said as we were getting ready to leave. "If you're okay with it, I don't mind helping out with the driving either, I could use some more highway driving practice." I felt my heart ache with pride.

My husband tried to be accommodating, putting little effort into helping and mocking the situation, unaware that his actions were driving us further apart. I tried to keep finding fault in myself but I was done with excuses. He pretended to be happy for us but I could tell it was fake and no longer cared. It no longer mattered. The man I had married, who had promised me so much when we first met, couldn't deliver. But that was okay, I understood it now.

And honestly, I needed to do this for myself. And I was ecstatic that right now, to share this with my boys. We said our goodbyes to hubby and headed out for our mother and sons' adventure.

The road trip was great: junk food, eating out, laughing, joking, telling stories and singing our favourite tunes at the top of our lungs. Arjan was a great back-up driver, so I could relax. What mattered most to me was that these monkeys were mine. Hanging out with them, all mature and capable, I couldn't recognize them.

These boys, what seemed like just yesterday were babies and so much work. Being so close in age, I had a lot to juggle. Diaper changes, breast feeding, disciplining, multiple activities, studying, temper tantrums, and mom guilt! Nights where I wish I could be anywhere else but in the midst of bringing these boys up. Sleepless nights, showerless days, caffeine as my only drug. Anxiously waiting to have a few moments to myself, where I wasn't tucking kids in, being pulled in three different ways, being yelled at, being vomited on and constantly needed. Not to mention all the stress of raising them right as they got older, doing the right thing, the right friends, the right sports, the right amount of homework, the list was endless. But I had made it through those years.

All my hard work had paid off. It wasn't a waste of time to be at home, I wasn't a worthless stay-at-home mom. I had used my time and talent and helped make these three stunning individuals into who they were today. They were strong, talented, handsome, kind, gentle, able and loving souls. It took me a while to recognize it but they were a reflection of me.

Race day was exhilarating. I looked at my three boys, standing side by side by side, with their personal hairstyles, lucky earrings, and tri outfits with race bibs on, standing beside their matching road bikes. They geared up, ready to compete—it was a very proud moment. I held onto the memory, trying to capture the moment forever. Of course, I started crying happy tears and the boys all came over and hugged me. Group hugs from these guys were the best. I took lots of pictures and we headed out. It was going to be a great day!

We all cheered each other on as each of us splashed while we swam, pedaled hard while we biked, and felt the breeze in our hair while we ran. We crossed the finish line with big smiles! Finishers medals hung from our necks! We took more pictures, walked about the town and bought souvenirs. Then we met up with some friends who were also in the area and all had freshly squeezed lemonade and poutine to celebrate. We went for dessert and when I suggested we share, the boys said, "Let's vote on it!" This was their trick, because although my vote "counted", I was always out voted, three to one!

When we got back home after our road trip, I called Carmen.

"I am so proud of you, girl! You did it! You raised three amazing boys and you triumphed and completed it on your own. I always knew you could do it."

"The trip was amazing—the boys even more amazing! I can't believe how strong they are, how capable they are and how much they took care of me. I can't wait to go again, with you. So, when are we planning our next trip?" I asked.

She always knew what to say, "Well, I am so glad you mentioned it. I just got us tickets to Wanderlust 108. I can't wait. You and me baby, we're going to Chicago in September! I'm hoping to get us tickets to Hamilton and reservations at "that" restaurant everyone has been raving about. The boys will be back in school, life will be back to routine and it will be the perfect time for us to get away. I can't wait to go shopping and check out the sites. It is going to be fabulous!"

"What!" I was a little shocked. I can't leave my kids. I felt my old insecurities creep in. Or could I? They were so grown up; they were taking care of me. Of course, I could. And my husband, he would have to be okay with it. Plus, we had missed out on spending most of the week together on this last trip.

"And besides, this is going to be a great way to celebrate my 29th birthday!" We laughed, as we both knew she was celebrating her 29th birthday for at least the third time!

Chapter 16

18 Months Later

Packing up a few last-minute items for my travel bag, I heard the doorbell. I opened the two-car garage door and I looked out to see my deep pink Audi RS5 parked in one spot and a mustard yellow sporty VW in the spot next to mine. The VW belonged to my very responsible part-time chauffeur, my 16-year-old son, Arjan.

"Hurry up kids, we're going to be late and if we're late, we are going to miss our flight. Your dad is waiting for us!" I yelled as I hustled the kids into the minivan.

I hugged my husband, greeting him kindly and gave him a light kiss.

“How come Baba isn’t going to come with us on the plane?” my youngest Arjev asked, yet again. I had already explained this to him but did it again, just to comfort him.

“Baba has to work. He is going to join us in a few days for the party. Not to worry, he won’t miss the festivities.”

“Is he going to get there as fast as he can?” he asked. He had this disappointed look on his face, all pouty and pretend sad.

“Yes, he is,” I reassured him. He was twelve years old and still the baby of the family. And he got away with it because he was my baby.

Eighteen months had passed since that road trip I had taken out west and so much had changed.

Once Carmen finalized her divorce, she flew to India for a few months to stay in an ashram in Rishikesh, India. As much I wanted to go with her, I couldn’t leave my children. Although I was sad that she went without me, she needed it to collect her thoughts and find herself again. She took one of my journals to record her journey. I would get updates and photos whenever she had access to wifi. She sent funny messages of things she saw and people she met. I missed her so much, but I knew she needed the trip and someday we would go together again. She had decided to do more teacher training and help out in the poorer areas.

She got to do a little touring and visited some of the holy temples and Hindu/Buddha sites. She visited the

Ganga River and sat under one of the largest Banyan trees in the world and meditated to the vibrations of singing bowls for eight hours. She would often wake up at sunrise, lead a simple life of labour: teaching, learning and often fasting. Some days were spent in complete silence. It sounded like paradise.

When she came back, she was a new woman. Her hair was even longer, tied up in a big messy bun on top of her head. She had malas (necklaces) and beaded bracelets. She had gotten slimmer and even stronger, living on "daal baath" (lentils and rice) all day. Her skin was smooth and tanned. She looked smarter, like she had gained all the wisdom of her travels from the yogis, holy men and children she had met.

Carmen was so motivated and inspired, she wanted to share her wealth of knowledge and help people. She decided to open her own hot yoga and workshop studio when she got back to Calgary. She called it the "Shanti Om" (Shanti means peace) and business was thriving. Her kind personality, strong skills and creative techniques for new fusion classes had people lining up at the door. Every once in a while, she would even let me teach a class, calling it "amateur night". I also got to help her with the business and marketing side of things while offering journaling and personalized workshops. Her husband had been more than generous to give her what she needed when they separated.

Marcelo flew back to Montreal after our time together and although we became closer friends, I hadn't seen him since. We still exchanged text messages: some were real, some were funny one-liners, most were kind. We still needed to go for scuba lessons, but we hadn't found the time to plan it. He was still traveling lots for work and although I kept telling him I would meet up with him one of these days in Miami, London, or Singapore, it never happened. I knew that I could count on him and, talk to him without complicating things. That kind of reassurance made our bond stronger. But at the same time, we knew we had given each other the best part of ourselves and needed to move on. He still had a little piece of my heart.

Not surprisingly, well, maybe a little, but not really, Carmen and Marcelo had decided to give their relationship a try. They didn't start dating right away, Carmen needed to sort her life out. Between her being in India and him in Montreal, they took it slow and the long distance helped them take it step by step. They both asked me permission, which I thought was adorable. Of course, it was their life to live. We still shared a special bond, but I was so glad they had found each other. I don't know if we could ever share that kind of connection again, but I knew I couldn't give either of them what they needed from each other.

As time went on, things got more serious. Carmen was visiting Montreal more often and Marcelo was coming out west to ski or golf. They were really fond of each other, balanced each out and made a charming couple. She would share little tidbits about how things were going: his texts, phone calls and visits.

I could tell when Carmen fell in love with Marcelo, she had that look in her eye and I knew he cared very deeply for her.

I never did tell my husband about the affair, I felt it wouldn't be fair to him, he honestly wouldn't be able to handle the truth and it would hurt him so much more. I was happy to keep my secret, I felt no shame. It wasn't about the trust; I just didn't want to burden him. He seemed fragile, more insecure and needed to be reassured and taken care of. I never felt guilty about what I had done. I didn't need to do that to him, I couldn't.

It wasn't because of the trip, Marcelo, Carmen, or anything specific. And yet, it was all of it. I was more of a free spirit than I was allowed to be in the confines of a marriage. I knew I didn't want to get married again. I wasn't even ready to fall in love because I still didn't know what it was and I needed to love myself first. I had been busy defining the limits of my life. I was understanding boundaries. Some, I needed to remove because they confined me; others I had to put up, to protect me. I wasn't about to give up on my kids, they would always be my priority, but I also couldn't pretend anymore.

Days had turned into weeks and weeks turned into months. I had promised myself a year to try to make the marriage work and to find my happiness. After the road trip, I had made it a point to no longer be used, controlled or manipulated by anyone, especially my husband. I stood up for myself and started putting my needs first. I found things to do that were important to me and my boys. I focused on connecting with friends and creating dependable friendships. I remembered all the things I enjoyed doing for myself and found new outlooks on life. I tried to include him, see past our differences, in hopes that he would come around. The more I planned, the more I realized, these things were for me. My husband partook, but he was content in his ways and although he wanted me in his life, he didn't want me. He wanted security but couldn't understand me. And if I did anything to rock that, he felt it was an attack on him, and I couldn't have that on my conscience. He enjoyed a quiet lifestyle and he wanted an obedient, dutiful Indian wife to take care of him.

As time went on, no matter what I did or how hard I tried, I could feel that we had disconnected. And there were still doubts, not accusations or anger, but more uncertainty about making each other happy. I didn't want to hurt him, but I needed to be happy. I also wanted him to be a part of the boys' lives in a healthy way. I couldn't pretend anymore to be something I wasn't. We were on different paths. It was time to move on and get closure while things were still amicable.

We eventually decided to separate and were on our one-year trial. I was reluctant to tell my Ma about everything that was going on, knowing she would see it as a failure. One day, when she showed up at my place with a pint of my favourite Haagen Dazs Cookie Dough ice cream, a case of beer for herself and a supportive shoulder to cry and lean on, I knew we were going to be okay. She had finally seen things through my eyes and accepted me for who I was, flaws and all. And I wasn't a total disappointment to her. We had a real conversation about life and after a long time, it was nice to need my mom and have her at my side.

I hadn't seen or dated anyone since. I was quite content and occupied doing my own thing. To feel that freedom, make my own decisions, focus on me when the kids weren't bugging me. I had never been on my own and although it had terrified me when I first thought about it, now, it was exactly what I needed. I wanted to know what it felt like to be alone and feel loneliness, not that it would really be possible with three boys, but I wanted a different kind of independence. I did have those intense achy feelings every once in a while, for Marcelo, but my memories seemed to be enough. I would also wear my tree pendant all the time. It kept him and Carmen close to my heart.

I had taken this time, inspired by Carmen, to launch my own business while still working for Rebecca. I also realized after the separation that all my careful saving and investing had paid off.

I had surprised myself. I thought I was weak, a worthless shell of myself that was stuck in a dissatisfied world. This past year, I had become so strong. My heart was open, my mind was spinning, my confidence was soaring and doors were opening. I was building my life into something I cared for, it had meaning again. Of course, I always had my kids, my friends, my family, but now I also had me.

I seriously delved into the world of journaling and created my first wellness journal. It was therapeutic for me to create them and even more beneficial to share them. I started creating online classes and going to organizations to promote my publications.

The recognition was great, building something was gratifying and helping people was life changing. It was all encompassing; the traveling, talking to, influencing and changing people. It was exactly where I needed to be.

I also had my girls, Tess, Jenna, Rebecca and of course Carmen who were always supporting me. We were trying new things as well, hiking, climbing, aerials and destination girls' trips.

As we boarded the plane to Montreal, I could feel myself getting giddy. Daryl was going to let us stay with him for the few days we were going to be there. He had no idea what he was in for when he had invited me and the boys but it was going to be an adventure. I had planned to take the boys to Old Montreal, to site see, and take in all the amazing things Montreal had to offer including the poutine and smoked meat sandwiches. From there we were going to go to Niagara Falls and check out the Mario Cart track and of course the falls themselves. Hubby was going to join us. I was so glad we were able to stay friends and not just for the kids' sake. We were better on a practical level than we could ever be in a marital level.

We were going to spend some family time together and once we got back to Montreal, I was going to stay back a few days and stay with Carmen and Marcelo while the kids went back with their dad.

We were also going to Montreal to celebrate! Marcelo and Carmen were officially engaged and they were throwing a party. I couldn't have been happier. Marcelo had decided to move to Calgary since Carmen's studio was there and he could work remotely from anywhere in the world. He also enjoyed skiing, which was a bonus when you lived close to the mountains. And he would be closer to me, so I was thrilled to have my two best friends within driving distance. He was going to keep his place in Montreal in case they decided to move back or at least visit. I planned to use it as my bachelor pad when I needed a break from the kids.

As the plane landed in Montreal, Daryl was there to greet us with his charming smile and sexy voice. His pleasing appeal with his tight embrace and gentle kiss on the cheek always made me feel wanted. Daryl crammed us into his tiny vehicle and we headed back to his apartment. I hadn't told him, wanting it to be a surprise, but Tess would be at the party.

It was an unusually warm weekend in early April, perfect weather for an engagement party. Carmen had found a castle in the countryside of Quebec to rent with a huge backyard, pool, and lots of space for an engagement party. When we got to the party, I let the boys have free reign of the buffet and the property. Daryl was also more interested in the open bar than the bride and groom to be.

"Daryl, there is more to life than an open bar you know?" I said nudging him and placing my finger on his cheek to turn the direction of his gaze towards a gazebo in the gardens.

"Well, when you are alone and surrounded by people in love…" he started to say, when he realized that Tess was standing in the gazebo, looking nervous and anxious.

"I wanted to surprise you. This is your chance, don't screw it up." I slapped his bottom and pushed him towards the gazebo. "Now, the rest is up to you."

I watched as he walked over to her as casually as he could, hands in his pant pockets, trying to hold his chest up and muster up the courage to talk to her. He gave her an awkward hug but an irresistible smile. I hoped Tess wouldn't mess it up either.

Walking through the enchanted castle, I made my way to the backyard where the festivities were going on. Tents, awnings, buffet, drinks, delicate decorations, twinkling lights, fragrant and colourful flowers, it was picture perfect. It took me a minute to find Carmen. She was in a gorgeous fuchsia coloured cocktail dress, backless, short and very pretty.

Marcelo was in a fitted dark blue suit, a shirt that brought out the colour in his eyes and a matching fuchsia coloured tie. He had his hand about Carmen's waist. I felt a distant connection as I reached up and felt around my neck. I was wearing my matching coloured pendant, like I was still a part of them. They were standing on the back foyer talking to other guests at the party. I stood there, taking it all in. I had seen plenty of Carmen, planning, traveling, working; but I hadn't seen Marcelo at all. He looked as charming as ever, those kind, gorgeous gray-green eyes, strong shoulders, long legs. I guess I wasn't quite over him, my healthy obsession now was observing him from a distance.

I walked over when there was a break between greeting guests. I felt myself hesitate when I made eye contact with him. There was no regret, no angst, no sadness. And yet, there was this pain. My heart still ached for him in a fairy tale kind of way. I still wanted him. But I knew he was never going to be mine. I was afraid to touch him, but when he reached out and hugged me, the electric intensity was gone. It was replaced with warmth and gentleness. We were friends, the kind that would grow old together.

I couldn't imagine a happier couple. They had decided on a short engagement and would be getting married a few months later. I couldn't be happier for them. I noticed Carmen wasn't drinking any zinfandel and her baby bump was just starting to show if you looked hard enough. She was due in the fall. It was the furthest she'd ever made it in one of her pregnancies and all her tests and ultrasounds showed a healthy baby. I was so excited for her, I could barely contain myself. I know how badly she wanted it and I had a really good feeling it was all going to work out.

They had planned a destination wedding in Belize and we were all invited. Carmen had decided to have the wedding of her dreams and had booked the nicest and fanciest resort she could find. And not just the resort, but the whole island. It was all inclusive and the perfect setting.

Of course, I was taking the kids and we were going to have an amazing time. I had a feeling that we were going to be one crazy, weird, big, happy family and I was the luckiest person in the world to be able to share it with so many people I loved.

I know I had said I didn't want to get to know Marcelo when we were on our trip, but life has a funny way of working out and he turned out to be one of my best friends. Nobody could ever replace Carmen, but he had become a close second. I thought I was giving up and losing everything, but it turned out, once I knew what I wanted and was true to myself, I got everything and more.

A few months later, we were on a plane to Belize. Nestled between the jungles of Central America and the Caribbean Sea, Belize was known for its islands, beaches, culture and beauty. Its barrier reef was rich with marine life was phenomenal for snorkelers and divers. The hundreds of low-lying islands known as cayes made kayaking and paddle boarding so much fun. The jungle was a backdrop for the many exotic animals that lived there and made it great for hiking. And the Mayan culture added a mysterious ancient feel with its archeological sites with hieroglyphs, tombs and temples.

We were chartered by ferry to a small island of paradise where we would be staying for two weeks. The boys were so excited to have a two week all-expenses paid vacation, with swim-up bars, boogie boarding and snorkeling trips. I was just happy to enjoy the sun and sand, and maybe a few spa treatments.

I had helped Carmen with the arrangements and helped her pick out her gorgeous, sea-blue wedding dress. She had real flowers in her hair, a touch of makeup and the highest heels she felt comfortable in with her protruding baby bump. It didn't really matter, because the ceremony was on the beach and she would have to be barefoot anyway. She looked so radiant and beautiful.

Carmen said, "Is it ironic that if it weren't for your overbearing husband taking you to Montreal, you never would've met Marcelo and if it weren't for my cheating husband, I never would've met Marcelo; so even though they are part of our past, they cosmically created our future."

I hugged her, "It doesn't matter because we are creating our future. You look so beautiful. I don't think I've ever seen you so happy. Everything has a way of working out, doesn't it? Neither of us would be considered traditional and we are happier because of it."

"And I don't think I have ever seen you so happy," she replied. "You've been through so much; you truly deserve happiness. I know you are in a way better place now but know that I'm always here for you."

Clicking our champagne glasses filled with virgin pina coladas, I winked at her. She was ready to get married.

My boys were part of the entertainment, playing the guitar, ukulele and bongos. I was her maid of honour. Daryl was the best man. It was a small wedding, forty-one people waiting in the audience, watching the bride as she walked down the aisle. The ceremony was perfect and, the weather was gorgeous. Everyone that was there loved the couple and couldn't be happier for them. It was a truly joyous occasion.

After the ceremony was over, Carmen had to get off her feet and relax. She found a table by the bar and put her feet up on a chair. She was sipping ice water and looking radiant and exhausted all at once.

Tess came over and gave me a big hug, squeezing me tight. She was not usually a hugger so I was worried. "What is going on with you girl, hugs and smiles. Has Belize gotten to you?" I asked.

She couldn't stop grinning as she held out her left hand, with a not so shiny rock on her finger. "It's no diamond, which is what I love, but a piece of the quartz from the house *we* are building."

"Did you say *we*?" I asked, surprised.

"Daryl and I are taking it slow, but I am so happy. We are designing a property together, which you will have to visit when it's complete. We want to make this work!"

Daryl had now joined us and I gave him a big hug, excited for my friends.

After mingling with a few of the guests, Marcelo made his way over to me. Arms outstretched, he held me in his embrace and gave me a long hug. He knew I was a hugger. "Thank you for everything. And thank you for Carmen. You will always be my person, but Carmen is my darling girl. And if it weren't for you, we never would've met—"

As he spoke, someone bumped into me and I almost fell over. Marcelo grabbed me and rescued me yet again, looking over at the guy who had hit me while holding me in his embrace.

"Hey, man! Awesome party! You are the best!" said an unfamiliar but suave and charming voice. He had a slight Italian accent.

Marcelo rolled his eyes and smiled at the same time. "Karina, this is one of my best friends and groomsmen, George. Let me formally introduce you. George, Karina; Karina, George. We grew up together and he's a lot of fun! He always finds ways to get me in trouble, in a good way. I'm sure he'll do his best to show you a good time in Belize."

I vaguely remembered seeing him at the engagement party and perhaps briefly when we first arrived at the island. But somehow, I hadn't been introduced to him.

"So sorry I bumped into you…" he said while giving me a big hug. He had no concept of personal space;

he pressed his body completely up against mine embracing me affectionately. Oddly, I hugged him back, enjoying the warmth of his touch. He pulled me in tighter. He had this way about him. He was smooth but not sleezy. He felt good and smelled even better. I picked up hints of coconut and pineapple.

He held my hand, kissed it and said, "Ciao Bella! You are the infamous Karina. So bellisima, beautiful! I must call you Kari, meaning 'dear' in Italian. You can call me Giorgio. I saw you at the ceremony and knew it was you from the way Marcelo described you. He has told me so much about you. I am thrilled to finally meet you. I can absolutely show you a good time." I couldn't tell if I should take him seriously. He was full of life; I could feel his energy and excitement. He was so different from Marcelo; vibrant and ready to go.

"Marcelo told me you like to dance, well now you can dance with a real dance partner!" He started moving his hips in a hypnotic manner while balancing his drink and pulling me in. He could definitely move his hips. He was charming and seductive, confident and sexy.

He looked over at Marcelo and thought he was whispering when he said, "I can see why you said she is a lot of fun! She has beautiful hips and stunning brown eyes! I can't wait to get her on the dance floor!" I looked over at Marcelo, surprised by the whole interaction and intrigued that he had talked about me to his friends.

“Oh yes! She’s amazing, and probably one of the only people I know who can keep up with you on the dance floor!” Marcelo was being too kind, as always.

Before I could say anything more, Giorgio was escorting me towards the beach bar and then to the white sandy beach. I awkwardly waved to Marcelo, hoping to catch up with him later. Giorgio had his arm wrapped around my waist and had pulled me tight into him.

Arjan, who was now a charismatic, even longer dark haired, tanned, well-built, strutting sixteen-year-old of a man came running up to us in his swim trunks wearing his aviator sunglasses, diamond stud earrings, and smiled sheepishly. “A bunch of us want to do some surfing lessons before going out onto the catamaran Marcelo chartered for us. Hope that’s okay? And yes, I will make sure my brothers are safe, have life jackets and are with me.”

I could see the other two, closer to the water’s edge, kicking and splashing around. Aryan had a slushy drink in his hand and Arjev was showing off his new corn rows hairdo while looking over at us in hopes of going surfing. I smiled. Arjan was so responsible and yet so good at doing his own thing. I also figured out a while ago that whenever he said, “a bunch”, there was usually a girl involved.

“Have fun sweetheart, stay safe and have a good time.” And off he went, giving me a thumbs up, indicating he approved of the man who was still holding onto me. I was surprised how okay the boys were with my separation from my husband. I think they saw how much happier I was and appreciated that being happy was important. I was so much more dedicated to them in a healthy way because I was making myself a priority. And they were happier too. I loved my boys.

Giorgio hadn't stopped talking since the moment he bumped into me. And what he had to say was interesting and captivating. He was charismatic and good looking in a more rugged than boyish way. He was well built, tall with broad shoulders, jet black hair and a nice tan. He was definitely Italian.

I guess Carmen was right, I had a type. I smiled as he continued to tell me about himself. He was an open book. I already knew so much about his job as an investment banker, his new hobby to enter a fitness competition and about his new "vacation property" in New York. He loved to work out, sail and spoil his friends. He was very into me. I couldn't tell if he was playing me or not, but I didn't care. I wanted to have some fun, and he was fun! It wouldn't take much for me to get swept away with this guy.

"So, this summer, you are coming to New York. And I won't take 'no' for an answer. This week, I am going to dazzle you with my charm and you will have no choice but to be under my spell." I couldn't tell if this was a line or just the way he talked. But I was willing to find out. He squeezed me a little harder as the warm sun caressed my skin. I looked out onto the teal-blue ocean waves, taking it all in. This was going to be a new life, a new beginning.

He continued, "I can't wait to show you my place and take you to Broadway and off Broadway. Marcelo promised to visit for a day or two as well." His hand moved down the curve of my back as he placed it liberally around my butt, giving it a little squeeze thinking I wouldn't notice. It was probably a little bold, but I didn't mind, I had missed the touch of an engaging and exciting man.

"That sounds fabulous, but I don't know..." I laughed, feeling uncomfortable and fascinated at the same time. I started to come up with an excuse but he cut me off, making me blush even more with what he said next.

"Please don't take this the wrong way, not trying to overstep, but I might've heard that you enjoy an adventure, have a playful side to you that you want to experiment. I would like to indulge you in all your fantasies: the clubs, the exotic vacations, the exclusive parties. If it's an adrenaline rush you seek, I will take you on an ice track experience in a Porsche or show you how to fly –" He said smiling, his dark brown eyes not able to hide his excitement.

Now I was really beginning to wonder what Marcelo had told him. I was curious to see what else life had to offer after being stuck for so long and perhaps this was my chance. I hadn't thought about my fantasies, exotic or otherwise or even realized I had any, but from Giorgio's approach and ease, I felt more confident about wanting to try new things.

"Whatever your heart desires, on your terms. I want to make you happy. I know, we've just met, but Marcelo has told me so much about you, I feel like I already know you. I have been waiting to meet you for a long time, Kari. I would love to introduce you to that world you have been craving and take care of you. Don't worry Kari Bella, I know how dear you are to Marcelo and he would kill me if I hurt you, so let me know what you want and I will make it happen!" He said.

Excitedly as he pulled me in and planted a kiss on the corner of my mouth, just grazing my lips. I had just met this guy, but he had a vibe about him which I was feeling.

Maybe it was the sun, sand and satisfaction of being on an island with my best friends, but I was getting excited by the idea of having this man in my life. Perhaps I just needed to get a little wild freedom out of my system. Either way, it felt good. I could really get used to this new me!

Marcelo and Carmen joined us on the beach. I gave Carmen a warm hug and squeezed her hand. I gave Marcelo a hug, he couldn't contain his grin from all the excitement. This is what happiness felt like. Standing shoulder to shoulder, we held each other, wrapping our arms around each other's waists while looking out at the ocean. Eventually Daryl and Tess joined as well.

Daryl told the man at the bar to crank some dance tunes and pulled Tess close while holding her hand.

Giorgio grabbed me around the waist and spun me in his arms, holding me from behind as we danced and watched the waves splashing over the beach. Marcelo held Carmen close, placing his hands on her big belly as they swayed gently to the music.

Carmen said, “To best friends and new beginnings…”

The End.

Acknowledgements

Although my love for writing has been a part of me since I have been a kid, I never thought I would get this far. Completing a novel. But I didn't do it alone. It started with an inspiration to write about something I was passionate about even if it wasn't conventional.

It was getting the support and strength from my sister, Pialee to pursue it. She pushed me out of my comfort zone and showed me a world I was too afraid to embrace. She helped me understand that there is happiness in pain if you know how to look for it.

It was the hesitant but understanding comments from Ma and Baba who were concerned about my openness. When they accepted the reality and beauty in writing a romance with raw emotion, there was appreciation. Although I don't know who teared first, me or my mom, her hugs made me realize it was worth taking the risk.

It was also my husband who always knew I had it in me to produce this kind of work but feared how the world would judge me and was secretly impressed by me for doing it. It was the love for my kids who are too young to understand the themes but curious and excited to read it one day. I hope to teach them more about their mom's different point of view and how unique life can be. These kiddos influenced the book in their unique way.

It was my many friends, some who are too humble for recognition that questioned, challenged and understood the journey. It was my one friend, Anjli, who was proud of me. She not only re-read the manuscript, but also cried and laughed with me and celebrated my tenacity and passion to produce an "amazing" book over margaritas.

I was surrounded by the talent of my editor India, who knew how to guide me, offend me, improve me and help me understand the art of editing. I was fortunate to have a friend like Simone, who I shared many moments of joy and sadness with to bring to life the cover art for the book. Her witty comments, sassy remarks and ability to steer me in the right direction has produced a work of art.

It was also for Carmen, Daryl, Tess, Brad, Jenna, and Rebecca, who have always been a part of my life but also came to life to make this story possible. I am honoured to have "shared" my journey with them.

It was for Marcelo, who in some ways was the fairy tale love of my life. His character opened a world of fantasy which was safe to play in. And finally, Karina, the girl I always saw in myself and trusted me to tell her story.

Serendipity

Karina's journey has just begun as she is about to embrace independence, new beginnings and living her life. Although not ready for love and not sure she still understands it, she is open to everything Giorgio has to offer. Never has a man pursued her, enticed her and desired her the way Giorgio does. He wants her and she's intrigued, but still unsure.

Carmen is about to embark on the journey of motherhood and all the joy it has to offer. Marcelo is a husband and to-be father and excited for all it has to offer. And yet his fiercely independent side of him is tugging on his need for autonomy. How will be balance and provide for his new family.

Daryl and Tess are also starting a new journey. Figuring out how to manage hectic schedules and be together while living at opposite ends of the country. Will they be able to make it work?

Everyone should live happily ever after...or should they? Even with new beginnings, old habits are hard to break. And when things are said and done, happiness is not what always what you expect it to be.

Will these friends find happiness?

Aka Naksha Journals

Check out these Aka Naksha Journals if you are looking for mindful techniques and inspiration or if you are on your own life journey.

Wellness Journal

Yoga Journal

Life Skills Organizer

Weekly Planner

About the Author

Bidisha Ganguli is always looking for a challenge in life, whether it be writing, raising a family, pushing boundaries or trying new things. Born and brought up in Canada, she loves the possibilities and experiences it has to offer and has learned a lot from her life which she has contributes to her writing. Travel, theatre and yoga are some of her favourite hobbies. She lives with her husband and kids and enjoys nature, baking, entertaining and writing whenever she can. She has a degree in Electrical Engineering and an MBA. Creating journals on wellness, life skills, yoga and relationships was what got her started. From there, she followed her passion to write not-so-ordinary romance novels. When she's not writing, she's sharing her ideas with friends, family and colleagues. For more information about her work, check out her website.

www.akanaksha.com

A Chance Meeting

Manufactured by Amazon.ca
Bolton, ON

23109117R00203